RALLY ROUND THE
FLAG, BOYS!

RALLY ROUND THE
FLAG, BOYS!

by

MAX SHULMAN

THE REPRINT SOCIETY LONDON

FIRST PUBLISHED 1958
THIS EDITION PUBLISHED BY THE REPRINT SOCIETY LTD
BY ARRANGEMENT WITH WILLIAM HEINEMANN LTD 1959

MADE AND PRINTED IN ENGLAND BY
HAZELL WATSON AND VINEY LTD
AYLESBURY AND SLOUGH

For
Carol
Dan
Bud
Pete
Martha

One

HERE begins a tale of action and passion, a guts-and-glory story of men with untamed hearts, of women with raging juices. There is violence, and torment, and raw, rampant power. But, withal, there is beauty—gentleness, occasional lulls in the storm, glades in the jungle, lambent moments to pause and reflect, to smile a bit, and—who can tell?—perhaps to blink back a tear.

At the vortex of this whirling drama, at the heart, so to speak, of the juggernaut, is one man. His name is Guido di Maggio. He is a tall young man, lithe as a willow wand and fair as the morn. He is by nature mild and merry, fond of lasagna, girls, and community singing. But unwarlike as he is, he wears the uniform of a second lieutenant in the United States Anti-Aircraft Artillery.

Our story begins, quietly enough, in the office of the post adjutant at Fort Totten, Long Island, on a grey winter day not so long ago. Second Lieutenant Guido di Maggio sat that day on a chair, straight, birch or maple frame, slot back, without arms, Type MIL-F-10091. In front of him was a desk, flat top, office, wood, oak colour, Type B-1-FED-AA-D-201. Behind the desk in a chair, swivel, with castors, artificial leather upholstered, oak, with arms, Type 1-D-FED-AA-C-311A, sat Major Albert R. McEstway, post adjutant.

"Fairbanks," said Major McEstway.

"Fairbanks?" said Guido.

"Fairbanks, Alaska," said Major McEstway.

"*Oh, no!*" shrieked Guido, clutching his cheeks.

"The exec up there got frostbitten, and they've asked for a replacement," said the Major. "You'll fly out in the first available aircraft, which ought to be at Mitchel Field in a—— What is the matter with you, Lieutenant?"

Guido seemed to be foaming somewhat at the mouth. "I can't go, Major!" he shouted. "I just can't!"

"I beg your pardon?" said the Major.

Guido reached across the desk and clasped the Major's hand in both of his. "Listen, Major," he pleaded, "you've got to get me an assignment in the States. In fact, it has to be right around New York."

The Major disengaged his hand gently. "May one ask why?" he inquired.

"I've got a girl," said Guido. "Wonderful girl. Pretty. Sweet. Educated. Plumpish. Not *fat*, you understand. About 120 pounds, I'd guess."

"How tall?"

"Five-four."

"Not a bit fat," agreed the Major.

"Plumpish," repeated Guido. "Toothsome, you might say."

"You might at that," allowed the Major.

"But stubborn. *Mamma mia*, talk about stubborn! A mule. A rock-head. You know how they get."

"Oh, do I not!" said the Major, rolling his eyes.

"Two weeks ago we had this little rumble, and I still haven't been able to square it. You ship me out of here now, and I'll lose her sure as hell."

"I see," said the Major.

"I knew you'd understand," said Guido.

"I do," said the Major. "Do you?"

"Understand what?"

"That you will leave from Mitchel Field on the first available military aircraft and report to the 998th Anti-Aircraft Battery in Fairbanks, Alaska. And don't go off the post. We never know for certain when a plane gets into Mitchel."

"But——"

"That's all, Lieutenant."

Guido groaned, rose, mumbled "Yes, sir," raised a limp salute, shambled out, shambled to the Officers' Club, found the bar not yet open, shambled out, shambled to the BOQ, oozed down on his bed, and reflected glumly on the vicissitudes of life.

Actually, Guido's life, until recently, had been singularly free of vicissitudes. He had been born and raised in the second vertical social stratum of Putnam's Landing, Connecticut. (As any journeyman sociologist can tell you, the commuting villages of Connecticut's Fairfield County—Westport, Darien, Stamford, Putnam's Landing, etc.—show three distinct social categories, vertically divided. First, there are the Yankees, descendants of the original settlers and still the wielders of power. Second, there are the Italians—like Guido's family—who initially came into Fairfield County as tracklayers for the New Haven Railroad and remained to become the storekeepers, artisans, mechanics, gardeners, police and fire departments. Third, there are the New York commuters, also called the lambs, or the pigeons, or the patsies.)

Guido's father, Vittorio di Maggio, owned a small but highly successful grocery store. On one side of Vittorio's store was an A & P, on the other a Grand Union, and down the block a First National. They all undersold him by a wide margin, but Vittorio's business continued excellent nonetheless. He carried one important item that his competitors did not—namely, charge accounts. Vittorio had made a study of commuters and had sagely concluded that a man who requires a four-bedroom house, a full-time maid, a part-time gardener, a second car, a power mower, riding lessons for his daughters, sailing lessons for his sons, a mink stole for his wife, and ten ounces of alcohol per day for himself is a man who must be chronically out of money. At the same time, having house, wife, children, maid, cars, mower, etc., he is not likely to decamp quietly on some moonless night. Skewered thus on the two horns of fixedness and cashlessness, could there be a better victim for a high-priced credit grocer?

So Vittorio prospered and—being prosperous, Catholic, and good buddies with his wife—proliferated. There were seven di Maggio children, of whom Guido was the last. They were all raised according to two simple precepts, one promulgated by the mother, one by the father. The mother said of child rearing: "Don't hit the kids unless you gotta—but when you gotta, hit 'em good." To this, the father added the unarguable dictum: "God never told nobody to be stupid."

Under these sensible rubrics, Guido, like his brothers and sisters, grew up to be smart, sunny, and obedient. He worked in the store, he sang in the choir at St. Thomas the Apostle, he fished and swam and clammed in Long Island Sound, he maintained a respectable B-minus average at school, he shot a passable game of snooker, and he left his virginity with a lady in Bridgeport.

He also played a lot of baseball—but not because he wanted to. Since his name was di Maggio, everybody naturally assumed he loved baseball and they automatically called for him whenever there was a game. Actually, he would have been much happier to stay at home, but he hated to disappoint people so he went along. Constant exposure made him, willy-nilly, a first rate ballplayer. In his last year of high school, he captained the team and hit a gaudy ·375.

After high school, he thought he might give college a whirl. He was the first di Maggio ever to entertain such an exotic notion, and Vittorio was quite taken aback when Guido broached the subject. *"College?"* he exclaimed, startled.

"Why not?" said Guido.

"Atsa right," replied Vittorio after some thought. "Why not?"

So Guido went off to the University of Connecticut. Why indeed not? He was a bright boy, his family could afford to send him, and they did not really need his help in the store. Besides, college would keep him out of the Army for a while. Guido, let it be emphasized, had no wish to shirk doing his bit, but neither was he in any tearing hurry.

College and Guido were friends from the outset. His respectable B-minus average stuck with him. He learned a smattering of literature, a smidgen of language, a dash of history. And, while trailing his fingers in the main currents of American thought, he also picked up some necessary graces: he joined a fraternity; he got a jacket with two vents in the back; he took up bongos; he bought a half interest in a Chrysler Airflow. And, of course, he played baseball. When Coach saw the name di Maggio on the enrolment list, he came pounding on Guido's door, and Guido, who wanted to play baseball like he wanted a third nostril, was, as always, obliging.

To keep the Army safely at bay, Guido joined the R.O.T.C. This took five hours out of his week—two of drill and three of classwork—but Guido considered the time well spent. It meant, in the first place, that he could count on four uninterrupted years of college, and, second, that when he was finally called he would go in as a second lieutenant.

His romantic activities on campus were lively, but non-specific. There was a series of assorted gropes, some moderately successful, some shut-outs. Once or twice, moonstruck or randy, he spoke careless words, but not too careless. God, he always remembered in time, never told nobody to be stupid. His SAE pin stayed firmly anchored to his baseball sweater.

Then, midway through his senior year, he met Maggie Larkin at a campus dance. Her hair was honey blonde and her eyes were Lake Louise blue. Her throat arched, her breasts billowed, her waist tapered, and her flanks were round and cunningly articulated. She was five feet four inches tall and weighed 120 pounds. Plumpish. Not *fat*, you understand. Plumpish.

Guido asked her to dance. Steering her round the floor, looking at her level eyes and excellent head, feeling her honest weight, Guido fell suddenly in love. It was about as pleasant as a judo chop. He felt weak and addled. His ears rang, his salivard ducts sludged up, his kneecaps vibrated like tuning forks. Smiling inanely, unable to speak, he danced with her again any again, and when the evening was over he hustled her into the Airflow.

Here, on home grounds, a measure of confidence returned to him. He drove to a moonswept hill, cut the motor, sidled skilfully towards her.

"No," she said.

"Aw," he said.

"Look," she said, "I am a normal girl with normal instincts, and you are a very attractive boy."

"Well then!" cried Guido, closing in.

She fended him off. "No."

"Maggie," he said truthfully, "if you're thinking this is just a pass, you're wrong. I don't know exactly what's happening, but you unsettle the hell out of me."

"I like you too, Guido," she replied, "but I have my work."

"What work is that?"

"Children."

"I'll be damned!" said Guido. "How many you got?"

She laughed, and Guido's heart leapt with every tinkle. "None of my own," she said. "I'm a teacher . . . That is, I'll be one in June when I get my degree. Right now I'm doing some practice teaching over in Willimantic—the second grade."

"I see," said Guido, then corrected himself. "No, I don't see. What's your teaching got to do with me?"

"I just don't have time for you, that's all. I mean I need every minute to prepare my lecture notes."

"For the second grade?" said Guido, looking at her askance.

"Guido, do you know what a teacher's job is?"

"Teaching?" he hazarded.

"Not the way you mean. Not just filling their little heads full of the three Rs. A teacher's job—no, a teacher's *sacred obligation*—is to repair the trauma that children incur at home!"

Guido regarded her shining eyes, her upraised fist, with some astonishment. Here, obviously, was a girl of passion and fire.

Now it remained to find out just what it was she was passionate and fiery *about*. "I'm not quite sure I follow you," he said.

"Do you love children?"

"What's not to love?"

"Exactly. How can you help loving those sweet, innocent little things, so full of trust and affection, so capable of perfect happiness? Now, why can't they *have* perfect happiness?"

"Well, it's a pretty tough world."

"Yes, it is. But why?"

"Wars, famines, H-bombs——"

"No, Guido, that's not it. The basic trouble in the world today is *emotional insecurity*. How can we ever hope to solve our political and economic problems when all our children are growing up with *deep psychic disturbances*?"

"They *are*?"

"Certainly they are! Didn't *I*? Didn't *you*?"

"Well, I——"

"Of course we did. Everybody does. And why?"

"Well, I——"

"Do you think insecurity is natural?"

"Well, I——"

"It's not! It's the most unnatural thing in the world. When you and I were born, we had no fears, no insecurities. Where, then, did we get them?"

"Well, I——"

"From our parents!" she said, ramming her forefinger into Guido's ribs with every word. "From the ignorance and malice of our parents!"

"Oh, no!" said Guido stoutly. "No, sir! I don't know what kind of folks you got, but mine are a couple of living dolls."

"Yes, yes," she said with a weary smile. "And I suppose, according to ordinary standards, mine are fine parents too. They fed me, they clothed me, they sent me to college."

"So what are you rapping 'em for?"

"Because they filled me full of insecurities."

"You don't look very insecure to me," said Guido honestly.

"No? Then why do I still have nightmares? Why am I afraid of snakes? Why can't I swim? Why won't I ever have an enema?"

"*Please!*" gasped Guido, going crimson.

"Don't you see, Guido? I've got all these fears—fears I was not born with."

"You've also got teeth you were not born with," he observed.

"You miss the point. My teeth came naturally. My fears were forced on me by my parents. Out of their deep, buried destructive impulses, they had to make *me* insecure too."

"Maggie, listen," he said earnestly, "try not to knock your folks any more, will you? It isn't nice. Really."

"Nice?" she cried. "The time for niceties is over. Action is what we need—and right now! A massive re-education programme! Mental health for parents! Clinics on every corner in America!"

"Fine," said Guido. "Now how about we go some place for ribs?"

"But it will take years to get a mental health programme started," continued Maggie, unheeding. "Meanwhile somebody has to try to repair the damage that parents are doing to their children at home. And that's where we come in—we, the teachers."

"This is all you talk about?" asked Guido with genuine concern. "Parents and kids and like that?"

"Could anything be more important? Why, do you know that in the United States—in this so-called enlightened democracy—there are still parents—today, mind you, in the twentieth century!—there are still parents who *actually physically strike* their children?"

"The hell you say!"

"Can you give me any reason at all why a grown-up adult should *actually physically strike* a child?"

"I'll give you several," said Guido with a reminiscent chuckle. "A) for busting a window; B) for jumping on the cat; C) for shoplifting at Woolworth's; D) for burning the curtains; E) for drinking up the Communion wine."

Maggie shook her yellow hair vehemently. "Those aren't reasons; those are excuses. There's only one reason why a parent strikes a child—only *one*—and that is because the parent subconsciously harbours a *homicidal hatred* for the child!"

"That does it," sighed Guido and started the Airflow.

"You taking me home?" she asked.

"As fast as I can."

She nodded philosophically. "Yes, this is what usually happens. But it doesn't matter. I've got no time for boys anyhow. I need all my time for teaching the second grade children of Willimantic that there is love in the world—not just fears and threats. Love! Patience! Kindness! Understanding!"

"Lots of luck," said Guido politely.

He dropped her at the Chi Omega house and went home and curled up in bed with a good book. "Boy!" he said to himself. "I am well rid of *that* one!"

"Too bad she's loony," he said to himself a little later, "because she sure is pretty. Those eyes! Those blue, blue eyes! And the teeth! Did you ever in your whole life see such teeth? Gorgeous! A woman like that wouldn't cost you a dime for dentist bills."

Still later he said to himself, "And what about the built? You think a built like that comes walking down the street every day of the week? In a pig's valise, buddy! A built like that comes along once in a life-time—if you're lucky, that is. *Mamma mia*, what a built!"

Toward morning he said to himself, "So she's a little overboard on the subject of kids. So what? She's been studying too much psychology and it went to her head. She'll get over it. And, anyhow, the whole thing does her credit. I mean this girl really loves kids. So nuts about 'em she can't think straight.

What a fine, big heart she must have! What a whale of a heart! There, now, is a parlay for you—those eyes, those teeth, that built, and a great big heart into the bargain! Am I going to let a package like that slip through my fingers?"

He did not. He courted her with skill and persistence, and he prevailed.

Naturally he had to do a bit of lying. He had to tell her with a perfectly straight face that he had reconsidered her views on child psychology and come to the conclusion she was absolutely right. Once she was persuaded of this, the rest came easy.

They went steady for the remainder of their senior year, and Guido was the happiest of men. There were, of course, occasional dead spots—usually on the days when Maggie received the latest psychopediatric bulletin and learned that asthma was nothing but interior crying or that Ivar Krueger's conduct was directly traceable to toilet training. On these occasions Maggie, her eyes bright with excitement, would run on for hours about permissive behaviour and ego-function and organ-language and birth-trauma, while Guido nodded and made intelligent grimaces and swallowed yawns.

But these seminars were fairly rare. Most of the time Guido and Maggie did just what any other lovers do: they danced and ski-ed and swam and went to movies and picnicked and clutched each other in moist, happy embraces.

In June of the year there accrued to each of them some parchment and some shiny, inexpensive metal. They both got their diplomas, Maggie got an engagement ring, and Guido got second lieutenant's bars.

There followed an exchange of visits to meet the folks. Guido travelled to Jessup Falls, a hamlet in the north-west corner of the state, to see Mr. and Mrs. Larkin. Mr. Larkin was a jolly fat man in the grain and feed game. Mrs. Larkin was a motherly type who baked her own bread. Mrs. Larkin cried and kissed Guido, and Mr. Larkin cried a little too and took Guido out in the garage and gave him a belt from a pint bottle of

Schenley hidden behind the skid chains. "If these people have deep, buried destructive impulses toward Maggie," thought Guido, "then I am Rex, the Wonder Horse."

After two jolly days at the Larkins', Guido took Maggie to Putnam's Landing to meet the di Maggios: Vittorio, the father; Serafina, the mother; Anna and Teresa, the sisters; and Pete, Bruno, Dominic, and Carmen, the brothers. The father cast an experienced Neapolitan eye on the lavish contours of his daughter-in-law-to-be and pronounced himself well pleased. The sisters pressed gifts of lace upon her. The brothers were amiably obscene. The mother made enough *pasta fazool* to feed the retreat from Caporetto. Everybody cried like crazy.

Three days later there were more tears; Guido got his induction orders. Guido and Maggie traded salty kisses and clung desperately and declared they would love one another for ever and ever. Then Maggie went home to dry her eyes and look over the numerous offers of teaching jobs for the following autumn, and Guido marched off to defend his homeland.

Guido had been graduated from college with a major in marketing and a minor in Spanish, so, naturally, the Army assigned him to a guided missile school. He reported to Fort Bliss, a parched and baleful post outside El Paso, Texas. Here he had thirteen weeks of OBC (Officers' Basic Course) in SAM (Surface to Air Missiles). This meant, of course, electronics, which was pure Choctaw to Guido. But it did not seem any more intelligible to any of his classmates, so he just sat and listened and, to his vast amazement, he found after a couple of weeks that he was able to tell an ohm from an oscillator. He was also able to do one hundred deep knee bends, shave in thirty seconds, and stay awake through a three-hour lecture on armature winding while the classroom temperature stood at 104 degrees.

After two weeks of lectures in mathematics and electronic theory, the class was introduced to the SAM—a liquid-fuelled missile with a solid-fuelled booster, the whole thing approximately twenty feet in length and one foot in diameter, needle-nosed, supersonic in speed, painted white, containing three warheads and many thousand electronic components, and officially designated as Nike.

Guido gasped when he saw the sleek and lethal Nike, and that was the last time at Fort Bliss he had time for a gasp. He was far too busy trying to master enough of radar and rocketry to fire a Nike if the occasion should ever arise. That's all the Army wanted of him. They did not expect him to repair a Nike or build a Nike or adapt a Nike or alter a Nike. All they hoped for was that he could learn what buttons to push and who to yell for if nothing happened. And that, when you are dealing with millions of parts, all frangible, and miles of wire, every inch of it whimsical, and radar, which is a training camp for poltergeists, is quite enough to learn in thirteen weeks.

His skull bulging and his eyeballs eroded, Guido finished the course and went off with his battery to the dismal hills of Red Canyon, New Mexico, to see if he had indeed learned what buttons to push. Here Guido actually fired the Nike. He took a long breath and banged the button and the Nike zoomed up and found the target plane in four seconds and filled the sky with kindling. *"Mamma Mia!"* whispered Guido. *"Carissima mamma mia!"*

There was a happy letter waiting for Guido at Red Canyon. Maggie wrote that she had chosen her teaching job for the autumn, and guess what it was? It was second grade in the Nathan Hale Elementary School in Putnam's Landing! So she would be right in Guido's home town, and wasn't that wonderful?

It was indeed—and doubly wonderful when Guido got his next piece of news: his battery had been assigned to Upper Marlboro, Maryland, which was just outside Washington, which was only five hours by train from Putnam's Landing or an hour and a half by air, which meant that Guido could be in Maggie's arms every single time he had a day off!

On his last day in Red Canyon, while Guido was sacked out

in his bunk thinking jolly thoughts about all the pleasing prospects ahead, the fly entered the ointment. One Clyde Greenhut, an officer in Guido's battery, a large young man with unsightly lumps of muscle all over him and a morbid addiction to athletics, came up to Guido, gave him a jolly whack, and cried, "Hey, di Maggio, let's play some ball!"

"No thanks, Clyde," said Guido pleasantly. "It's too hot out there."

"What? A hundred and ten is hot? Come on!"

"No thanks, Clyde. I really don't feel like it."

"Ah, come on! Who ever heard of anybody named di Maggio who didn't feel like playing ball?"

So, responding to the familiar call, Guido went out to the ball field. In the top of the fourth inning, with Guido playing shortstop, the batter hit a sharp ground ball to the second baseman. There was a runner on first, so Guido dashed over to second to get the double play. The second baseman whipped the ball to Guido. The runner came charging in to break up the throw to first. The runner was Clyde Greenhut. He barrelled into Guido, knocked him into short left field, and divided his ankle into two unmatched pieces.

So Guido went into traction instead of Upper Marlboro. For weeks he lay in his hospital bed and cursed steadily, cheered only slightly by the bubbly letter which arrived every three days from Maggie. She was now in Putnam's Landing, which she loved, and had found a darling apartment, which she adored, and was busy teaching the second grade at Nathan Hale Elementary School, which was composed of the most fetching and cuddlesome little organisms ever begotten.

Glum tidings were awaiting Guido when, all healed, he finally got out of the hospital; his lovely assignment to Upper Marlboro was no longer available. Another officer had replaced him during his confinement. Guido was told to report to area headquarters at Fort Totten, Long Island, where he would receive a new assignment. He took some consolation, however, from the fact that he was allowed to go home for a week's leave before re-porting to Fort Totten.

Guido's family was gathered on the station platform when he arrived in Putnam's Landing. It was a raucous reunion, full of wet kisses and shrill endearments. Then Guido asked about Maggie, and a strange thing happened. The festive mood vanished abruptly. Dead silence descended on the clan. They all avoided Guido's eyes with great care.

Guido looked at his family with perplexity. "Didn't you hear me?" he said. "I asked how Maggie was."

The silence deepened.

Guido turned to his father. "What is it, Pa? What happened to her?"

"I don't know," muttered Vittorio. "Don't aska me."

"Ma——" said Guido.

"I don't wanna talk about her," said his mother.

Guido turned frantically to his brothers and sisters. "For God's sake, what is it? Is she sick or what?"

For a moment nobody answered. Then Bruno spoke. "She ain't sick," he said curtly.

Dominic gave a short nasty laugh. "Don't be so sure," he mumbled.

There was a cab stand at the station platform. Guido wheeled abruptly from his family, raced to the stand, got in a cab and gave the driver Maggie's address. He was there in five minutes. He ran into the building, rang Maggie's bell, pounded on her door, threw it open, and burst into a tiny two-roomed flat.

Maggie was in the kitchenette washing dishes. She uttered a cry of delight, gave her hands a quick wipe, and ran to Guido. "Oh, darling, you've come!" she said exultantly. "I knew you'd stick by me!"

"What?" said Guido, blinking in bewilderment. "Stick by you? What have you done?"

"Only my duty, dear," she replied and kissed him soundly. "Oh, I'm so glad you're here to help me fight this thing!"

Guido took her shoulders and gently disentangled himself. "Maggie baby, I've been on a train from New Mexico for the last four days. Would you mind filling me in?"

"That's right. You couldn't know about it."

"About what?"

"I've been fired from my job."

"Fired? From the school? For what?"

"For trying to let a little light into the darkness!" declared Maggie, lifting a fist. "For trying to clean out the ignorance and sickness of centuries!"

"Could you be a little more specific?"

"I gave," said Maggie, "a talk on sex."

Guido's jaw plopped open. "To the *second grade?*" he whispered in horror.

"Of course."

"*Are you out of your goddam mind?*" shrieked Guido.

Maggie jumped back in alarm.

"Have you gone completely off your rocker?" he roared bearing down on her. "What the hell do second grade kids know about sex?"

"But that's just the point, darling. They don't know anything. Somebody has to tell them. Do you want them to grow up repressed? Traumatized?"

"So you had to go and tell them?"

"Well, they asked me to. One day they came back from recess and asked me where babies came from. I decided the best thing to do was to give them a simple, truthful, straightforward explanation."

"I don't suppose you left out anything?"

"Certainly not."

"All the details, huh?"

"Everything."

Guido clapped a hand on his forehead. "Oh, my back!" he moaned. "Oh, my aching, breaking, cruddy, bloody back!"

"Guido, I don't understand you at all." There was an edge of anger in her tone. "Whose side are you on?"

"Oh, yours, of course!" said Guido with a low bow. "What right-thinking American wouldn't be?"

"Well, I'm glad to hear that anyhow."

"What are you going to do now—go back home?"

"Certainly not!" she said ringingly. "I'm going to stay here and fight for reinstatement."

"That's what I figured," he said morosely.

"Do you think I'm going to let Mr. Vandenberg get away with this?"

"Who?"

"Mr. Vandenberg—the principal. He's the one who found out about my sex lecture."

"Oh, grand! What'd he do—walk in while you were talking?"

"No. As a matter of fact, he didn't come in till after the class. But, of course, the pictures were still on the board."

"*You drew pictures?*" screamed Guido.

"How else do you explain anything to seven-year-old children?" answered Maggie hotly. "And don't you raise your voice to me. I'm beginning to think you're not on my side at all."

"And I'm beginning to think that you're a public menace!" Guido shot back. "Good God! Dirty pictures in the second grade! What's your next project—marijuana?"

"Guido di Maggio," said Maggie, trembling with fury, "you get out of here and never come back again. Never! You're just as ignorant and benighted as the rest of them. Out! Out!"

Guido, seeing his love going glimmering, was suddenly drained of anger. "Now, Maggie honey," he said placatingly.

But she wasn't having any. "Out! Out!" she repeated. "You're not on my side. You never have been, have you?"

"Now, Maggie, let's not be hasty——"

"Of course you haven't. You lied to me. Lied from the beginning! I can see that now. Oh, get out of here, you vile, awful man—and take this with you!"

By "this" she meant her engagement ring, which she now yanked off and slapped into his startled hand.

"Maggie, this is ridiculous——"

"Out! Out!" she screeched, hammering him randomly on the head and shoulders with both fists.

"I'll come back when you're calmer," he said and fled.

He came back, but she got no calmer. Not toward him, at any rate. He was outside her door every day for the seven days of his leave, but not once did she speak to him. She did, however, kick him three times.

Then, lorn and sick at heart, he had to report to Fort Totten, where, as we have seen, the *coup de grâce* was administered by Major Albert R. McEstway, post adjutant, who, unmoved by Guido's tragic circumstances, put him on a shipping list to Fairbanks, Alaska.

And now, a broken man, Guido lay on his sack in the BOQ and contemplated his frigid future. For hours he lay, a lifeless hulk, a mound of anguish. At last he stirred.

"*Che sarà*," he said, forcing a ghastly smile, "*sarà*."

Two

HARRY BANNERMAN stood at the bar in the club car of the 5.29. In his hand was a bourbon and water, his second since leaving Grand Central Station twenty minutes earlier. Harry was not ordinarily a bourbon drinker—scotch was his tipple—but he had discovered that bourbon made him more drunk more quickly. That, in recent months, had become an important consideration.

Harry was a typical commuter of Putnam's Landing, Connecticut, which is to say that he was between thirty-five and forty in age, married, the father of three children, the owner of a house, a first mortgage, a second mortgage, a grey flannel suit, a bald spot, and a vague feeling of discontent.

Though he loved his wife and children, though he enjoyed his house and had hopes of reforesting his bald spot, though he was, all in all, not dissatisfied with his lot, just the same, from time to time, a sort of helpless feeling took hold of him—a feeling that he had no control over the forces that shaped his life, that he was merely a puppet in the hands of some dimly understood power. Namely, his wife.

Make no mistake: he loved her. Grace was handsome, fair, supple, and bright, and he had wanted to marry her the minute he had clapped eyes on her. It had been right after the War. Harry had just been mustered out of the navy and had returned to New York where he had found a job on the "Talk of the Town" section of *The New Yorker*. Grace was an assistant in the same department. When she saw Harry walk in wearing his pre-war civvies, his wrists and ankles sticking out like Huck Finn's, she promptly burst into laughter. But it was warm, friendly laughter, and Harry did not mind a bit. He told her that if she *really* wanted some laughs, she should see him in his tuxedo. So they went to dinner that night, and then they had a lot more dinners and rode in hansom cabs and listened to jazz at Condon's and took trips on the Hudson River Day Line and pressed their noses against Cartier's window and got married.

Harry's idea of married life was simple: you rented an apartment in Greenwich Village and sat on a pouf and listened to Rodgers and Hart records and drank wine from wicker-covered bottles and held each other very tight.

Which is just how it was for the better part of a year. They lived in a high-ceilinged two-roomed apartment on Bank Street with a mattress, a box spring, a corduroy throw, a red and blue pouf, an electric percolator, a hot plate, and a phonograph without a changer. That was the only thing Harry lacked to make his happiness complete—a changer for the phonograph.

Grace's ambitions were rather larger. "Darling," she said to Harry one night, "don't you think people ought to start their families when they're young so they can grow up with their children?"

"Yes, I suppose so," he replied casually, and the next thing he remembered, his son Dan was upon him.

(That was Grace's idea of a conference. She was always coming up to Harry and saying something like "Wouldn't it be nice to have panelling in the basement?" or "Don't you wish we had more closet space?" and he would answer absently "Yeah," or "Uh-huh," and the next time he came home from work the house was teeming with carpenters.)

So now they had their son Dan. He did not do much for the first six months except cry and spill things, including a bottle of cod liver oil on Harry's bed, and if you have never slept on a mattress reeking of cod liver oil, you have never known anguish. But Harry got a new mattress and eventually the boy turned fat and pink and no trouble to anyone.

One night after this satisfactory child had been put to bed and Harry and Grace were curled up on the red and blue pouf, she said to him, "You know, it must be terribly lonely to be an only child. Don't you think so?"

"I guess it is," he replied absently, and before you could say twilight sleep, he was the father of another boy.

After Bud (for that was his name) joined the family, there were no longer enough poufs to go around, so, of course, they had to move to a bigger place. "Why not buy a house in the country?" suggested Grace. "It's just as cheap as paying rent, and it'll be so wonderful for the children."

"Well——" said Harry, and while he was scratching his head, he became the owner of a house on a hill in Putnam's Landing, Connecticut.

For Grace and Putnam's Landing, it was love at first sight. Almost before she was unpacked, she had another baby, bought a large brown dog, joined the PTA, the League of Women Voters, the Women's Club, the Red Cross, the Nurses Aids, the Mental Health Society, and the Town Planning Commission. "How wonderful," she would cry, slinging Dan on one hip and Bud on the other, tucking young Peter under her arm, putting the dog on a leash, and rushing out on errands of mercy, "to live in a town with real community spirit!"

Harry's enthusiasm for Putnam's Landing was kept under somewhat tighter control. He liked the place, mind you. It did have, as Grace said, real community spirit, and the people were interesting—writers, artists, actors, ad. men, TV executives, and other such animated types—and there was a pleasant patina of New England upon the winding lanes and rolling land. But living in Putnam's Landing was a blessing not entirely unmixed. For one thing, it cost more money than Harry was making. For another, it required more hours than there were in a day.

Once, on a dullish afternoon at the office, Harry set down a time-table of a typical day in his life. It looked like this:

6.30 A.M. Rise, shave, shower, breakfast.
7.00   Wake Grace to drive me to station.

7.10	Wake Grace again.
7.16	Grace starts driving me to station.
7.20	Grace scrapes fender on milk truck.
7.30	Arrive station.
7.37	Board train for New York.
8.45	Arrive Grand Central.
9.00	Arrive *New Yorker Magazine*.
5.18 P.M.	Leave *New Yorker Magazine*.
5.29	Board train for Putnam's Landing.
6.32	Arrive Putnam's Landing. Grace waiting at station.
6.51	Traffic jam at station untangles. We start home.
6.52	Grace tells me sump pump broken.
6.56	I ask Grace what is sump pump.
6.57	Grace tells me sump pump is pump that pumps sump.
6.58.	I say "Oh."
7.00	Grace tells me Bud swallowed penny.
7.02	Grace tells me Dan called his teacher an "old poop."
7.04	Grace tells me Peter is allergic to the mailman.
7.06	Grace tells me she signed me up to work all day Saturday in Bingo tent at Women's Club Bazaar.
7.12	Arrive home.
7.13	Dan, aged 8, Bud, aged 6, and Peter, aged 4, looking at television. Dan and Bud want to look at Looney Tunes. Peter wants to look at John Cameron Swayze. (?) Grace rules in favour of Peter. Bud swallows another penny.
7.30	Grace puts children to bed. I go out on lawn to pick up toys.
7.38	Dinner.
8.01	Mrs. Epperson, baby sitter, rings doorbell. I ask Grace what we need with baby sitter. Grace says tonight is PTA meeting. I remind Grace we just went to PTA meeting three days ago. Grace says

that was regular meeting, tonight is special emergency protest meeting. We go to special emergency protest meeting.

8.32	Arrive special emergency protest meeting. Special emergency protest seems to be about a hole in the school playground. Chairman of Board of Education, a conservative Yankee type, says no appropriation in budget for fixing hole. Grace rises and demands special appropriation. Chairman of Board calls this creeping socialism. I doze off.
9.51	Grace jams elbow in my ribs, wakes me to vote on motion to refer hole to Special Committee to Study Hole in Playground. Motion carried.
9.52	Meeting adjourned.
9.53	Grace and I go to Fatso's Diner with O'Sheels and Steinbergs, fellow PTA members. Women discuss hole further. Men yawn.
10.48	Leave Fatso's Diner.
11.25	Arrive home. Grace asks Mrs. Epperson, baby sitter, if everything all right. Mrs. Epperson says Bud woke up once and started crying but she gave him some pennies and he went back to sleep.
11.58	Grace and I go to bed.
12.04	Grace says she hears animals around garbage can. I go out.
12.05	Grace is right. There *are* animals around garbage can. I go back in.
12.53	Animals finish garbage.
1.10	I sleep.

And so passed the days of Harry Bannerman's years. If it wasn't a meeting, a caucus, a rally, or a lecture, then it was a quiet evening at home licking envelopes. Or else it was a party where you ate cubes of cheese on toothpicks and talked about plywood, mortgages, mulches, and children. Or it was amateur theatricals.

Or ringing doorbells for worthy causes. Or umpiring Little League games. Or setting tulip bulbs. Or sticking decals on cribs. Or trimming hedges. Or reading Dr. Spock. Or barbecuing hamburgers. Or increasing your life insurance. Or doing anything in the whole wide world except sitting on a pouf with a soft and loving girl and listening to Rodgers and Hart.

It was more and more on Harry's mind—the pouf, the phonograph records, the long, languorous nights. He would look at Grace in a nubby tweed skirt and a cardigan with the sleeves pushed up, rushing about dispensing civic virtue, wisps of hair coming loose, her seams crooked—and he would remember another Grace in pink velvet lounging pyjamas, curled up like a kitten next to him on the pouf, in one hand a cigarette lazily trailing smoke, the other hand doing talented things to the back of his neck.

He would look at his house—the leaks, the squeaks, the chips, the cracks, the things that had to be repaired, recovered, rewired, replaced, remodelled—and he would recall the days when all you did when something went wrong was phone the landlord.

He would look at his children. He would watch them devouring sides of beef and crates of eggs; poking toes through stockings and elbows through sweaters; littering the yard with balls, bats, bicycles, tricycles, scooters, blocks, crayons, paints, tops, hoops, marbles, bows, arrows, darts, guns, and key bits of jigsaw puzzles; trailing mud on the rugs; breaking off the corners of playing cards; eating watermelon in bed; nailing pictures of athletes to walls; leaving black rings in the tub; getting carsick. He would observe this arresting pageant and he would think, "Yes, they are fine children, they are normal, I love them very much, and I will guard and keep them always . . . But, oh, how sweet and satisfactory those golden days on the pouf!"

Sighing, Harry ordered another bourbon. "You know something?" he said to the bartender. "You know who saved more marriages in Fairfield County than the church, the state, and the psychiatrists all put together?"

"Who?" asked the bartender.

"Pat McGinnis," said Harry.

The bartender looked at him incredulously. "You mean the Pat McGinnis who used to run the New Haven Railroad?"

"Yes, sir," said Harry vehemently. "Oh, I know he ran a godawful railroad. The trains were late and the cars were filthy and the service was miserable. But, by God, he did one thing that every wife in Fairfield County ought to get down on her knees and thank him for every night!"

"What's that?"

"He put club cars in the commuter trains," said Harry. "Do you think us poor slobs could face what's waiting for us at home if we had to get off this train sober?"

"Putnam's Landing!" called the conductor, opening the door of the car. "This stop is Putnam's Landing."

Harry tossed off his bourbon and, less anæsthetised than he would have liked, walked slowly towards the door.

Three

GRACE BANNERMAN had been sitting in her station-wagon
beside the platform for ten minutes before Harry's train arrived.
She always got there ten minutes early; it was her only chance
during the day to enjoy an uninterrupted cigarette. As she had
recently written to her mother, "What with cooking and keeping
the house and shopping and chauffeuring the children all over
town and trying to stay abreast of current affairs and going to
meetings and helping out at the Red Cross, the hospital, the
school cafeteria, etc., it seems as though I just don't have a
second to myself any more. I'm beginning to wonder if I
shouldn't cut down a little."

"*NO!*" her mother had written back in underlined capitals.
"Don't you cut down one tiny bit! Just remember that we
women have to make a life of our own, because men are only
interested in *ONE THING!*"

Grace had laughed at first, but now she was beginning to
wonder whether there might not be a trace of truth in her
mother's contention. Harry was, of course, interested in many
other things besides sex (they did not, for the moment, leap to
mind) but it had to be admitted that his advances were as hot and
importunate as ever. In fact, they seemed to be coming these
days even when circumstances were most unpropitious—like
when there was a turkey to baste or a meeting to attend or a child
in the tub.

Grace did not, mind you, find Harry's attentions a cause for
complaint. She was a smart girl—smart in her slim, mature good
looks and smart in her head—and she recognised that after ten
years of marriage, ardour in a husband was no small tribute.
Moreover, when there were no turkeys to baste or meetings to

attend or children to bathe, she had a good strong honing for
Harry too. She was a woman of robust appetites, responsive and
inventive, and she loved her husband very much.

But everything in its place. Love to Grace was not something
that had constantly to be demonstrated. Love was basic, that is,
it was the base, the foundation. As such, it had to be firmly
established. But once established, as Grace's and Harry's was, it
could thereafter be safely ignored. It required no further fussing,
tending, or bolstering. The time had come to turn the attention
away from love and concentrate instead on love's accretions—
the children, the home, the community.

Grace had often developed these views to Harry, and though
he had not argued, he had yawned rather a lot. But Grace had
not been dismayed. She knew there was nothing fundamentally
wrong with Harry; he was just a little slow to mature, that's
all.

As the years flew by and maturity continued to elude Harry,
Grace was still undismayed. Annoyed—yes. Piqued, vexed,
chagrined, furious, rabid, homicidal—yes. But not dismayed.
"He *will* grow up," she kept telling herself. He is a good man, an
intelligent man, and some day soon he is bound to realise that he
is no longer Childe Harold, nor I Pola Negri; that it is just as
important to know the annual budget of the school board as the
lyrics to *My Funny Valentine*; that making love on a pouf gives
you a very sore back.

"And when maturity overtakes him at last, when that blessed
day comes, we will be husband and wife again, just as we were in
the early days. We will recover the togetherness that has been
so long, so painfully, missing. . . . Yes, I have been unhappy.
Too often I have seen the stamp of boredom on Harry's face—
at meetings, at parties, even at home—and my heart has grown
heavy. Why, I have wondered, can't he enjoy the same things I
do? Have I made a mistake? Have I pushed Harry into a kind
of life that is wrong for him?

"But how can that be? How can anything be wrong which is

so solid, so basic, so full of real, lasting values? Can good, healthy, happy children be wrong? Can a fine, well-kept house be wrong? Can an alert, enlightened community be wrong?

"No, of course not. All these things are right. The fault is in Harry, and time will cure it.

"He will grow up. He will lose the silly, romantic notions that still plague him. He is sad now because he thinks youth and adventure and love have gone out of his life. How foolish he is! His youth still lives in his children. Adventure—*great* adventure —can still be found in building a better community, a better world. And love—doesn't he understand that he has more love now than he ever dreamed of? My love! The children's love! The love of the community, if he will only make an effort to earn it!

"He will grow up, my darling Harry, because he is good and kind and intelligent. Meanwhile, I will be patient. I will continue to love him, continue to expose him to the true, the important, the abiding things—home, family, community. I have led my horse to water; he will drink."

Grace's horse, having drunk six ounces of I. W. Harper, cantered slowly off the train, spotted his 1954 Plymouth station-wagon alongside the platform, whinnied softly, and headed towards it with a hobbled gait. Grace, watching him from behind the wheel, was filled with a sudden surge of affection and pity. How bedraggled he looked! How glassy! How brackish! How unloved! "Hello, darling!" she cried as he stepped into the car. "Hello, sweetie-face!" she cried and threw her arms around him and gave him a long, lush, passionate kiss.

"Well!" said Harry, registering surprise and delight.

"I missed you," said Grace, nuzzling his cheek.

"Well!" said Harry again.

Grace started the car and joined the traffic moving sluggishly out of the station parking lot. She took Harry's hand, squeezed it lovingly. "Did you have a good day, honey?" she asked.

"Fair," he replied, removing his hand, suddenly wary. "Is there something on your mind, Grace?"

"Not a thing," she said. Then, suddenly, she corrected herself. "Yes!" she exclaimed. "Yes, there *is* something on my mind and I just thought of it this minute. . . . Harry, how would you like to go away for a couple of days—just the two of us?"

His face lit up like a sunburst. "Great idea! Great! Let's leave right away. You get a sitter. I'll call Sig Harris to take over for me tomorrow. We'll start driving about seven-thirty, go over the Bear Mountain Bridge to the Catskills, check into the Concord Hotel, then tomorrow morning we'll have one of those wonderful Concord breakfasts, and then——"

"Oh, no, darling," she interrupted. "We can't leave tonight."

"Why not?"

"You know why not. There's a town meeting."

"Let's skip it."

"I wish we could, dear, but tonight we're voting on the garbage disposal plant. '

"Oh, for Christ's sake!" snarled Harry. "I talk about the Concord, and you talk about garbage!"

"I'm sorry, dear, but it's terribly important. Betty O'Sheel has been slaving for months on this project, and she needs every vote she can get."

"We'll give her our proxies."

"You can't do that, Harry. And, besides, I have to be there tonight. I'm speaking for the Committee to Reinstate Maggie Larkin."

"Who?"

"That school teacher who got fired for giving a sex talk to the second grade."

"Well, I should think so!" he said indignantly.

"Now, darling, don't be medieval."

"Okay," he sighed. "So we can't leave tonight. How about tomorrow morning?"

"Fine!" said Grace.

"Tell you what," said Harry, cheerful again. "We'll get to the Concord around noon, have one of those wonderful Concord lunches, then spend the afternoon ski-ing, and then have one of those wonderful Concord dinners. How's that sound?"

"Oh-oh!" said Grace.

"What's the matter?"

"I just remembered. Tomorrow I'm in the Bloodmobile."

"The *what*?"

"The Red Cross mobile blood unit. I can't very well skip that, can I?"

Harry sighed once more. "I guess not. . . . How about Saturday?"

She looked at him with utter horror. "You're not serious?" she whispered.

"Huh? What'd I do?"

"Are you trying to tell me you don't know what Saturday is?"

"No. What?"

"Only your son's birthday, that's all!"

"Which one?"

"Oh, Harry, you're awful! Just awful!"

"Which one?" he insisted. "I've got a right to know."

"It's Bud's—and I'm thoroughly ashamed of you!"

"Okay, I'm a no good rat. . . . What about Sunday?"

"Sunday's the birthday party."

"But you said his birthday was Saturday."

"I know, but Dickie Sutphen and Billy Nye have a dancing lesson Saturday, so we decided not to have the party till Sunday."

"I see," said Harry tonelessly. "Now tell me why we can't go on Monday."

"Oh, Harry, you know Peter's getting his bite-plate fitted on Monday."

"Listen," said Harry, his voice rising several decibels, "I want to ask you just one question. Since you know we're never going to get away, why the hell did you bring up the idea in the first place?"

Stung by Harry's tone, Grace wheeled and replied in kind. "I'll tell you why: because you looked so mangy and pathetic coming off the train that I felt sorry for you."

"I see," said Harry through tight lips. "Throw the poor dog a bone."

"Exactly!" snapped Grace.

They drove for a while in silence, each stoking his anger. Grace opened up first. "And I'm getting damn good and sick of it!"

"Of what?"

"Of you staggering off that train drunk every night. Don't think I don't know why you do it. It's because you can't face what's waiting for you at home. . . . Well, the hell with you, Harry Bannerman!"

"Thank you!"

"What are those terrible, dreadful things you can't face?" she demanded. There were tears in her eyes, and her voice was quavering. "What evil, awful things are waiting for you at home? Three beautiful, bright, sweet, good children. A house that's clean and comfortable and snug and homey. A fine lawn. A wonderful garden. . . . And a wife—" she was sobbing now— "a wife who tries her best to take care of you and the house and the children, who tries her very, very best!"

Weeping openly, copiously, piteously, she sprawled across the steering wheel, her eyes blind with tears, her body racked. "Oh, God, what more can I do?" she wailed, pounding the wheel with both fists. "In Heaven's name, what more can I do?"

"You can pull over to the kerb," suggested Harry, "before you get us both killed."

She headed the car into the kerb and cut the ignition. Turning away from Harry, she collapsed in the corner of the seat, tears flowing undiminished, shoulders heaving erratically.

Harry looked on for a moment, troubled and indecisive. Tears were not Grace's weapon. He had seldom seen her cry, except during pregnancy, but then, as everyone knows, all women are unhinged. "Honey," he said, putting a gentle hand on her shoulder. "Honey, please."

Angrily she shrugged off his touch.

He tried again, more firmly this time. He gripped her arms and turned her around. Murmuring softly, he laid her face on his shoulder, kissed her hair, her brow, her salty cheek. "Don't cry, darling. Don't cry, sweetheart," he said over and over.

The tears ebbed. The shoulders were still. "I'm sorry," she said.

"It's all right." He smiled, then kissed her tenderly on the lips. "I love you," he said quietly.

"And I love you," she answered. "That's what's so frustrating. Why can't I make you happy?"

"I'm happy. Honest!"

"No," she insisted. "Not until you grow up."

"That again."

"Yes, that again. You've got to get rid of those romantic fancies of yours."

"Why?"

"Because you and I, let's face it, are not newly-weds any more."

"I see. We're decrepit. It's impossible that romance would still dwell in a couple of old wrecks like us."

Grace grinned. "It dwells," she said. "But not on the main floor. Up in the back bedroom maybe."

"No, sir," said Harry with a vehement shake of his head. "I'm not ready for the pipe and slippers yet. I'm a young man, still full of fire!"

"Fireball," said Grace, taking his hands in hers, "I love you. Right now, full of booze and nonsense as you are, I love you so much I can hardly stand it. You're a romantic idiot and I love you for it. But I love you for other things—important things, like being chairman of the hospital fund drive last year, like building that bookshelf in the den, like teaching Dan how to ride his bike."

"Bookshelves and bikes!" he said bitterly. "The story of my life."

"I'll tell you a much sadder story," said Grace. "No bookshelves and no bikes. Just emptiness."

"Emptiness? When two people have each other?"

"But that's only a beginning," Grace said. "What do you think love is—a sensitive plant you must nurture and protect all your life? Well, it isn't. Not our kind. Ours is a rock to build on."

"Yeah, and we've built all over it," he complained. "We can't even see it any more."

"It's there. If it wasn't, everything would come tumbling down." She looked at him searchingly. "Don't you understand that?"

"Well——"

"Don't you?"

"Yes, Grace, I understand it. Believe it or not, I understand everything you say. I always have. . . . But there's something *you* don't understand. For me, romance has not retired to a back bedroom. It's still in the front parlour and wide awake!"

"I'll remember," said Grace.

"See that you do."

"Yes, sir."

"Now kiss me."

"Yes, *sir*!"

She put up her lips, and he gave her a businesslike kiss, then worked his way across her cheek and under her ear. "We don't really have to go to that town meeting tonight, do we?" he whispered, munching on her lobe.

"Good Lord, we're going to be late!" she cried. She pushed him away, started the car, and zoomed out from the kerb.

"How about next weekend?" asked Harry.

"For what?"

"For the Concord Hotel—just the two of us?"

"Oh, sweetie, we can't next weekend."

"Why not?"

"The Randrigoraths are coming."

"I beg your pardon?"

"Don't you remember? It's United Nations week. We invited that Hindu couple to stay with us."

"Perhaps we could double-date," said Harry with a thin smile.

"Oh, Harry, you're a scream."

"I'm a regular Joe Penner."

She reached over and squeezed his hand. "Don't worry, darling. We'll go away soon. I promise."

"When?" he asked. "After the children get married?"

"That reminds me! I've got to pick up the sitter for tonight. Where's Nutmeg Lane?"

"First corner past the light. But that's not where Mrs. Epperson lives."

"I know. It's a new sitter. And much better."

"Who?"

"Maggie Larkin."

"The sex fiend?" asked Harry.

"Oh, stop it."

"You know," he said thoughtfully, "I might stay home myself tonight. This Larkin girl sounds pretty interesting."

Grace gave him the back of her hand smartly across the navel. "You just stow that kind of talk, mister," she warned.

"I'm only fooling," Harry said, stroking her nylon knee. "I don't want anybody but you."

"You better not," she said menacingly.

"I really don't," he assured her. "I don't want anybody but you. And some day—some day when we don't have to go to a meeting or a rally or a lecture or a caucus—some day when the lawn doesn't need cutting and the trash doesn't need burning and the hinges don't need oiling and the stairs don't need runners and the faucets don't need washers and the weatherstrips don't need tightening and the drawers don't need loosening and the children don't need bite-plates—some day, Grace, some day, mark my words, I'll get you yet!"

Four

COMFORT GOODFAOTURE oat at her deck in her father'o otudy with her homework in front of her. She was a large girl of sixteen years with creamy haunches and a fast-rising bosom. Occasionally one of her male colleagues at Webster High School, made reckless by desire, would undertake to lay hands on those haunches or that bosom. For his pains he would receive a clout that sometimes required stitches. Comfort, no matter how she jiggled and jutted, was still unawakened.

She opened her textbook in geometry, found a clean sheet of paper, uncapped her pen, furrowed her alabaster brow, and began to write. "Dear Elvis," she wrote. "Well, I suppose you are wondering what happened at the last meeting. Elvis, it was the most! Betty Ann Steinberg had this absolute gasser of an idea. Instead of playing the whole album like we always do, we only played one song—*Hound Dog*, of course. We played it 38 times and I'm here to tell you everybody went ape! I mean it was Wigsville, USA, till my father came in and tore the arm off the phonograph. Man, was he p.o.'d! Well, afterwards something happened that was so beautiful that I still get misty when I think about it. This girl Gloria Coleman was at the meeting. I never wrote you about her before because this is the first meeting she ever came to. She hasn't been a bit well. She ran into this lobster pot when she was water ski-ing last summer, and she had to have bone grafts and everything. She's all right now, but she sure is a changed person. I mean, before her tragedy she was always hacking around and yocking up a storm, but now she's very quiet and spiritual if you know what I mean. Well, anyhow, she said she wrote this poem which she wanted to read. Of course, everybody groaned and pretended they were shutting their ears, but she read it anyhow and, Elvis, I'm here to tell you when she finished, there wasn't a dry eye in the house. So we passed a resolution for me to send you the poem which hereinafter follows:

> *I dreamt I saw James Dean last night*
> *A-sitting lonely on a cloud,*
> *And I said, 'What are you doing?'*
> *And he said, 'I watch the crowd.*
>
> *'When I see them digging Elvis,*
> *When I hear that rocking strain,*
> *When I feel that rolling rhythm,*
> *I know my life was not in vain.'*

Well, Elvis, I know how you must feel after reading this, so I will close now. The girl who wrote the poem's name is Gloria Coleman, and it would be very nice if your agent could send her a little note or something, because when a person has had bone grafts they can always use a little cheering up. I will write you again after our next meeting, and meanwhile the girls all join in wishing you many more golden platters, and may the Big Fellow in the Sky continue to watch over you and your meteoric career.

Your Fan,

Comfort Goodpasture"

She addressed the letter, put it away, and turned with a martyr's groan to her geometry book. At the end of a half-hour, with Pythagoras holding a commanding lead, the uneven match was interrupted by the entrance of her father. "Hi, Daddy-O," she said, looking up at him in an unfrightened manner.

Comfort was not intimidated by Isaac Goodpasture, but there were plenty who were. Isaac was a long, dark, craggy Yankee with eyebrows like hanging gardens. He had an abrasive wit and a place to exercise it: he was editor and owner of the *Putnam's Landing Gazette*, a weekly newspaper which had belonged to his family since 1834.

Isaac and Comfort lived in a tiny, tidy pre-Revolutionary clapboard house, located unfashionably near the centre of town. There were just the two of them. Comfort, an only child, had been left motherless when she was twelve, and it had fallen to Isaac to guide her through puberty. He had, in his opinion, done a reasonably good job. True, her speech was an execrable mish-mash of teen-age patois, and the clothes she wore were sometimes grounds for arrest, and her marks in school took no prizes, and she thought Elvis Presley shaded Abe Lincoln as the greatest American of all time—but, on the other hand, he had success-fully kept her out of the white slave trade. And that, in this rock-and-roll era, he regarded as no minor achievement.

He stood now in his study and looked down at Comfort, in-congruously pink and voluptuous behind his austere Early American desk. "Good evening, Comfort," he said.

"Daddy-O," she said, pointing at her geometry text, "I don't dig this Pythagoras cat."

"Try a little harder," said he. "But try up in your own room, will you please? I need the study. Some people are coming in."

"All rootie," she said agreeably. She picked up her book and papers and, humming the largo from *Hound Dog*, she started out of the study.

"Comfort!" he called sharply.

"Yeah?"

"Must you walk like that?"

"Like what?"

"Like *that*!"

"But, Daddy-O, that's the way I walk," she said innocently.

"*Nobody* walks that way," he declared. "Or, at least, nobody did until Marilyn Monroe invented it."

"Gee, I can't help the way I walk."

"Yes, you can—and, as a matter of public safety, you better had," he said grimly.

Comfort broke into a delighted giggle. She came back to

Isaac and planted an affectionate kiss on his cheek. "Daddy-O," she said, "you're square as a bear, but I dig you the most."

"I appreciate that," he said drily. "Now get upstairs and do your homework. . . . And do it right. One more report card like the last one, and I'm putting you to work in the steam laundry."

"Har-de-har-har," said Comfort, vastly amused.

"This is no laughing matter, my girl. You're going to start tending to business and stop running around with those hot-rod Romeos. What in the world do you do with those boys anyhow?"

"I cope," she replied.

"Successfully, one hopes?"

"Are you kiddin'?" she snorted derisively. "Why, those little twerps at Webster—I can handle 'em with my pinkie!"

"For this relief much thanks," he murmured.

She giggled again. "You stone me," she said fondly. "I mean you drive me ape."

She gave him another kiss and went to her room. Isaac watched pensively as she ascended the stairs. "If she gets any rounder," he thought, "I will have to post guards."

Nature had been more than ordinarily whimsical to give a daughter like Comfort to Isaac. He was everything she was not —bony, dry, tough, unfrivolous. He had only one passion—the preservation of the *status quo*. In the *Putnam's Landing Gazette* he stood foursquare and fearless against change of any kind. Each week, as the Yankees nodded approval and the commuters had conniption fits, he wielded his editorial axe against new schools, new roads, new sewers, new parks, and other such, as he had once called them, "toboggans into the murky valley of deficit financing."

Now, as Comfort sat upstairs making feckless lunges at Pythagoras, Isaac, in his study, broke out a bottle of blended whisky and a box of dime cigars. A few visitors were coming to help him shore up the *status quo*. Tonight was town meeting night in Putnam's Landing, and Isaac was holding his usual small caucus at home before the meeting.

The town meetings of New England, Isaac would agree in principle, were an excellent thing. Every voter could attend, could rise and could be heard, could cast his ballot. It was democracy in the grand old Yankee tradition.

But—and here, for Isaac, was the heart of the matter—it was a tradition that could work *only* for Yankees. Or, at any rate, only for adherents to the Yankee financial philosophy. Isaac had no prejudices of a religious or racial nature. When, for example, the Italians moved into Putnam's Landing and he saw that underneath their swarthy volatility they had a healthy respect for the dollar, both private and public, Isaac was well pleased to have them. But the commuters were something else again. In this instance, too, he had no objections on grounds of prejudice; it made no difference that so many of them were Jews, copywriters, Barnard alumnæ, vodka drinkers, dextrose eaters, Kafka readers, Democrats, and other such exotics. But what he found utterly and totally unconscionable was that these people earned an average of ten to twenty thousand dollars a year and *failed to live on it*!

And, instead of decently hiding their shame at home, they came pouring into the town meeting each month to make fervent speeches for more schools, more parks, more traffic lights, more everything—precisely the same kind of lunatic over-extension they practised in their homes!

It was to save Putnam's Landing from these fiscal idiots that Isaac held his caucus before every town meeting. He called together a few prominent citizens, Yankees all, men of his own sober political persuasions, and together they laid plans to meet the menace of the commuters.

The members of the caucus arrived promptly at eight. They took seats in the study, accepted White Owls and one and a quarter ounce shots of Three Feathers. (In point of fact, two of them did not smoke or drink, but as a matter of principle they never turned down anything free.) There were five of them in all. Reading from left to right, they were, first, George Melvin, a rosy, plausible real estate dealer who had got rich selling housing sites to commuters. George's success was largely attributable to one fact: he had mastered the art of nomenclature. When, for instance, he bought the swamp behind the old Penniman place, he named it "Powderhorn Hill" and sold it off in a twinkling. Forty acres of salt meadow south of the tracks were re-christened "Flintlock Ridge" and sold with equal dispatch. Perhaps his boldest stroke was "Upper Meadow"—formerly a gravel pit. No pangs of conscience disturbed George's peace. Maybe his customers' cellars did leak a bit, but, by golly, when a fellow has been living, say, on 68th Street, it sure made him feel mighty proud when he could call his friends and say, "How'd you like to run up to Flintlock Ridge this weekend?"

Next was Waldo Pike, a direct beneficiary of the leaky cellars spawned by George Melvin. Waldo owned the local hardware store and did a booming business in wall sealers. And when, after hideous expense, the cellars were finally snug and dry, Waldo promptly persuaded the homesteaders to fill them with work benches, power saws, jigs, lathes, drills, sanders, and a huge gleaming variety of tools. This took no great persuasion, for, as Waldo gleefully knew, the average commuter was queer for tools. After dealing exclusively with abstractions from Monday to Friday at CBS, BBD&O, or Doubleday, he felt a frantic compulsion to restore the balance by working with his hands on weekends.

Which redounded directly to the enrichment of the third member of Isaac's caucus, Dr. Emmett Magruder, who could always count on a brisk trade with needle and suture on Saturdays and Sundays. And, to his great surprise, he was busy all the rest of the week too. Doc, now nearing seventy, had received his M.D. from a Boston diploma mill in 1909 and had successfully avoided learning any medicine since. The Yankees of Putnam's Landing knew the extent of Doc's training and never troubled him with anything a talented Boy Scout could not fix. But the commuters flocked to his office in droves. After New York with its high-pressure doctors and their high-gloss equipment, they found it downright refreshing to come to a twinkly old man in a creaky old swivel-chair. Like a Norman Rockwell painting it was good; simple; *American*! They were further gratified to learn that Doc was not given to glib diagnoses. Unlike his arrogant Manhattan colleagues who would never admit themselves at a loss, Doc would more often than not make a frank, cheerful confession that he hadn't a clue as to what ailed them, but whatever it was, it would probably go away. "What a fine, honest old gent!" they would say about him later, those who lived.

The fourth member of the caucus was Minton Evans, landscaper, from whom never was heard a discouraging word. Was Minton called to make a lawn where soil was too sandy? Too silty? Too sour? Did the land lie in the path of every spring freshet? Was the sun blocked off from seven a.m. to nightfall? Were the moles holding a track meet underneath? Was the forest nibbling on the edges? . . . Well, never mind. Minton would do the job, no matter how much muscle, manure, and money were required. And when the job had to be done again, Minton was available again. And again. And again. "One good thing about Minton," the commuters told each other. "You can always get him."

Manning Thaw completed the caucus. Manning was the first selectman of Putnam's Landing. The office was equivalent to mayor, and, in fact, Manning had long wanted the name changed officially to mayor. But George Melvin, the expert on nomenclature, had argued strenuously that "first selectman" had just the kind of quaint, cottage-cheesy quality that kept New Yorkers moving to Putnam's Landing, and so the name was retained.

Manning was a drab, sallow little man, sixty years old and precisely five feet tall. He was about as unlike a politician as a politician can be. He shook no hands, clapped no backs, kissed no babies, granted no interviews, made no public speeches. No private speeches either; he was as thrifty with words as with money, and that was thrifty indeed. On his selectman's salary of $4,200 a year, he supported himself, kept an aged mother in St. Petersburg, operated a 1951 Chevrolet, gave a tithe to the Congregational Church, paid his taxes, and bought three shares of AT&T each year. He was a bachelor and lived in a furnished room over Da Costa's drug store. His *objets d'art* were two—a framed sampler over his bed which said:

> MAKE IT DO,
> WEAR IT OUT,
> USE IT UP,
> DO WITHOUT.

and a framed sampler over his desk at Town Hall which said the same thing.

Isaac Goodpasture, having fulfilled his obligations as host, capped the Three Feathers, closed the White Owls, and began the business of the evening. "Boys," he said to all assembled, "we've had some tough town meetings before, but tonight's is going to be a bitch-kitty. First of all, that demented O'Sheel woman is coming in with a recommendation for a garbage disposal plant. She says we can't keep dumping in Haskins Hollow and covering it with gravel."

"Why the hell not?" demanded Minton Evans, the landscaper, who sold the town five yards of gravel each day to cover the garbage.

"Why, it's a wonderful system," declared George Melvin, the real estate dealer, who had an option to buy Haskins Hollow once it was filled and covered.

"And very sanitary," added Doc Magruder, who had three inbred cousins, otherwise unemployable, who were now on salary as custodians of the dump.

"You don't have to convince *me*," said Isaac. "I don't want to throw away a half million dollars on a garbage disposal plant. But the O'Sheel woman is coming in loaded for bear this time. She's got some brand-new gimmick, and she's also got a lot of people on her side. We better think of something."

Manning Thaw had been silent to this moment. Now he said two words: "Forget it."

They all turned and looked at him askance. "*Forget* it?" said Isaac incredulously. "Manning, I tell you she might have the votes to push it through."

"Forget it," repeated Manning.

Isaac looked at him narrowly. "Manning, do you know something we don't?"

"Yup," said Manning.

"You going to tell us?"

"Nope."

"Why not?"

" 'Cause it's a long story, and I got to tell it at the town meetin'. No sense tellin' it twice."

"I see. But we're not to worry about the garbage disposal plant?" Isaac pressed him.

"Nope."

"All right," said Isaac. "If you say so. . . . Now here's item number two: another wild woman with a mission. Laura Beauchamp wants the town to sponsor a folk-drama on the Fourth of July."

"What in tarnation is a folk-drama?" asked Doc.

"Nothing small," Isaac replied. "It's a historical pageant. This one will have a cast of a hundred people."

"Doing what?" asked Minton.

"Re-enacting the landing of the British on Ram's Head Beach in 1778," said Isaac. "And, believe me, the original British landing was a good deal cheaper. She's asking for fifty Redcoat uniforms, fifty Minute-men costumes, a hundred muskets, a hundred sabres, three longboats, two field pieces, and God knows what else will pop into her feeble mind!"

"Forget it," said Manning.

"This too?" asked Isaac.

"Yup."

Isaac gave him a close scrutiny. "You're sure?"

"Yup."

"Positive?" asked Isaac.

"I *said*, didn't I?" snapped Manning.

"All right, Manning. On to the next item. Still another one of our busy young matrons—Grace Bannerman—is making a motion to re-instate that teacher who taught the second grade how to copulate."

"Anybody supporting this motion?" asked Minton incredulously.

"Every so-called enlightened housewife in town," Isaac answered. "They've been ringing doorbells, writing leaflets, passing petitions, making speeches, all week long."

"Forget it," said Manning.

"All right, Manning," said Isaac firmly. "What's this big secret of yours?"

The others crowded around the first selectman.

"Yeah, Manning, what's up?"

"What's been going on?"

"What makes you so cocky?"

Manning rose. "Possess your souls in patience," he said primly. "Come on, time to get to meetin'."

He started out with the others close behind him, wagging their heads in bewilderment. As they passed the staircase, Isaac stopped suddenly. "Go ahead, boys," he said to his cohorts. "I'll meet you outside."

When they had gone, Isaac shouted up the stairs: "Comfort!"

"Yes, Daddy-O?"

"I'm going to town meeting now."

"That ought to be yells."

"Do your homework, do you hear?"

"Yes, Daddy-O."

"And don't go running around."

"I dig you, Daddy-O."

"Good night."

"Crazy, man!"

Wincing, Isaac went out to join his friends.

"The square on the hypotenuse of a right triangle is equal to the gizmo on the rillera of my blue suede shoes," said Comfort and flung her geometry text peevishly into a corner.

"Dullsville," said Comfort, lying on her back and regarding her toes. "Everything dullsville. Geometry. Town meetings. Her dad. Her toes. Everything."

Suddenly from beneath her window there came a roar of dual exhausts, a screech of brakes, the blast of a klaxon. "Oh, *no*!" she groaned. "Not *him* again!"

She looked out of the window. At the kerb behind the wheel of a make-it-yourself automobile sat Grady Metcalf, the leading juvenile delinquent of Putnam's Landing. (The term "juvenile delinquent" is here used loosely. Grady was not the lean, hard, Sal Mineo type. He was more on the well-fed, spongy side. The tenement that spawned him was a $40,000 ranch house on two well-kept acres. Grady was a member of the new school of juvenile delinquency, the You Too Can Be A Rebel School. The head masters were Elvis Presley and the spook of Jimmy Dean, and the entrance requirements were completely democratic. A boy was no longer excluded from the glamorous ranks of the delinquents simply because he had had the rotten luck not to be born in a slum; all he had to do was *look* as though he had. If he would wear his hair in a duck-tail cut and his sideburns at nostril level, forsake grammar, dress in black khaki trousers with the cuffs narrowed to fourteen inches, never do his homework, and spit a lot, his origins, no matter how respectable, would not be held against him.)

"Go away!" said Comfort, leaning out her window. Of all the gropers at Webster High, this one was far and away the stickiest. Only last week she had given him a fat ear, and here he was again! "Go away!" she repeated.

Unheeding, Grady stepped out of his hot-rod. He took out a cigarette, struck a kitchen match on his thumbnail, lit the cigarette, tilted his pelvis, half-lowered his eyelids, hooked his thumbs in his wide, studded belt, and expressed some saliva. "Whaddya say, hey?" he said to Comfort. "Let's do some cruisin'."

"I've got homework," she said.

"Homework's for squares. Come on, we'll have a few chuckles."

"Chuckles with *you*?" she hooted. "Oh, flake off, little man!"

"You're fighting me," he said reproachfully.

"You are a ninety-handed idiot," said Comfort, "and I hate you like death!"

"No, you don't," he said positively. "I figured it out, see? I drive you ape, and you just don't trust yourself with me, that's what it is."

"Har-de-har-har!" replied Comfort.

"And I'll tell you somethin' else," he continued. "In exactly three months, you and I are gonna be goin' steady."

"Man, *what* are you smoking?"

"It's a fact, hey. No doubt about it. Because in exactly three months, I'm gettin' somethin' that's gotta swing it."

"Plastic surgery?" asked Comfort.

"A motor-cycle," said Grady.

"Hm!" said she thoughtfully. This *did* put rather a new aspect on the situation. "Why do you have to wait three months?" she asked.

" 'Cause it'll be my eighteenth birthday, and the fossils promised to buy me a Harley if I pass math."

"Then you're dead," she said flatly. "I've been knocking myself out all night with this Pythagoras cat, and I'm nowhere."

"Maybe if we kind of helped each other?" suggested Grady.

"Well, maybe," she allowed. "Come on in."

"No, you come out. We can cruise while we're studyin'—maybe get a hamburger or like that."

Comfort sighed. So it was going to be another evening of groping. . . . Oh, well, what did it matter? She'd have no trouble handling this busy little man, and anything was better than laying around this dullsville house all by herself.

"I'll be right down," she said.

Five

SOME said it was metal fatigue, some said it was electrical failure, and some said it was plain old-fashioned pilot error. But all anybody knew for sure was that in four widely separated areas of the world—Utah, West Germany, Okinawa, and Natal—four U.S. Air Force C-124 transport airplanes had crashed within a single week.

The Air Force began an immediate investigation. Pending the results, orders went out grounding all C-124s everywhere. One C-124, bound from Mitchel Field to Fairbanks, Alaska, was actually in the air when the grounding orders came through. The pilot made a 180 degree turn, headed back to Mitchel, landed, taxied to the hangar, and out came a passenger named Guido di Maggio, smiling the profound smile of the reprieved.

"It's the hand of God!" cried Guido thirty minutes later as he rushed into the office of Major Albert R. McEstway, post adjutant at Fort Totten. "It's what I keep telling you: I am not meant to go to Alaska. Sir, if you send me now, you're flying in the face of Providence!"

"I'll risk it," said the Major.

"Sir, look at me," said Guido earnestly. "Have I got a pleasing personality? Am I bright? Alert? Agreeable?"

"You are all of those," allowed the Major, "and persevering into the bargain."

"Right! So why don't you send me to New York? Boston? Washington? Are you going to waste officer material like me on the frozen tundra?"

"That I am," said the Major comfortably.

"Sir——"

"There will be another plane any day now, and you will be on it."

"Sir——"

"Good night, Lieutenant."

"Okay, I'll leave," pouted Guido. "But don't expect a salute."

He left the adjutant and went to the nearest phone booth. He called Maggie Larkin in Putnam's Landing. This was a rite he had been performing twice daily since his arrival at Fort Totten, and always with the same outcome; when Maggie heard his voice she slammed down the phone. Tonight, however, was different: as Maggie was out baby-sitting at the Bannermans', Guido got no answer at all.

Muttering ripe expletives, Guido stomped over to the Officers' Club. Seething with frustration and rage, he stormed into the bar-room. It was deserted except for the bartender and a solitary captain, hunched over a highball at the end of the bar. Guido had never laid eyes on the Captain before; nonetheless, he strode directly over to him and said, without preliminary, "Let's get one thing straight, Captain. I'm in no mood for any conversation tonight. Okay?"

"Suits me," said the Captain, regarding Guido incuriously. The Captain was a large, muscular man of forty. His chest was decorated with three banks of combat ribbons of Korea and the World War. His hair was cropped, his neck was thick, his jaw was strong, his eyes were pale blue and glittered like two bits of ice.

"No offence, see?" said Guido, his tone softening a little. "I mean, it's nothing personal. It's just there's things on my mind."

"Okay." The Captain turned back to his drink.

"My name's Guido di Maggio," said Guido.

The Captain sat motionless over his drink for a moment, then turned back to Guido. "I'm Walker Hoxie," he said.

Guido extended his hand. Walker Hoxie considered it

briefly, then decided to shake it. This done, he turned back to his drink.

"You're new here, aren't you?" asked Guido.

Walker Hoxie sighed. He turned back to Guido. "Lieutenant," he said softly, "I'm glad you don't want any conversation tonight, because I don't want any either."

"Well, that simplifies things, doesn't it?" said Guido, flashing Walker Hoxie a winsome smile. No smile was forthcoming in return. Guido looked at Walker Hoxie's flat, hard face, his corded neck, his bulging sleeves, his big, blunt hands, his battle ribbons. Guido felt a small chill. "See you," he said hastily and retreated to a stool at the other end of the bar.

He ordered a rye and ginger ale. As he drank, he stole a glance at Walker Hoxie sitting motionless over his glass, his head down, his shoulders sloping inward, looking as hard and sharp and lethal as a projectile. Guido suppressed a shudder. "Boy," he said to himself, "there is one guy I am never going to get mixed up with!"

Somebody Up There chuckled.

Six

THE four clocks on the wall of Oscar Hoffa's office said, respectively, 7.01, 6.01, 5.01, and 4.01, indicating the time in the Eastern, Central, Mountain, and Pacific zones, and indicating also that Oscar was a television executive of the first magnitude. Lesser executives had to get along with only one clock; it is said, in fact, that on poorer networks, they sometimes had to share a clock between two of them.

Ignoring all four clocks, Oscar shot back his cuff, looked at his wrist-watch, and punched a button on his desk. Instantly a thirty-one inch television screen on the wall across from him flickered into life. A rocket ship swooshed across the screen. The sparks from the exhaust arranged themselves into flaming letters that spelled: THE ADVENTURES OF CRUNCH CRANDALL—SPACEMAN!

Never taking his eyes off the screen, Oscar snatched open the lid of a mahogany cigar box. His hand swooped in, seized an Upmann Monarch like an eagle seizing a lamb, carried it to his mouth. His teeth closed like a trap, ripping a ragged inch off the end of the cigar. He struck a match, puffed furiously, shook the match out, flipped it on the rug.

Oscar was a bow-legged, barrel-chested man with a skin head, gimlet eyes, bushy nostrils, oversize mouth, and a thirty-dollar suit, purplish-brown in colour, and the breast pocket full of mechanical pencils. This antithesis of a Madison Avenue tycoon had started his television career roundaboutly at the age of sixteen when he was hired as a skull-cracker by the circulation department of a New York tabloid. He advanced steadily in the circulation department until his knuckles gave out, and then he moved over to the business department. When the paper bought a radio station, Oscar went along. Then he went to another radio station, and another, and then to television, spiralling ever upwards, and now he was a four-clock executive sitting with an Upmann cigar and watching Crunch Crandall, Spaceman, save the fair Skarlotta, a Martian lass, from the foul clutches of "It," the nameless monster of Ursa Minor.

Oscar watched intently until the show was over. Then he snatched up the speaker of his dictaphone. "Memo to sales," he barked. "Main title runs too long. Cut ten seconds and sell it to Philip Morris. . . . Memo to costume: More cleavage on Skarlotta. Let's see those knockers. . . . Memo to casting: Get a new monster. This one's a faggot."

There was a buzz from the intercom on his desk. He flipped the key impatiently. "Yeah?"

"Mr. Hemming is still waiting," said his secretary.

"Oh, for Christ's sake!" snarled Oscar.

"He's been here since five-thirty."

"All right, all right. Send him in."

The door opened and admitted Mr. Hemming, who would have been very angry at having to wait two hours in the outer office, but he was an agent and could not, therefore, afford to get angry. "Good evening, Mr. Hoffa," he said, smiling whitely.

"What's on your mind?" asked Oscar, not rising.

"As you know," said Mr. Hemming, "I represent Lanier Mott, who, I believe I may say without fear of contradiction, is one of our truly great writers."

"If he's such a great writer," asked Oscar, "what does he need with television?"

"Well now," said Mr. Hemming, somewhat unhorsed, "it isn't that he *needs* television——"

"On the other hand," interrupted Oscar, "what does television need with him?"

"Now, Mr. Hoffa," said Mr. Hemming reasonably, "surely television can use a Pulitzer prize winner—a Critics' Circle prize winner—one of America's really *important* writers."

"Important writers!" sneered Oscar. "Listen. The yucks who look at television don't know the difference between Ernest Hemingway and Huntz Hall. What do they care about important writers? What they want is shows where one guy kicks another guy in the belly while a dame leans over 'em with her cakes falling out of her négligé. Or domestic comedies where the whole family gets together to screw gruff old Dad. Or quiz shows where people get put in isolation booths and develop coronary occlusion before your very eyes.... Important writers! Remember when NBC tried to beef up their Sunday nights with important writers? Plays by Robert Sherwood—Thornton Wilder—Ferenc Molnar. Important enough for you? ... So what happened? I'll tell you what: forty million people nearly broke off their dials turning back to Ed Sullivan to watch a dog fart *The Star-Spangled Banner*!"

The intercom buzzed. Oscar flipped the key. "Now what the hell?" he asked angrily.

"Mr. Wexler calling from production centre," said his secretary.

Growling with exasperation, Oscar picked up the phone. "Yeah?" he snapped. "Yeah. . . . Yeah. . . . No. . . . No! . . . No, goddamit, you cannot put the *Mayflower* in the tank; Esther Williams is in there!"

He slammed down the phone and returned to Mr. Hemming. "Now then, what's this important writer of yours got to sell?"

"It's a play," said the agent. "Ordinarily, of course, my client writes only for the legitimate theatre. But in this instance, because of the scope of the work, he feels that television may be a more suitable medium."

"So everybody on Broadway has turned it down," said Oscar. "Well, all right, send it over. I'll have a look."

"Just a moment, Mr. Hoffa. I want one thing understood clearly. My client has instructed me that there is to be no deal unless he retains strict control over the commercial announcements."

"In your hat!" replied Oscar promptly. "You get no control over the commercials. We're in business for one reason—and it's not to entertain or enlighten or enrich or educate. It's to *sell* —and, buddy, nobody tells us how or when."

"My client doesn't mean to be unreasonable," said Mr. Hemming placatingly. "He is perfectly willing for you to have commercials at the beginning and end of his play. But he feels very strongly that the mood, the dramatic continuity, will be shattered if you interrupt the play with a commercial in the middle."

"No deal," said Oscar flatly. "I just finished spending a quarter of a million dollars on a survey of viewing habits. I am up to my belly-button in charts and graphs—including graphs on what happens to the time between shows. I mean those three minutes when you get the closing commercial on one show, the station break, and the opening commercial on the next show. You know what happens during those three lousy minutes? We lose 71% of the audience, that's what! Where do they go? I can tell you that too: 24% of 'em go to the can, 21% go to the ice-box, 19% go see if their kids are covered, 16% nap, 9% read two pages in a book or magazine, 7% play a hand of gin rummy, and 4% just stand like idiots and spin the goddam dial. . . . So don't tell me about beginning and end commercials, buddy. I want 'em smack in the middle when we got the yucks glued to the chair!"

The intercom buzzed again. Oscar slapped down the key. "Who now, for Christ's sake?"

"It's Mrs. Hoffa, sir."

"Here?"

"No, sir. On the phone from Putnam's Landing."

"Tell her to wait."

Oscar swung back to the agent. "That's the deal, buddy. Take it or leave it."

"I will talk to my client," said Mr. Hemming, "but I'm afraid the answer will be no."

"We'll survive," said Oscar. "Good night."

The agent went off to kick somebody smaller, and Oscar lifted the phone to speak to his wife.

"Angela? What do you want? . . . What do you mean, why ain't I home? I'm flying to Hollywood tonight, didn't I tell you? . . . Well, didn't anyone tell you? . . . All right, I forgot. . . . Of course, I have to go. That Ivy League idiot out there is going to put on *Oedipus Rex* if I don't stop him. Always some sonofabitch trying to drip culture into the network. . . . No, it can't wait. . . . What the hell do I care about a goddam town meeting in Putnam's Landing? . . . Can't you go without me? . . . Okay, baby, I'll see you in a few days. . . . No, I don't know just when. As soon as I fire a few of them college bastards who keep trying to tone up the industry. . . . All right, Angela. Goodbye."

Angela Hoffa hung up her pink telephone and muttered a blue word. She walked over to the bar, poured herself a shot glass full of White Label, and tossed it off. Then she sat down, unclenched her fists, and with a conscious effort of will, forced the anger to subside within her. "You get mad, you get lines around the mouth," she told herself. "And lines around the mouth, I got enough."

There were, it is true, a few lines around her mouth and also some vague crow's feet at her eyes, but nothing that would not yield to Max Factor. At thirty-eight, Angela was a tall, white-skinned, black-haired, ripe beauty. A bit of the bounce had gone out of the pectorals, and there was an extra handful around the hips, but she could still count on a gratifying response when she appeared on Ram's Head Beach in the summer.

But it was not summer; it was winter. And she was not on the beach being ogled; she was at home being stupefied by boredom. Out of the last thirty nights, Oscar had been home exactly six; the rest of the time he had been away swelling the unemployment rolls in Los Angeles, Chicago, and New York. And even when he was home, he was not exactly what you would call company. An evening with Oscar was seven straight hours of television, with an occasional break to fetch him a new belt for the dictaphone beside his chair.

"Do you want a divorce?" Oscar would ask when she made one of her frequent complaints. "If you do, you can have it. I got no time to argue."

But Angela did not want a divorce. Or, to be more accurate, she *did* want a divorce. She would have been tickled pink to get rid of Oscar and wall up the television set. But then what? Then she would be a thirty-eight-year-old woman living in Putnam's Landing without children and without a husband. There could be no more extraneous condition. In a town like Putnam's Landing, fiercely dedicated to the perpetuation and protection of the home, only wives had status. Widows and divorcees were tolerated, provided they had children, but a childless, unfettered adult female was regarded, at the very best, as a second-class citizen, and, in the case of one as decorative as Angela, as an enemy agent.

No, she could not stay in Putnam's Landing, not unless she was looking to get her eyes scratched out. Nor could she move back to New York. This, for her, would be like Joe Louis returning to the ring when he didn't have it any more. New York had once been Angela's arena, and she had been a champ. She had touched cheeks with Mr. Billingsley, Mr. Perona and several Mr. Kriendlers. She had sat between Row C and Row J at all the openings and against the wall at Sardi's afterwards. She had sighed to Piaf, hummed to Dyer-Bennett, clicked to Greco. She had done the champagne-and-stout bit, the Westhampton bit, the French poodle bit. She had even had the accolade: Joe E. had sniped her drink during his act at the Copa.

But that was long ago. Other, younger, firmer buttocks nested on the zebra-covered banquettes today; prettier faces twinkled back from the bar-mirrors; springier arches cha-cha'd till the small hours. At thirty-eight years of age Angela was not fool enough to come back into the ring against such young, tough, heartless competition.

And, anyhow, she had her fill of New York. The reason she married Oscar in the first place was that she had been bored silly with the flits and lushes of café society. She had wanted to find a man—a hard-working, hard-bearded, woman-oriented, honest-to-God man—and live with him in a country house and be his country wife. Oscar had been, beyond cavil, a man, and she had managed after some difficulty to get him into a country house, but then television came along and pulled him right out again, and that was the end of Angela's sweet dream of domesticity.

But the dream did not die. Angela still wanted to be a wife— a full-time wife with a full-time husband. But where would she find one? Not in New York, where the pickings were too slim and the competition too heavy. And not in Putnam's Landing, where bachelors were as rare as unicorns.

Married men, on the other hand, were plentiful in Putnam's Landing, and Angela had often toyed with the idea of picking off one of the more loosely-attached specimens. But she had always rejected the notion. It was, she told herself, not neighbourly.

Tonight, however, sitting on a chintz love-seat in a pecky cypress living-room, looking out from a picture window at two acres of closely barbered lawn, thoughtfully sipping another hooker of Scotch, Angela began to wonder whether her ethics might not be misplaced. Here she was, a woman with a great untapped reservoir of wifeliness. And around her were dozens of discontented husbands, men who found their wives inadequate, unsympathetic, even hostile. What was Angela's higher duty in these circumstances? To stay aloof and let the poor souls suffer? Or to choose the most deserving, take him to her bosom, and be to him wife, helpmeet, tender comrade, guiding star, and all the other things he had so poignantly been longing for?

Angela rose and paced the room. She had never before analysed things in quite this way. It sure put a new face on the situation. Taking somebody's husband—somebody's *dis-*

contented husband, that is—was not thievery; it was *liberation*! Like John Brown going into Harper's Ferry, kind of. Angela smiled, pleased with the notion of herself as Old Pottawatamie. And it wasn't so far-fetched either, thought she with a righteous nod. Wasn't she, too, going on a slave raid? Wasn't she going to find a man in bondage and set him free? Of course she was. That was *exactly* what she was going to do—release a poor captive, sever his shackles, unyoke his shoulders, heal his welts, and guide his faltering feet down Freedom Road!

Satisfied that she was doing the Lord's work, Angela got down to details. Who in Putnam's Landing needed liberating? Well, the closest was Willard Beauchamp, who lived just a quarter of a mile down the road. Willard was in thrall to his wife, Laura, a broth of a woman standing just under six feet high, weighing a rock-hard hundred and sixty pounds, and filled with energy in the megaton range. This energy was directed chiefly into amateur theatricals. Currently she was rehearsing *A Sleep of Prisoners* at the Congregational Church, *The Dybbuk* at Temple Israel, *Dear Ruth* at Webster High School and *A Kiss for Cinderella* at Nathan Hale Elementary School—and, at the same time, making preparations for a Fourth of July folk-drama, a reenactment of the landing of the Redcoats on Ram's Head Beach. To cast her plays, Laura roamed Putnam's Landing like a one-woman press gang, collaring anybody who did not see her first, dismissing their objections with jovial thuds on the back, dragging them into rehearsals by main force. Willard, being ready-to-hand and a good deal smaller than she, was, of course, an actor in all her productions. With a rush of pity, Angela remembered the last time she had seen him perform. It was an outdoor production of *A Midsummer Night's Dream*, in which Willard, wearing a short Grecian tunic, came cavorting miserably across the village green in the teeth of a frosting March wind, brandishing a lath sword, and declaring that he was Oberon, king of all the fairies.

Yes, thought Angela, Willard definitely needed liberating.

But, after brief consideration, she dismissed him and went on to the next prospect. After all, Willard was sixty years old, and who knew what shape his heart was in after all those theatricals? No use liberating a man if he's going to fall dead at your feet.

Angela now turned her thoughts to David Coleman. David drew a comic strip called *Pudgy and Spot* which ran daily and Sunday in two hundred and ten newspapers. He was young, handsome, strong, and clearly a discontented husband, as anybody could testify who had heard him make his "Anchor" speech. In this speech, which was delivered whenever David was drunk, he developed the interesting thesis that his wife was an anchor. He, on the other hand, was a ship—specifically, a four-masted schooner. Once upon a time he had sailed the ocean bravely and freely, charting no course, heading only for the horizon. Then he got married. His wife, with her insatiable demands for luxuries—like three meals a day and a dry bed—had forced him to give up painting true and beautiful pictures (the proof of it was that nobody would buy them) and instead pervert his talent into making a living. The ship, in other words, had acquired an anchor—an anchor that moored him to the slimy shoals of success. More anchors accrued to him—children, a house, cars, furniture, maids, cooks, gardeners—and now, his talent betrayed, his soul besmirched, he was stuck with $80,000 a year instead of decently starving to death.

No, thought Angela, passing him by. Not David. People who wear cashmere jackets shouldn't beat breasts.

She turned next to Henry Steinberg. Henry had been a perfectly contented husband until his wife insisted on breeding their Harlequin Great Dane bitch. "It will be so wonderful for the children watching the miracle of birth," declared Henry's wife, and he had allowed himself to be persuaded. So the children had watched the miracle of birth, and had gone promptly into traumatic shock. Two of them were still under treatment. And the pups—eleven of them—were now going on four months old, without one single buyer having appeared in spite of ads every week in the *Putnam's Landing Gazette* and every day in the *New York Times*. So there was Henry, stuck with eleven great, clumping, spotted, ungainly creatures, eating their own weight daily, knocking over priceless vases, teething on the Chippendale, crying all night long, and making a stench that beggared Air-wick.

Yes, Henry was discontented. But it was not really serious. All he needed was eleven escaped lunatics to come around and buy his Great Danes, and his marriage would be as good as new.

Angela riffled through some more names, rejecting each in turn. One was a drunk, one liked sports-cars better than girls, one lived on blackstrap molasses, one was a television producer.

Then she came to the name of Harry Bannerman.

She grew very, very thoughtful. This, now, could be pay dirt. Harry Bannerman was without doubt a discontented husband. He had all the earmarks—the stricken face, the glazed eyeballs, the dragging feet. And, if she needed any more evidence, his lushing on the 5.29 was matter of record.

Discontented he surely was. Now to the next question: was he worth liberating?

Yes. Indeed, he was. Wasn't he personable? Presentable? Intelligent? Trustworthy? Employable? Certain of his gender? Yes! To all of those, yes. Harry Bannerman was a good man, and good men do not abound.

Angela picked up the pink telephone. She put it down again, struck by a sudden flurry of conscience. A picture of Grace Bannerman came into her mind—sweet, decent Grace. Was this a friendly thing to do to Grace—honest, seemly Grace?

But, thought Angela, probing deeper, that was not the point at all. This had nothing to do with Grace; this had only to do with Harry. He was a good man; he deserved to be happy; Grace had failed him; now Angela must try. That was the American way.

Angela picked up the pink telephone and dialled resolutely. "Hello, Grace? . . . Grace, honey, this is Angela Hoffa. . . . Are you and Harry going to the town meeting tonight? . . . I know this is too tiresome of me, but would you mind picking me up? Oscar's off on one of his things again. . . . Thank you, lamb. Just honk. I'll come a-running. . . . Bye."

Angela put down the pink telephone and went to gird up her loins.

Seven

GRACE BANNERMAN hung up the phone. "That was Angela Hoffa," she said to Harry. "We're picking her up on the way to the meeting."

"Oh, for Christ's sake!" said Harry. "She's 'way to hell over on the other side of town."

"Now, dear," said Grace reprovingly.

"All right, all right," he sighed. "Let's get going then. You ready?"

"In a minute. You go say good night to the children."

"Yes, ma'am," said Harry.

He hung up the towel with which he had been helping Grace dry the dinner dishes. He walked out of the kitchen area, around the breakfast bar, through the utilities area, across the dining area, past the activities area, over the family area, and up the stairs. The Bannermans lived in a modern-type house in which the first floor was one single sweep, divided only by waist-high counters, planters, and shelves. This arrangement saved steps, increased space, promoted cleanliness, and made it flatly impossible for a man to hide from his family.

This progressivism did not, however, obtain on the second floor. Here walls decently separated the four bedrooms and two baths. Harry walked into the bedroom of his eldest son Dan. He found all his sons seated on the floor, listening to Maggie Larkin, also seated on the floor, reading to them from *The House at Pooh Corner*.

Dan, Bud, and Peter Bannerman, aged respectively eight, six and four years, were three of a kind; each was sweet, soft, round, trusting, and vulnerable. Sometimes Harry would look at them, and his heart would be so full of love that tears would rush to his eyes. Other times he would look at them and gnash his teeth and wish fervently that there was just a little touch of guile about them, just a *soupçon* of meanness. Every child, including Harry's, needed a firm hand from time to time, but how did you apply a firm hand when your kids looked like three Kewpie dolls wearing "Kick Me" signs?

Dan leapt up and kissed his father's cheek. "Good night, Papa," he cried.

Bud kissed the other cheek. "Good night, Papa," he cried.

Peter kissed him full on the lips. "I love you, Papa," he cried.

Maggie Larkin observed this demonstration closely. There was not, as you might expect, an approving smile on her face; instead there was a small frown. "Mr. Bannerman," she said, "I wonder if I might talk to you for a minute."

"Certainly," he said.

Maggie rose and went out in the hall with him, closing the bedroom door behind her.

"Yes?" said Harry.

"I hope you won't think I'm interfering," said Maggie earnestly. "It really isn't any of my business, and if you don't want to talk about it, I'll surely understand."

"Talk about what?"

"Your children."

"What's wrong with them?"

"Let me ask you the same question, Mr. Bannerman. What *is* wrong with them?"

"Why, nothing," said Harry uneasily. "Nothing that I can see."

"Do they tell lies?" asked Maggie. "Do they steal? Do they bully other children?"

"Certainly not!"

"Aha!" said Maggie wisely.

"What do you mean—aha?" demanded Harry.

"Mr. Bannerman," said she, laying a hand on his sleeve and looking frankly into his eyes, "do you think that's normal?

Don't you realise that in this stage of their emotional growth, they are primarily interested in themselves? All that matters is to gratify their own wishes, their own desires. In this period children are *normally* selfish, *normally* inconsiderate. They see nothing wrong in lying, cheating, stealing, if it helps them gratify their desires."

"I see," said Harry, running his finger nervously inside his collar band. "Well, that's very interesting, Miss Larkin. Now if you'll excuse me——"

Maggie's grip tightened on his sleeve. "That's what worries me about your children, Mr. Bannerman. They are *too* good, *too* honest. Something has repressed their natural, normal drives."

"Yeah. Well——"

"But you can't bottle up things like that," continued Maggie, holding tight. "They're bound to come out somewhere—maybe as hay fever or asthma, maybe as migraines, maybe as colitis. When a child feels something he cannot express, his body will express it for him!"

"Oh, come now, Miss Larkin——"

"No, Mr. Bannerman, it's a fact! It's a scientific fact. Why, only last month Sigafoos at Johns Hopkins proved that 87% of arthritis patients first suffer the symptoms in the hand they used to masturbate with."

Harry gulped. "Is that so?" he said weakly.

"So you see, Mr. Bannerman, this is a very serious thing. I hope you won't resent my saying it, but your children need help."

"Yes, Miss Larkin," said Harry, removing his sleeve from her grasp. "I'll get help for them first thing in the morning. . . . But let's not try anything tonight, okay? I mean, for tonight, could you just kind of leave 'em alone? Okay, Miss Larkin? Huh?"

"Of course."

"That's a good girl. Just read 'em a story or something and put 'em in bed. Okay?"

"Certainly."

"I appreciate that," breathed Harry. "Good night."

"Good night."

Dashing perspiration from his brow, Harry joined Grace downstairs. "Listen," he whispered urgently, "you can't leave the kids with that girl. She's cuckoo!"

"Now, Harry—"

"Don't give the 'Now Harry' bit. I tell you this girl is a certifiable maniac!"

"Yes, yes, I know," said Grace calmly. "She gave me the statistics on arthritis and masturbation too."

"And you're not afraid to leave the kids with her?"

"Of course not."

"And tonight at the town meeting you're making a speech to have her reinstated?"

"Harry, listen to me," said Grace, taking his arm and leading him outside to the car. "She's a young girl, and her head is full of half-digested information about child psychology. . . . But she is also a *good* girl. She is basically very intelligent, and she loves children. With a little time, a little seasoning, she'll make a wonderful teacher. And in days like these, with such a terrible shortage of teachers, I'm not going to let this town throw away a prospect like Maggie Larkin!"

They were at the car now. Harry opened the door for Grace, then went round and got behind the wheel. He backed out of the driveway and started down the street.

Grace watched him shaking his head darkly as he drove. "It's all right," she smiled. "It'll work out."

"Yeah," he mumbled, unconvinced.

"And one more thing——"

"Yes?"

"When we pick up Angela Hoffa, try to be nice to her, won't you? I mean, don't ignore her, the way you always do."

"Perhaps she could sit in my lap," suggested Harry drily.

"No cracks, Harry. I feel very sorry for Angela. What kind of life can she have—being married to Oscar?"

"The mind trembles," he replied.

"So do be nice to her, won't you, dear?"

"Yes, Grace, I'll be nice to her."

"That's my Harry," said Grace, kissing his cheek. "That's my sweet Harry."

Harry picked up her near hand and licked each fingertip thoughtfully. "You sure we have to go to this meeting?" he asked.

She took her hand back. "Yes, you old goat," she said. "I'm sure."

Eight

An American flag hung over the door. Three hundred folding chairs stood on the unslanting floor. Across the front of the room ran a low platform on which there was a lectern for the Moderator, as the chairman of the town meeting was called.

The Moderator was not yet at the lectern—it was still five minutes to meeting time—but the room was already jam-packed. All three vertical social strata of Putnam's Landing were represented. In the front rows were the commuters, tweedy and fervent, chock-full of civic virtue, prepared to give without stint of their talent, their articulateness, their yeasty imagination. Directly behind them sat the Yankees, waiting grimly for the onslaught of rhetoric and ready with plans to table, delay, sidetrack, and defeat. In the last rows were the Italians, who voted most of the time with the Yankees, but enjoyed the meetings a whale of a lot more. As Guido's father, Vittorio di Maggio, had once pointed out, "Town meeting, itsa like opera. First one fella singsa aria, then another fella sticksa knife in his back!"

At the hub of the commuters' sector, poised on the threshold of her shining hour, was Betty O'Sheel, head of the Study Committee on Garbage Disposal. Betty, a stolid, modest matron of thirty-four, had never expected to reach such heights in politics, and she had worked prodigiously to deserve the honour. For weeks her husband and two infant daughters had lived on Spam and made their own beds while Betty had pored over United States Public Health Service Bulletins on the disposal of putrescible and non-putrescible wastes; had sent questionnaires to sanitation commissioners all over America; had made field trips to dumps and sewers throughout Fairfield County and Long

Island. Her labours had been rewarded. Unlike several earlier garbage disposal plans which had been voted down as impractical or too expensive, the proposal that Betty held in her hand to-night was—her friends all agreed—a dead-sure winner.

Grace Bannerman sat next to Betty, working over her as a second works over a fighter before a bout. She soothed Betty's jumpy nerves, assured her that victory was in the bag, promised to deal personally with any cute parliamentary tactics the Yankees might try to spring. Grace had more than a normal interest in Betty's success tonight, for it had been Grace's idea to pull her out of obscurity and give her this major assignment. Other, more qualified ladies had been suggested for the job, but Grace had said, "No, girls, let's give it to Betty O'Sheel because Betty O'Sheel is a fat girl and fat girls need lots of love and approval." The others had, of course, seen the keen logic of Grace's position. Now they could all congratulate themselves not only on making possible a splendid report on garbage disposal, but also on lifting a sagging psyche.

Next to Grace was Harry Bannerman, who sat and wished glumly that he was at a PTA meeting instead of a town meeting. At the PTA meetings the seats had arms, and a man could safely fall asleep. Here, in these lousy folding chairs, you were liable to topple over and crack your skull.

Seated beside Harry was Angela Hoffa. She looked at his clouded eyes, his slack jaw, and she thought, "Oh yes, this is indeed a discontented husband! Oh, yes, there is work for me here!" She shifted a bit upwind to give Harry the full benefit of her Bellodgia.

The Bellodgia wafted back a couple of rows to where First Selectman Manning Thaw was sitting. His long white nose twitched barely perceptibly; otherwise no expression quickened his features. On either side of him sat Isaac Goodpasture and George Melvin, the real estate dealer. They stole frequent glances at Manning's face, both wondering what secret lay locked there, why Manning had assured them so positively that tonight the Yankees had nothing to fear from the commuters. But Manning's face told no tales.

The Moderator mounted the platform, took his position behind the lectern, and called for order. The Moderator, a tall, bespectacled man of sixty, was a sort of hybrid—a Yankee who commuted. Born and bred in Putnam's Landing, he now practised law in New York City. With one foot thus fixed in each camp, he was not too broad for the Yankees and not too narrow for the commuters, and he was currently serving his tenth consecutive term as Moderator.

"Meeting will come to order," he said. "First item on the agenda is a report from Mrs. O'Sheel of the Study Committee on Garbage Disposal. . . . Mrs. O'Sheel."

But before Betty could rise, Manning Thaw was on his feet. "Mr. Moderator!" he called.

"Yes, Mr. First Selectman?" said the Moderator.

"Before we get talkin' about anything else," said Manning, "I've got a very important announcement to make."

Isaac Goodpasture and George Melvin exchanged a knowing smile. Good old Manning! He sure wasn't wasting any time springing his trap! Good old Manning! Shrewd old buzzard!

Betty O'Sheel turned distraughtly to Grace Bannerman. "Oh, dear!" she cried, biting her knuckles. "He's up to something! If he wrecks my garbage report, I'll just *die*! Oh, stop him, Grace! Stop that terrible old man!"

"Don't you worry," said Grace grimly. "I'll fix *him*!"

Grace sprang to her feet with a mighty bound, startling Harry considerably. He had always found her animated at meetings, but never what you would call *physical*. "Mr. Moderator!" she shouted in tones that rang like a gunshot through the chamber. Harry sat up straighter; this was a Grace he had not yet seen.

"Yes, Mrs. Bannerman?" said the Moderator.

"I don't know what kind of trickery the first selectman is up to," said Grace heatedly, "but I do know this: he's dead-set against the new garbage disposal plant and he'll go to any lengths to stop it! Well, let him try! In fact, I *dare* him to try! But *not now*! I should like to remind you, Mr. Moderator, that this meeting is conducted according to parliamentary procedures, and the first item on the agenda is the report of the garbage disposal committee. Manning Thaw can talk later if he likes, but right now the floor belongs to Betty O'Sheel!"

The commuters' section broke into a great salvo of hand-clapping, with scattered cries of "Bravo!" from the more travelled members. Harry sat and looked at Grace in pop-eyed wonder. Was this his wife? Or was it some tigress, some fire-brand, some wild, leaping thing? Whatever it was, he wanted it.

Angela Hoffa looked at Harry. "How wistful his eyes," she thought, "how full of longing! Oh, poignant yearner," she thought, "cease from pining, for I shall soon fill the hole in your heart!"

The Moderator addressed Manning Thaw. "Mrs. Bannerman is right, Mr. First Selectman. You'll have to wait your turn."

Without a word Manning sat down. Isaac Goodpasture and George Melvin traded a nervous glance. The first selectman's torpedo, whatever it was, had so far turned out to be nothing but a wet firecracker. "Well, Manning," whispered Isaac, "do you still think we're going to lick 'em?"

"Yup!" snapped Manning. There was not a hint of doubt in his icy eyes. Isaac shrugged and turned his attention to the speaker.

Betty O'Sheel stood on the platform, a sheaf of notes trembling in her hand. She took a deep breath, pressed her fat knees firmly together, and, unaccustomed as she was to public speaking, began to deliver her report loud and clear. "Garbage disposal methods," said she, "can be divided into three broad classifications. First, there is the so-called sanitary landfill method, which is now being used in Putnam's Landing. This method, as we all know, is unsatisfactory because it is not truly sanitary, it results in malodorous odours and it requires a constant search for new dumping grounds as old ones are exhausted.

"Second, there is the incinerator method. This is a much more efficient method than the sanitary landfill method, but Putnam's Landing has several times rejected proposals to build an incinerator because of the great cost and expense of construction.

"The third method is what I like to call 'The Garbage of Tomorrow Method.' This is the conversion of garbage into fertilizer. This is not only highly efficient and very cheap, but it is also of vast benefit to the farmers and gardeners of America. There are now several large companies in the United States which are in the business of converting garbage into commercial fertilizer. One of the biggest of these companies is the Garba-Crunch Corporation of Great Neck, Long Island. I have had several meetings with Mr. Emil Wetkus, vice-president and general manager of Garba-Crunch, and I am pleased to report that he has surveyed our garbage problem in Putnam's Landing and he feels confident that Garba-Crunch can handle it.

"Mr. Wetkus has offered to build a plant here which will grind up our garbage and then convert it by means of bacterial action into fertilizer. He guarantees that there will be no unseemly noise or malodorous odours. Garba-Crunch will charge the town three dollars a ton for processing garbage, which is a clear saving of 42% over our present cost of garbage disposal. Also—and *mark this well*—the Garba-Crunch Corporation will build their plant at their own expense! Putnam's Landing will not have to provide a penny. All we have to do is to give them the land on which to put the plant.

"I'm further pleased to report that I have found a perfect site for the plant—the old Yarbro place, consisting of four acres on the Shore Road. I therefore move that we buy the old Yarbro place and turn it over to the Garba-Crunch Corporation and begin a new and brighter era in garbage disposal for Putnam's Landing! Thank you."

Before Betty O'Sheel was seated, George Melvin was on his feet. "Hold on! Hold on there! Now hold on!" he cried in panic. For the Yarbro place belonged to George, and he had no intention in the world of turning it into a garbage disposal plant. This, by God, was shore-front property, as valuable as platinum, even if it did dwindle somewhat at high tide. You take a lot like the Yarbro place, and give it an attractive name— Pilot's Knob, for example—and you could get maybe $15,000 an acre!

If the O'Sheel woman had to have some land for a garbage plant—and at the moment George could not think of a single way to stop her—then he had plenty of bogs and fens that would do just fine.

"Now, Mrs. O'Sheel," said George with his most ingratiating smile, "I'm going to be perfectly frank with you. The old Yarbro place is no good for a factory, what with tides and all. What you want is something high and dry—and I've got just the place for you."

"No, sir," replied Betty. "It has to be the old Yarbro place."

"Why?" asked George nervously.

"Because it's on the shore and it's got a good anchorage," said Betty. "Mr. Wetkus and I looked at several places before we settled on this one. As I said before, the Garba-Crunch Corporation is in Great Neck, Long Island, which, as we all know, is on the north shore of Long Island. They are going to come across the Sound and pick up our fertiliser in barges, which means that they have to have a place on the shore with a good anchorage."

"For God's love, do something!" hissed George at Manning Thaw. "You said we didn't have a thing to worry about. Now look at the mess we're in!"

Manning rose. "Mr. Moderator!" he called.

Grace Bannerman sprang to her feet. "Mr. Moderator!" she cried. "Point of order!"

"Yes, Mrs. Bannerman?" said the Moderator.

"Mrs. O'Sheel has made a motion," said Grace. "Does the first selectman rise to speak to the motion?"

Harry looked with admiration on his wife. This keen, in-

cisive, forceful creature—was she really his? And if so, was he
ever going to get to prove it?

"Your point is well taken, Mrs. Bannerman," said the Moderator. "Mr. First Selectman, do you rise to speak to the motion?"

"We're talking about buyin' land, ain't we?" said Manning.
"Well, that's what I want to talk about—buyin' land."

"Proceed, Mr. First Selectman," said the Moderator.

Manning walked to the front of the room, turned and faced
his constituents, and said matter-of-factly, "The United States
Army is buyin' a hundred acres of land in Putnam's Landing.
They're puttin' in one of them guided missile sites. Nike, it's
called."

A complete, absolute, stunned silence fell upon the assemblage.
Mouths plopped open, eyes blinked. Not one word was uttered
for a full minute.

"Great balls of fire!" thought Isaac Goodpasture. "No wonder Manning was so sure that nothing would get done at the
meeting tonight! What a piece of news! What a staggering,
crushing, stupefying piece of news!"

It was the Moderator who spoke first. "Mr. First Selectman,"
he said, "did I understand you correctly? The Army is putting
a guided missile site here in Putnam's Landing?"

"Yup," said Manning.

"Why?" asked Rodney O'Sheel, husband to Betty. "Why
should they put a guided missile site in a quiet little village like
this? We have no industry, no shipping, no targets of any
military value."

"I know it," said Manning. "But Bridgeport has. The way
the Army fella explained it to me this afternoon, we're part of a
ring around Bridgeport. They're puttin' Nike bases in Westport
and Fairfield too. An overlappin' defence pattern, he called it,
in case enemy planes try to bomb the factories in Bridgeport."

"Where's the Army buying this hundred acres?" asked
George Melvin.

"Johnnycake Hill," said Manning.

"Eek!" said George Melvin and fell heavily into his seat. Johnnycake Hill was a two-hundred-acre residential site owned by George. With the Army taking a hundred acres to shoot rockets, thought George, moaning aloud, who'd build houses on the other hundred?

"But surely," said Henry Steinberg, the Harlequin Great Dane breeder, "the Army can find some place besides Putnam's Landing for a base. Why do they have to put rockets and gasoline and high explosives and maybe atomic warheads right smack in the middle of our town?"

"The children!" cried Grace, bounding to her feet again. She turned and faced the entire audience. "Listen to me, my friends," she said in a voice choked with emotion, "listen to me, all of you. We have our differences here, it's true, but on one thing we are all agreed: we love our children. Are we going to sit by and let them be scorched and blasted and scared out of their wits by rockets zooming all over the place? *No!* We must fight this thing! We must close ranks and all work together to keep this terrible, dangerous weapon out of our town! We must protect the children we have brought into this world!"

For the second time that evening Grace got a round of applause, but this time it came from all over the hall, not just from the commuters' section. Grace stood erect through the ovation, her eyes bright with tears, her cheeks kindled, her head high, her shoulders back, her breasts jutting defiantly. "A goddess!" thought Harry, awe-struck. "A goddess of fire and passion and thrust!"

He took her hand and pulled her gently down beside him. "Listen," he said in a low, urgent voice, "I know you're in the Bloodmobile tomorrow, and Saturday is Bud's birthday and Sunday is the birthday party and Monday Peter gets his bite-plate. . . . How about Tuesday?"

"What?" said Grace, not really hearing, her attention on the excited speeches now pouring from everywhere with no semblance of order.

"How about Tuesday?" repeated Harry. "I mean for you and me to go up to the Concord Hotel. Okay?"

"Harry, for Heaven's sake——"

"Okay?" he insisted. "Okay?"

"Okay!" she replied impatiently. "Now, pay attention, will you?"

George Melvin was making himself heard over the general roar. "What's this going to do to real estate values?" he demanded. "I've got two hundred acres at Johnnycake Hill. The Army takes a hundred. Now who's going to buy the rest of it? Who wants a house next to a rocket launcher? And don't think I'm the only one who'll suffer. You're all home owners here; you've all got investments to protect. What do you think your homes will be worth when the Army turns this town into a shooting gallery?"

"And what of our daughters?" cried Laura Beauchamp, the amateur theatricals lady. She rose now and threw her arms dramatically upwards. "What of our young, innocent daughters when the town is full of sex-starved soldiers, crazed with drink!"

"I'll tell you what the biggest irony of all is," said David Coleman, the comic strip artist. "The biggest irony of all is that Nike doesn't even work! A couple of Air Force guys I know told me that Nike couldn't hit the side of a barn! It's just a big boondoggle for the Army; they're trying to get the guided missile programme away from the Air Force."

"Then why must we have it?" shouted Laura Beauchamp. "It will ruin our daughters, ruin our homes, ruin our town, and it doesn't even work!"

"What's all the talkin' for?" said Manning Thaw mildly. "If the Army says we're gettin' it, we're gettin' it."

"We'll see about that!" said Laura Beauchamp grimly. "Mr. Thaw, who's in charge of this Nike and where do we find him?"

"It's a Colonel Thorwald," replied the first selectman. "He's over in Long Island—Fort Totten."

"All right then," said Laura Beauchamp. "I move that we appoint a representative to visit Colonel Thorwald and tell him in the strongest possible terms that he cannot put his rockets in Putnam's Landing!"

"Good idea," agreed George Melvin. "Let's pick someone with a flair for words—like a writer."

"Yes!" cried Grace, leaping up. "My husband is a writer—and a darn good one! Harry, you'll draft the protest, won't you?"

"Huh?" said Harry, blinking rapidly.

"Excellent!" exclaimed Laura Beauchamp. "I know you'll do a fine job, Mr. Bannerman. But time is of the essence. How soon can you get it done?"

"Well——" said Harry, still blinking.

"He'll do it over the week-end," said Grace, "polish it up on Monday and deliver it to Fort Totten on Tuesday."

"Tuesday!" yelped Harry.

Grace looked at him askance. "Yes. Why not?"

"But don't you——" Harry began, and then abruptly stopped. What was he going to do—tell the whole town that he had made a date to sleep with his wife on Tuesday? And, worse, that his wife had forgotten all about it?

"Tuesday's all right, isn't it?" asked Grace.

"Yeah," he mumbled and sank into a snit.

Angela Hoffa noted his condition, and rubbed her hands. No doubt about it; this apple was ripe for plucking. All that remained now was to find the time and the place.

"Folks," said Manning Thaw, "things bein' how they are, hadn't we better call it a night?"

"Second the motion," said George Melvin.

"Golly," said Betty O'Sheel to Grace Bannerman. "How about the garbage thing?"

Grace waved her hand impatiently. "Next time, Betty. Not tonight."

"I guess you're right," said Betty bravely.

"A motion to adjourn has been made and seconded," said the Moderator. "All those in favour——"

"Aye," came the cry.

The meeting broke up into little swirls. The O'Sheels, the Steinbergs, the Beauchamps, the Colemans gathered around Grace. "Let's go over to Fatso's Diner and kick this thing around come more," said Rodney O'Sheel.

"By all means," said Grace. "Come on, Harry."

"I don't want to go to Fatso's Diner," said Harry in a black pout. "I want to go home."

Angela Hoffa heard the brisk knock of opportunity. "As a matter of fact, sweetie," said she to Grace, "I'm pretty brushed myself. I'll grab a cab and go home."

"Don't be silly," said Grace. "Harry will be glad to drop you—that is, if he's going home. Are you, Harry?"

"Yes."

"You're sure you don't want to come to Fatso's?"

"Yes."

"All right, dear." She rose on tiptoe and kissed him quickly on the cheek. "Don't worry about me. I'll get a ride home with somebody. . . . Good night, Angela."

"Good night, honey," smiled Angela. "Thanks for the use of your husband."

Nine

"COME in for some coffee."

"No, thanks, Angela, I've got to be going."

"A drink?"

"No, thanks."

"Brandy?"

"No, honestly."

"What can I tempt you with?" said Angela in mock despair. "Raisin cookies? Eskimo pies? My beautiful white body?"

"Ha, ha!" said Harry uneasily, a vision of Angela's white body scampering lewdly across his brain-pan.

"Oh, come on in!" she said, taking him firmly by the arm. "Your wife is at Fatso's Diner, my husband is in Hollywood, and we could both do with a little booze and sympathy."

"I guess we could at that," he allowed and followed her into the pecky cypress living-room.

"I know this is going to sound awful corny," said Angela, "but would you excuse me while I slip into something more comfortable?"

"Of course," said Harry, feeling a sudden twitch of excitement. He had been to enough movies to know what ladies meant when they said they were going to slip into something more comfortable.

"You fix the drinks," said Angela. "I won't be a minute."

Harry studied her buttocks switching up the stairs. In his ten years of marriage he had, like any red-blooded American boy, had an occasional letch for a woman other than his wife. But these seizures were not so much carnal as contemplative—just a kind of quiet, non-urgent speculation as to what kind of bed-mate this one or that one would make. *Scholarly*, you might call it.

But now, watching Angela's shimmering bottom, a tremor of unease shot through Harry. This, it suddenly occurred to him, might not be in the realm of academics. This might be *available*.

His first impulse was to bolt. He had an unbroken record of fidelity to Grace—not because of any high moral principle, but simply because he had honestly never wanted anybody else. Why smirch the scutcheon tonight?

Oh, but this was ridiculous, he told himself, moving over to the bar. Not only ridiculous, but libellous. There had never been a breath of scandal about Angela. By what right did he assume that she was a pushover tonight? . . . No, he was 'way off base. All the woman wanted was, as she said, a little booze and sympathy.

And supposing, thought he, pouring himself a White Label and water, supposing she wanted more than a little booze and sympathy? Supposing she came slinking down the stairs in a transparent négligée and pinned him to the hearthrug. Was that such a dismal prospect? Was there anything better waiting for him at home? In fact, was there anything *at all* waiting for him at home?

He took a long, angry pull on his drink. If he should end up in the hay with Angela tonight—he wouldn't, of course, but just *if* then Grace would have nobody but herself to blame. If she hadn't run off to Fatso's Diner, he wouldn't even be at Angela's right now. And, what's more, if she wasn't so goddam busy being a homemaker, clubwoman, and patriot, then he wouldn't be thinking about getting his jollies elsewhere!

It was Grace's fault. Whatever happened, it was clearly Grace's fault. He didn't want Angela. He didn't want anybody. All he wanted was his wife. But, for Pete's sake, it was like trying to get tickets to *My Fair Lady*!

Having fixed the blame where it belonged, Harry turned with a good conscience to the problem at hand—namely, what to do when Angela came downstairs in her peek-a-boo peignoir.

It had been a good long time since Harry had done anything

in the seduction line, and, truth to tell, he had never been any great shakes at it. But this much he knew: soft lights and sweet music were *de rigueur*. He walked now around the room and doused every light not necessary for minimum visibility. Then he went to the phonograph, rummaged through the albums, selected some rape-tempo Rodgers and Hart, and switched on the turntable.

A fire, thought he, would lend a nice sexy glow. He knelt and lit the birch logs in the fireplace.

Next he swung the sofa around to get the full benefit of the fire. He fluffed up the cushions, arranged pillows artistically in the corners.

Finally he mixed two drinks—for himself a weak one so he could stay alert; for Angela a double so she could not. He lit a cigarette, assumed an insouciant pose, and awaited his quarry.

Then he heard Angela's footsteps coming down the stairs, and panic closed around him like a big clammy fist. "Well, I guess I better be going," he croaked, licking his dry lips and plunging towards the door.

He stopped at the foot of the staircase. There stood Angela, not in a filmy négligée, but in a pair of pink velvet toreador pants and a blue silk blouse, both perfectly opaque.

She looked at Harry in astonishment. She looked around the room, noting the dim lights, the soft music, the fire, the re-arranged sofa. She burst into peals of laughter. "Oh, no!" she cried. "Oh, no, you can't go home! Not now. Not after you've gone to all this trouble to set the scene for a seduction!"

Harry felt his neck and face turn crimson.

"And a blush too!" exclaimed Angela delightedly. "An honest-to-goodness blush! Oh, Harry lamb, I'm tempted to throw myself right in your arms and yell 'Take me!' "

"Small favours gratefully accepted," said Harry in what he hoped was a tone of light badinage. It came out more like panting.

Laughing, she walked over to him and patted his cheek. She

sat down on the sofa, curled her legs underneath her, and pointed to the cushion at her side. "Sit down."

He sat.

She lifted her drink off the coffee table and tasted it. "A double, huh? You weren't taking any chances, were you?"

"I'll get some more water," he said sheepishly.

"No, it's all right." She took a slow sip, looking at him with amusement over the rim of the glass.

"Well," he said uncomfortably, "I'll be going."

"Not just yet." She held his hand lightly. "Let me ask you something. Don't think I'm not flattered, but what put these hot little thoughts in your mind tonight?"

"Well——"

"Well?"

"Well, you said you were going to slip on something more comfortable——"

"Ah!" said Angela. "So you thought I was going up to do the kimono bit!"

"Well, that's what it sounded like," he said defensively.

"New at the game, aren't you, son?"

"Yeah."

"Believe it or not, so am I."

"I believe it," he said.

"Now tell me, after I came downstairs in this diaphanous wrapper, what was your plot—to hop in bed with me, hop right out again, and get home before Grace does? Wham, bam, thank you, ma'am?"

"Something like that," he mumbled.

She shook her head. "I'm surprised, Harry. You never struck me as the Wham-Bam type. You know how I see you? Slow and easy and romantic—a satin dressing-gown—a white scarf at your throat—champagne cooling in a silver bucket—caviar and thin rye toast—gleaming linen—candlelight—a balcony looking out over the sea. . . . Do you like the picture?"

"Very much," said Harry. "There's only one thing missing."

"What?"

"A girl!"

"Do I detect a note of bitterness?" she asked.

"Listen, I better hit the road."

"Oh, relax. You came in for booze and sympathy, remember? You want to cry on my shoulder?"

"It's a very nice shoulder but—no, thanks."

"Okay," said Angela cheerfully. "No sympathy. But let me get you some more booze."

"I'll get it."

But Angela was on her feet. "You sit still. There's nothing I like better than *doing* for a man."

She went quickly to the bar in her pink toreador pants and came quickly back with a Scotch and water. She gave Harry the drink and sat down beside him. "Put your feet on the coffee table," she said. "Loosen your tie."

He put his feet on the coffee table. He loosened his tie. He leaned back. The fire was warm. The lights were low. The drink was balm. The lady next to him was round and fragrant. The phonograph was playing *Small Hotel*.

"Another drink?" said Angela.

"No," he answered. "Are you a good dancer?"

"One of the best. Are you?"

"Airy like a fairy. Come on."

They rose. Gracefully, lightly, they skimmed around the room as the phonograph played *Small Hotel* and *Blue Moon* and *Bewitched, Bothered, and Bewildered*. Angela was soft and weightless in his arms, and her thighs pressed pleasantly against his, and she smelled wonderful.

"What are you smiling at, Harry?"

"Nothing. It's just that I thought I'd never feel young again."

"But you *are* young."

"You're goddam right I am!" he said vehemently.

"All right, Harry," she answered in a placating tone. "I said you were, didn't I?"

"That's right, you did," he admitted. "You're a very nice girl, Angela. And pretty too."

"Thank you. And you are a fine figure of a man."

"And *young*," he reminded her. "Don't forget young."

"You're a boy, Harry. That's what you are—a darling, dashing, impetuous boy."

He nodded his agreement. "Listen," he said. "Do you want to kiss me or anything?"

"That sounds jolly!" said Angela.

He looked at her to see if she was kidding. She was not. She ran her hands lightly over his cheeks. Carefully, deliberately, she drew his lips down to hers and gave him a long, busy kiss.

"I better go now," he said thickly.

"You've got a few minutes."

"Now," said Harry. "It's either go or Wham-Bam."

She disengaged herself quickly. She linked her arm in his and walked with him to the door. "Good night," she said softly.

"Good night," he answered, looking at the dimly lit room, the cheery fire, the luxurious sofa, the creamy lady beside him. "I don't want to go very badly," he said.

She squeezed his hand. "Harry," she said, "you know what we were talking about before—candle-light, champagne, a balcony overlooking the sea?"

"Yes?"

"There's a lovely old hotel called the Miramar in Port Jefferson on the North Shore of Long Island. Have you ever been to Port Jefferson?"

"No."

"You're going to be."

"Me? When?"

"Next Tuesday. Don't you remember? You have to go to Fort Totten about that Nike business. Port Jefferson is only a few miles away."

"Yes?"

"Maybe," said Angela, averting her eyes in a maidenly

manner, "maybe when you're through at Fort Totten, you could go over to Port Jefferson. Maybe I could be waiting for you there."

Harry suddenly felt his ardour ebb away and his heart grow chill. It was one thing to put horns on your wife when it happened quite unexpectedly; then you could chalk it up to a temporary derangement, a lapse of the moment. But when *premeditation* came into the picture—when you laid plans, booked hotel rooms, took trips—you were clearly out of the novice class; you had won your "A" for sure.

"Gee, Angela, I don't know," he said doubtfully.

"All right, darling, let's forget it."

"Maybe we better."

"Sure . . . Good night, Harry."

"Good night, Angela."

He stood indecisively, wondering whether in these circumstances protocol called for a good night kiss. His problem was settled as Angela suddenly threw herself in his arms and gave him a fierce, probing kiss. "Oh, darling, let me make you happy!" she whispered and stood without moving as his hands flew eagerly over her body.

"Hotel Miramar," she said softly in his ear. "Port Jefferson."

She opened the door, let him out, pointed him at his car, closed the door and returned to her drink. "He'll be there!" she said aloud, smiling confidently into her glass.

"Like hell I will!" said Harry aloud, driving through the night.

Ten

"My teeth," said Guido di Maggio.

"Your *teeth*, did you say?" asked Major McEstway, post adjutant.

"Yes," said Guido. "Look." He leaned forward across the Major's desk and opened his mouth wide.

"In a minute," said Major McEstway and turned his attention to a crop-haired, angry-faced captain wearing a chest full of ribbons who had just come into the office. "Yes, Captain," he said.

"I'm Walker Hoxie," said the newcomer. "Colonel Thorwald sent for me."

"Hello, Captain Hoxie," said Guido, looking up at him with a tentative smile.

The Captain regarded Guido blankly.

"I'm Guido di Maggio," said Guido. "We met briefly at the club the other night. Remember?"

Walker Hoxie gave Guido an ill-tempered grunt and turned abruptly back to the Major. "Okay to go in?" he asked.

"Go ahead," said the Major.

Walker Hoxie went past the adjutant's desk and into the office of Colonel Thorwald, battalion commander. Guido, watching him, suppressed a shudder. Mean looking bastard, he thought. "Who's this guy Hoxie?" he said to Major McEstway.

"He's going to command one of the new bases," replied the Major. "But never mind him. Get back to your story. I'm fascinated!"

"Where was I?" said Guido.

"You were explaining why you couldn't go to Alaska," the Major prompted. "Something about your teeth."

"Oh, yes." Guido opened his mouth and leaned towards the Major. "Look here," he said, pointing at his molars. "See all those fillings?"

"Yes."

"Morbidly sensitive to cold, every one of them. Know what happens if I eat ice cream?"

"No," confessed the Major.

"Agony!" declared Guido. "Wild, screaming agony!"

"Pity!" murmured the Major.

"What's it going to be like when I get to the frozen North?" said Guido.

"Agony?" ventured the Major. "Wild, screaming agony?"

"Right!" said Guido. "I'll be no use at all to the battery. I'll be in the dentist's chair all day long."

"Tell you what," said the Major brightly. "We'll have all those teeth pulled before you go!"

"Very funny!" muttered Guido, casting the Major a baleful look.

"Lieutenant," said the Major, chuckling, "I'm going to miss you."

"Sir, you're making a big mistake!" cried Guido. "How can you send me to Alaska? I'm an Italian. For a thousand years my family lived in sunny Napoli. Couldn't you find a Swede?"

"I want you to know, Lieutenant," said the Major, clasping Guido's hand, "that when I ship you out, I will count it as a great personal loss. In these last couple of weeks, you have brought bushels of joy into this dreary life. Now get out of here so I can get some work done."

Guido started disconsolately for the door, but before he reached it, in walked a civilian, a tall man of thirty-some years. Guido looked at him curiously. Somewhere he had seen that face before; he would take his oath on it.

"Can I help you, sir?" said Major McEstway to the civilian.

"I'm Harry Bannerman," said the civilian. "I have an appointment to see Colonel Thorwald."

"Go right in, sir," said Major McEstway.

Ah! thought Guido. Now he remembered. Harry Bannerman of Putnam's Landing. They didn't exactly move in the same social circle, but Guido had seen him around town a few times. What, thought Guido, was he doing here?

Then another question crossed Guido's mind. The Major had told him that Captain Hoxie was going to command a new base. Then along came Harry Bannerman from Putnam's Landing. Could it be more than a coincidence? Was it possible that the new base would be at Putnam's Landing?

But why speculate? Why not find out?

He walked quickly out of Post Headquarters, around to the back of the building, squinched down under Colonel Thorwald's open window, and listened.

Captain Walker Hoxie was not angry all the time—only in peacetime.

In wartime a professional soldier—like Captain Walker Hoxie—had stature. He was *somebody*; he got respect from people. But what did he get in peacetime? Hind tit, that's what.

Coolie wages, that's what, and sweat-shop hours, and assignment to holes that would appal a gopher . . . But never mind all that. What really griped Captain Walker Hoxie, what churned and ground down his back teeth, was that the average American civilian regarded the professional soldier as an out-and-out bum! If a man was able to make a living any place else, asked the average civilian in a tone that brooked no rebuttal, why in the world would he choose to stay in the Army?

Such an assumption in the case of Captain Walker Hoxie was a plain canard. Walker was a guided missile expert—a category woefully short in the Army, but even more woefully short in private industry. He could have resigned his commission any day and gone to work for a fancy salary at some missile or electronics factory, but the hateful thought never crossed his mind. He flatly did not want to be a civilian. He had never had a good day with civilians in his life. His father, a civilian in the moonshine line in Searcy County, Arkansas, had walloped him daily until he ran away from home at the age of sixteen. For the next two years he had drifted around, riding the rods, picking a little fruit, piling up a goodly collection of vagrancy raps, and getting his skull banged regularly by yard bulls, deputies, and turnkeys—all civilians. In 1934, aged eighteen and seeking a place to lie down till his ears stopped ringing, he walked into an Army recruiting office and signed up.

He loved the Army from the very beginning. For one thing, people stopped hitting him on the head. For another, his life finally took on a meaning. He had a mission at last, and not a small one: to protect and defend the United States of America.

He was a sergeant when World War II broke out. He came back from overseas with a battlefield commission for gallantry. In Korea he won the Bronze and Silver stars. After Korea, harking to the Army's urgent need for missile officers, he transferred to Fort Bliss, overcame an extensive inacquaintance with mathematics, took up a full year's course in Nike, and ended up an expert technician.

Then, to his unspeakable disgust, he was sent to Fort Totten, Long Island. It was not Fort Totten which disgusted him. Fort Totten had, after all, acres of dusty drill fields, rows of ugly barracks, hordes of milling troops; it was, in short, *homey*. What raised Walker's gorge was that the assignment was only temporary: he was scheduled to leave shortly to take command of a new Nike installation at some place called Putnam's Landing. It would not be a *post*, mind you, not a base, not even an encampment—but just a tiny enclave of troops entirely surrounded by *civilians*!

And now it gave him a conspicuous lack of pleasure to be sitting with one of those very same civilians—a man named Harry Bannerman—in the office of Colonel Thorwald, battalion commander.

Colonel Thorwald, on the other hand, was wreathed in smiles. The Colonel was a portly, patient West Pointer of sixty years who had learned that the only way to run a Nike command was to keep smiling. You could never find a community that wanted Nike; you could never find enough qualified officers to run a battery. This left you two choices: smile or mental discharge.

"How do you do, Mr. Bannerman," said he, smiling. "I am Colonel Thorwald, battalion commander. This is Captain Hoxie. I have asked him to join us because he will be in charge at Putnam's Landing when we build the base. . . . Now then, Mr. Bannerman, we are delighted that you are here because the only way we will get our little differences settled is by honest, friendly discussion. Have a seat, sir, and tell us what is on your mind."

What was on Harry's mind was to get out of this ridiculous situation forthwith. But Grace was depending on him, and after his recent session of slap-and-tickle with Angela Hoffa, he felt that it might be well to play the dutiful husband for a spell.

"Well," said he, trying hard to conceal his sheepishness, "we feel that the Army should reconsider putting a Nike base in Putnam's Landing. Surely you can find a more suitable place than a quiet little residential town like ours."

Walker gritted his teeth silently. "Lousy civilians," he thought. "They are all alike. You go in and try to save their stinking skins, and what do you get? The back of their hands, that's what you get."

"What I mean," said Harry, wishing fervently he were somewhere else, "is that a Nike base will upset everything in our little community—social equilibrium, real estate values, things like that."

A column of red climbed rapidly up Walker's neck. "Lousy, maggoty civilians," he thought. "Pudgy palmed, shifty-eyed, grey flannel crud."

R.F.B.—4

"So," concluded Harry with a wan smile, "now that you see our side of it, I feel sure that you will look a little harder and find some other place."

"Thank you, Mr. Bannerman," said the Colonel courteously. "What you say is very interesting, and, of course, we quite see your point. Don't we, Captain Hoxie?"

"Yes, sir," said Walker. "We see the point, all right. The point is that Putnam's Landing is full of yellow-livered, money-grubbing, fat-bellied feather merchants, and if I had my way, I'd line 'em up against the wall and shoot the whole sickening lot of 'em!"

"Aghast" is the word for the Colonel's face at this point. Unmistakably "aghast."

Walker bounded out of his chair and stuck his nose, quivering with fury, an inch away from Harry's. "What's all this crap about real estate values?" he demanded. "Your country is in danger. The *United States of America* is in danger! Are you an American? Or are you some kind of commie rat bastard?"

Now Harry was on his feet too, every bit as outraged as Walker. "Just a minute!" he shouted. "I'm not going to stand here and have my patriotism impugned. It so happens that I did my bit in the last war!"

"Sure," sneered Walker. "You were drafted. If you're such a hotshot patriot, why didn't you re-enlist?"

A moan escaped the Colonel's lips and his mind turned longingly to the good old days when officers were gentlemen. Now they were technicians, and when you had one as good as Walker, you had to count yourself lucky. If he happened also to be a churl and a boor, all you could do was keep smiling and thank God he wasn't a geek.

"But no!" Walker was yelling at Harry. "*You* wouldn't re-enlist. Defending USA ain't good enough for high class guys like *you*. That's for slobs like me and the Colonel here . . . Well, all right, mister. We'll save your bacon for you. We always have and we always will. But just don't be getting in our way. Don't be telling us where we can put our bases and where we can't. That's *our* business!"

"What the Captain means," said Thorwald with a conciliatory smile, "is that——"

"I don't give a damn what the Captain means!" bellowed Harry in a blind fury. What the hell was he doing here anyhow? What did he care if Nike came to Putnam's Landing? How did he ever get into this horrid situation? . . . *How?* He knew damn well how. Grace, that's how!

"You see, sir," said the Colonel pressing on gamely, "we have made a careful study of defence requirements——"

"You sure as hell haven't made a study of public relations," retorted Harry hotly. "Or of common courtesy, for that matter!"

With that he wheeled and stormed out of the office. He had left a cab waiting in front of Post Headquarters. He flung himself into the back seat and slumped in a corner, trembling with anger.

"Back to the railroad station?" said the driver.

"Yeah," growled Harry, full of black bitterness. "Thank you, Grace," he thought savagely. "Thank you very much for this pleasant excursion. And for all the other joys you have brought into my life. Thank you for the rollicking days in the Bloodmobile, the enchanting evenings at the PTA. Thank you for making a pygmy out of what used to be a man."

"Driver!" shouted Harry suddenly, so suddenly that the driver almost lost the wheel. "I don't want to go to the railroad station. I've changed my mind—and high time, by God!"

"Where do you want to go?" asked the driver.

"Do you know the Hotel Miramar in Port Jefferson?"

"Sure."

"Take me there," said Harry with determination. "Let the revels begin!"

Guido di Maggio, listening underneath Colonel Thorwald's

window, was struck with the most brilliant idea of his entire life.

He scampered quietly away from the Colonel's window, ran around to the front of the building, and burst into the office of Major McEstway, post adjutant.

"Major," he cried breathlessly, "I have to see Colonel Thorwald right away!"

"What you have to do right away," said the Major, "is go pack your gear. I just got a call from Mitchel Field. There's an airplane waiting for you."

"No, no!" said Guido frantically. "I can't go! I have to see the Colonel!"

A steely edge came into Major McEstway's voice. "All right, Lieutenant, it's been fun, but playtime is over. Go get packed, and be back here in fifteen minutes."

"Yes, sir," said Guido glumly. This left him no alternative. He walked out of Major McEstway's office, out of Post Headquarters, around to the back of the building, over to Colonel Thorwald's open window, put his hands on the sill, and vaulted into the office.

Colonel Thorwald and Captain Hoxie whirled and looked at Guido in pop-eyed wonder.

Before they could recover, Guido started talking at machine-gun rate: "Colonel, sir, I know this is a little irregular, but believe me, sir, you'll thank me when you hear what I got to say. . . . Colonel, sir, let's face it, sir, when you send Captain Hoxie to Putnam's Landing, you are going to have yourself one hell of a public relations problem. True?"

Still stunned, the Colonel nodded dumbly.

"Colonel, sir," continued Guido, pressing his advantage hard, "I got a way to lick it. What you need is an executive officer for Captain Hoxie who can not only perform all of an exec's technical and administrative duties, but who can also conduct a public relations campaign. . . . Me, for instance, Colonel, sir, I was born and raised in Putnam's Landing and I know everybody in town and I was in the Scouts and the school police and I tell you the honest truth, Colonel, sir, there is not a soul in Putnam's Landing who does not have the highest esteem for me. You send me up there, Colonel, sir, and I guarantee you I will put on a public relations programme that will have the whole town clasping us to their bosom!"

Walker Hoxie found his tongue first. "Colonel," he said, "what do you want me to do with this lunatic?"

"Just a minute," said Thorwald to Walker. To Guido he said, "What kind of public relations programme?"

"Well, sir," replied Guido, his fine Italian mind racing, "first I'd call a special town meeting and explain to the people that Nike is perfectly safe. Then I'd go around town and make friends with all the important organisations. I'd speak to the Kiwanis and Rotary and Lions. I'd sign up with the Red Cross blood bank. I'd ask the clergy if they needed anybody for their choirs. I'd enlist the men in the volunteer fire department."

"Colonel, you're not really listening to this guy?" asked Walker incredulously.

"As a matter of fact, yes," answered the Colonel. "And, what's more, I'm liking what I'm hearing. Continue, Lieutenant."

"Yes, sir," said Guido, ideas flooding into his brain as his confidence mounted. "I'd do a lot of work with kids, because kids are the No. 1 industry of Putnam's Landing. I'd station soldiers at school crossings. I'd show films at assemblies. I'd give camping lessons to the Scouts. I'd manage a Little League team."

"Oh, for Christ's sake!" snarled Walker.

"Captain," said Thorwald, turning patiently to Hoxie, "this boy has ideas about public relations. Do you?"

"Certainly not!" cried Walker, deeply offended.

"That's what I figured," said Thorwald. "Captain, I'm afraid my course is clear. I must admit I have certain reservations about an officer who comes leaping through my window, but just the same he does have a public relations programme for Putnam's Landing—and with you in command, God knows we'll need one. I'm sending him along as your exec and P.R.O."

"Now wait a minute——"

"That," said the Colonel mildly, "is an order."

"Yes, sir," said Walker through clenched teeth.

"Oh, thank you, Colonel!" cried Guido ecstatically. "You'll never regret it."

"See that *you* don't!" warned the Colonel, a new and menacing note coming into his voice. "*Him*"—he nodded at Walker—"I can't replace. But *you*"—he pointed an ominous finger at Guido—"I damn well *can*!"

"Yes, sir," quaked Guido.

"I'll have no nonsense from you," said Thorwald, fixing Guido with a bird-colonel's glare. "No jumping through windows, no cutting up, no goofing. You're going to Putnam's Landing to do a job, and, by God, you better deliver!"

"Oh, I will, sir!" declared Guido. "I will!"

"What's your name?"

"Guido di Maggio, sir."

The Colonel frowned thoughtfully. "Aren't you on a shipping list to Alaska?"

"There's been some rumours," shrugged Guido. "Nothing definite."

"Well, I'll tell you something definite," said Thorwald. "I'll give you time to get things organised in Putnam's Landing, and then I'm coming up to inspect . . . and if I don't see results, you'll be in Alaska the very next morning, I promise you!"

"Yes, sir," quavered Guido.

The Colonel gave Guido a final scowl and flipped the key on his inter-office squawk-box. "Major McEstway?" he said.

"Yes, Colonel," came the voice of the adjutant.

"I'm assigning Lieutenant Guido di Maggio to Putnam's Landing," said Thorwald. "Cut some orders."

The squawk-box was silent for several seconds.

"Are you there, Major?" asked Thorwald.

"Yes, sir," came the voice.

"What are you doing?"

"I am taking my hat off to Lieutenant Guido di Maggio," said the Major reverently.

Eleven

VITTORIO, the father; Serafina, the mother; Anna and Teresa, the sisters; and Pete, Bruno, Dominic, and Carmen, the brothers, were all in festive array on the station platform when Guido arrived in Putnam's Landing the next evening to start Operation Friendship.

They greeted him *con amore*, kissed him *allegro*, whacked him *fortissimo*, and then Vittorio grabbed him by the arm and headed him towards the delivery truck that served as a vehicle when the di Maggios travelled *en famille*. "Come on," said Vittorio. "Letsa go home."

Guido freed his arm. "You go ahead, Pa. I have to make a stop first."

"Ah, come on!" cried Serafina, the mother, giving him a two-handed thump on the back that sent him reeling into the tailgate of the truck. "Come on home. We gotta big surprise!"

"What do you want to go to Maggie Larkin's for?" said sister Anna. "She hates you."

"Sure," said sister Teresa. "Better you should come home and see the surprise."

"Listen——" said Guido, but the four brothers, two at each side, grabbed his elbows and lifted him into the truck. Then everyone else got in, and Vittorio started the motor and home they went.

The first thing that Guido noticed when he came into the house was how tidy the living-room was: not a cigar butt, not a stray sock anywhere. Then, walking forward, he saw that the dining-room table was covered with the good lace cloth and set with the hand-painted Trylon and Perisphere dinner plates.

"Gee, Ma, this is great," he said, touched. "But you didn't have to go to all this trouble just for me."

"Who says itsa for *you*?" asked Vittorio.

The others thought this was a mighty fine joke and laughed and winked and nudged each other with great gusto.

"Is somebody else coming?" asked Guido.

This, too, was considered wildly hilarious. At length Vittorio raised his hand for order. When all was still, he called, "Okay, surprise. You come out now!"

The swinging door to the kitchen opened slowly. Out stepped Maggie Larkin, demure in a navy blue dress with a little white collar and little white cuffs. A pretty blush was on her cheeks, a tentative smile on her lips.

"Hello, Guido," she said shyly.

"But——" said Guido. Then he said, "What——" and "Er——" and "But——" a few more times.

"Hey, dumb!" said Vittorio, giving him the elbow. "Go kissa you girl!"

"But I don't understand," said Guido. "I mean, what—when—how——"

"Don't talk so much," said Serafina.

"Yes," said Maggie Larkin. "Come kissa you girl."

She held out her arms and, trancelike, he walked into them. He gave her a timid kiss, but she pulled him close and made a job of it.

"Brava!" cried the di Maggios, applauding thunderously. "Bis! Bis! Brava!"

"Okay!" called Serafina. "Everybody sit down. Eat, eat, eat!"

Anna and Teresa went into the kitchen with Serafina to fetch the dinner. Maggie tried to go along to help, but Vittorio grasped her firmly and put her in a chair. "You sit," he said. "You guesta honour. Guido, you guesta honour too. Sit."

"Yes, Pa," said Guido, still in a daze. He took a chair on Maggie's right, Vittorio sat on her left, and the brothers took their accustomed places.

"Shesa good girl, you Maggie," said Vittorio, giving her round young arm an affectionate tweak. "She wasa pretty craze, but shesa all right now."

"Look," said Guido to Maggie. "I don't want to pry, but what happened?"

"Well," said Maggie, but she got no further because the women came out of the kitchen staggering under an assortment of platters, bowls, tureens, and serving dishes. Fragrant clouds of steam rose from each plate and merged into a single heady effluvium of pepper, garlic, oregano, olive oil, and parmesan. "Ah!" said the di Maggio men, their nostrils widening with honest appreciation.

Vittorio filled glasses from a wicker-covered bottle of Chianti. "To the guestsa honour!" he said, raising his glass.

Maggie looked into Guido's eyes and smiled and squeezed his hands as the others drank the toast.

"You gonna tell me what happened?" asked Guido.

"Have some *scungilli*," said Teresa, passing a plate to Maggie. Maggie took some. "Delicious!" she exclaimed. "What is it?"

"Snake," said Bruno.

The smile left Maggie's face; the fork stopped halfway to her mouth.

"Itsa not snake!" said Serafina indignantly.

The smile came back to Maggie's face; the fork continued upwards.

"Itsa conch," said Serafina.

The smile went away again, but she chewed bravely.

"Try some *frittura piccata*," said Anna.

"What is it?" asked Maggie warily.

"Cat," said Carmen.

"You shut up!" said Serafina. "Itsa veal and ham."

Maggie took a helping. "Oh, divine!" she cried. "But it must be terribly hard to make."

"Nah," scoffed Serafina. "You take a nice veal cutlet, see, and you slice him very thin and——"

"Ma," said Guido, "do you think you could give Maggie a cooking lesson some other time? I'm trying to find out what happened."

"Well," said Maggie, "do you know Mrs. Bannerman?"

"Harry Bannerman's wife?" asked Guido.

"That's right."

"Yes, I know her. Funny you should mention her. I ran into Harry Bannerman only yesterday."

"Where?"

"At Fort Totten."

"Oh, of course," said Maggie. "He spent the night there last night."

"He *did*?" said Guido sceptically.

"Yes," said Maggie. "You see, I was supposed to sit with the Bannerman children last night—the Bannermans were going to a hospital fund meeting—but after I got over there, Mr. Bannerman phoned and said he had to spend the night at Fort Totten."

"I see," said Guido, shrugging. None of his business where Harry Bannerman spent his nights.

"Well," continued Maggie, "Mrs. Bannerman decided not to go to the meeting, but she asked me to stay anyhow because she wanted to talk to me. So we made coffee and had a long talk, and Guido, it was one of the most wonderful experiences of my whole life!"

"What did you talk about?"

"Children. . . . And do you know what, Guido? Mrs. Bannerman knows more about child psychology than I do!"

"*No!*"

"Yes! Why, she made me feel like a neophyte. I believe I learned more child psychology last night than I learned in the whole rest of my life put together!"

"Have some *gnocchi*," said Pete.

"No, thank you," said Maggie.

"So where do you stand now?" asked Guido.

"I stand corrected," replied Maggie. "Oh, how wrong I've been—how foolishly, ridiculously wrong!"

"You wasa pretty craze, all right," said Vittorio.

"Yes, I was," said Maggie forthrightly. "But no more. As I told Mr. Vandenberg this morning, from now on I am going to be completely sensible and practical about children. No more wild theories!"

"Mr. Vandenberg, the principal?" asked Guido. "You mean you're back at school?"

"That's right. I had a good, frank talk with him this morning, and he was perfectly wonderful about it, and tomorrow I start teaching again."

"Maggie," cried Guido, his face luminous with joy, "I love you!"

"And I love you," said Maggie simply.

"Atsa nice!" said Vittorio, and then everybody sighed and blinked back a tear and finished the scungilli and frittura piccata and gnocchi and manicotti and zucchini parmesan and finocchi and red bean salad and garlic bread and maritozzi and bocca di dama and coffee and Strega.

Then Guido took Maggie away and drove with her to a public park called Tall Walnuts—a lovely spot with lovers' lanes and secret glades and towering walnut trees as ancient as the hills. He parked the car upon a moon-bright knoll and took his soft and ample true-love in his arms—not *fat*, you understand; *plumpish*—and kissed her lips and throat and hair and two blue eyes.

"Dear God," he said, "if I gotta go, take me now because I'll never be this happy again."

"I love you," said Maggie.

"And I love you," said Guido.

"And you forgive me for being such a fool?" she asked.

"Everybody makes mistakes," said Guido generously. "The important thing is that you've learned your lesson."

"Yes, dear. And we'll never, never fight again."

They kissed happily for a spell.

"But we haven't talked about you yet!" exclaimed Maggie suddenly. "Oh, darling, I think it's just wonderful that you're going to be stationed here in Putnam's Landing."

"It's only on a trial basis," cautioned Guido.

"Oh, pooh!" said Maggie lightly. "You'll make good."

"From your lips to God's ears," said Guido devoutly.

"Tell me all about your job," said Maggie.

"Well, I'm the executive officer, but my particular field is public relations."

"Gee!" said she, impressed.

"What I'm going to do is call a special town meeting, make contacts with all the important organisations, and generally establish a good relationship with the town."

"My goodness, it sounds like a lot of work."

"Yes," he admitted, smiling bravely. "But there'll be some fun too. For instance, we're going to sponsor a team in Little League, and I'm going to manage it."

He felt her plumpish body stiffen.

"What's the matter?" he asked.

She broke out of his embrace and faced him with shocked eyes. "Guido, you're not serious?"

"Serious about what?"

"Managing a Little League team."

"Sure. Why not?"

"I'll tell you why not," she said vehemently. "Because Little League is the greatest single menace to the mental health of America's children, and I am not going to let you be a party to it!"

"Oh, *no*!" groaned Guido. "Not again! Not so *soon*!"

"All that emphasis on winning!" cried Maggie. "All that tension! All that pressure! Never mind playing the game. Just *win*! Let the nerves crack. Let the heart break. But *win*!"

"Maggie——"

"And the bleachers full of parents acting out their thwarted aggressions, screaming at their children—Fight! Fight! Win! Win! Never mind the trauma. Never mind the——"

Guido banged the horn of his car, stopping Maggie in mid-sentence. "Damn it, Maggie," he said sternly, "didn't you just finish telling me you were all through with your crazy theories about child psychology?"

"But——"

"But nothing! You're starting all over again, aren't you?"

Maggie fell silent. She nodded sheepishly. "I guess I am," she said in a tiny voice. "I'm sorry, sweetheart."

"Okay. . . . But let's don't let it happen again, huh?"

"Yes, dear."

"All right. Now where were we?" He resumed his embrace. He sought her lips. But she was talking.

"You go right ahead with your Little League team," she said.

"Thank you," he said.

"And I'll help you," she said.

Guido felt a warning tremor. A simple equation came to mind: Maggie plus children equals trouble. "Oh, that's all right, honey," he said, patting her shoulder. "I can manage."

"No, dear. I'll help," she insisted.

"But what can you do?"

"Keep score. Encourage the boys. Arrange little picnics. Things like that."

"I see," said Guido glumly. "Well, that's very nice, dear, but, honestly, you don't have to."

"I *want* to, darling."

"But——"

"Oh, talk, talk, talk!" said Maggie. "Come kissa you girl!"

And placed her palm on Guido's nape and pulled him to her red, red lips, and there all doubts were stilled, all misgivings softly laid to rest.

Twelve

HARRY BANNERMAN, boy adulterer, sat in the smoking-car of the 7.37 and pressed his fevered forehead against the cold window. More than a week had passed since his night of candle-light and yum-yum with Angela Hoffa at the Hotel Miramar, and there had not been the slightest repercussion. Grace had never questioned his explanation that he had stayed overnight at Fort Totten; nobody had recognised him at the hotel; Angela had discreetly kept her distance afterward.

Why then, wondered Harry, should he feel so miserable? In the first place, it was Grace's fault, not his, that he had strayed from righteousness. In the second place, the session with Angela, once he had ingested enough champagne to still his fluttering ganglia, had been a jolly amalgam of lyricism and know-how. And in the third place, he had gotten away with it clean as a whistle. He should be congratulating himself, not sitting around with a conscience like a big, steaming rock.

All this he told himself as the 7.37 pulled out of the Putnam's Landing station and headed towards New York. All this he had told himself hourly since he broke the Commandment. But it failed signally to help. He still felt an excoriating rush of guilt every time he looked at Grace, and when he saw his children, their faces turned up like three fat roses dewy with love, he felt positively leprous.

Now as he sat and rolled his hot brow against the cool window pane, his *Angst* was suddenly interrupted by a voice in the seat beside him saying explosively, "Jesus H. Christ!"

A few minutes earlier when somebody had taken the seat next to his, Harry had not turned to see who it was. Now he did. The blood rushed out of Harry's head. His sweat ducts opened and his salivary glands closed and his heart banged crazily against his ribcage. "Hello, Oscar," he whispered hoarsely.

"Look at this!" cried Oscar Hoffa, pointing with his clear Havana at the obituary page of the *New York Times*. "Same goddam thing every morning! Guys dropping dead like flies. And look how old they are!" His Upmann stabbed around the page as he picked out various obituaries. "Wilson T. Fleming, broker—52. Morris Rosenthal, ladies' ready-to-wear—45. Ancel Drobny, composer—49. William J. Klein, lawyer—48. Grayson Wing, actor—54. T. O. McFetridge, publisher—61. . . . Wonder what the hell kept McFetride alive so long."

"Yeah," mumbled Harry, wildly uncomfortable. It seemed to him that horns twelve feet long were jutting out of Oscar's forehead. Could it be possible that Oscar didn't notice them?

"I defy you!" cried Oscar, his Upmann coming within an ace of setting the *Times* on fire. "I defy you to find one *woman* on this obit page. Go ahead. Just find me one stinking woman who let herself get pried loose from life!" He thrust the paper at Harry, but yanked it back immediately. "Don't waste your time. You won't. I been reading the obit page for twenty years, and I haven't found one yet."

"Really?" said Harry, licking his dry lips. Oscar apparently did not know he had been cuckolded, but Harry felt no relief. In fact, he felt worse than ever. In his current state of guilt, pistols at sunrise would have seemed a welcome way out.

"No, I'm wrong," said Oscar. "I did see a woman's obit last week. I remember it clearly: 'Mrs. Rutherford B. Hayes, widow of the nineteenth president, died yesterday at the age of one hundred and seventy-four while topping a Douglas fir in North Conway, New Hampshire. She is survived by six daughters, eighty-eight grand-daughters—and her mother.' "

"Ha, ha," said Harry with a sickly grin.

"Why the hell *should* they die?" asked Oscar. "They've got it licked. They've turned the goddam country into a goddam matriachy. All they need from a man is money and stud. You take the average slob on this train. What's his day like? He crawls out of bed at six a.m., goes to New York and works his tail off all day, comes stumbling home at seven o'clock, more dead than alive, and then his wife tells him he has to work a little harder because she's decided to put a new wing on the house. No wonder the poor bastards drop dead at forty! And I'll tell you something else: half the guys who keel over dead aren't even sick, they're just taking the easy way out."

"Very interesting," said Harry. "Would you excuse me, please? I'd like to get a drink of water."

"You take television," continued Oscar, unheeding. "When I plan a programme, do you think I even consider what *men* want to look at? Like hell I do! What for? From six p.m. to nine p.m. a man looks at the programmes his kids want to see. From nine to midnight, the wife picks the programmes. And at midnight the poor sonofabitch has to go to bed because at six in the morning he's got to get up and go to work and make some more money so she can build another wing on the goddam house!"

"If you'll just kind of move your legs a little so I can squeeze by——"

"Television! Christ, what a way to make a living! I bet I've got more flying time than Rickenbacker. I just came back from Hollywood last night, and where do you think I'm going this afternoon? That's right—Hollywood! Just keep watching the obit page, pal. I'll be there soon!"

"Oscar, I hate to be a bother," said Harry, laying a firm hand on his knee, "but I really do have to get a drink of water."

"Why didn't you say so?" said Oscar and moved his legs.

Harry went to the cooler and had four quick glasses of water, but his throat was still parched. Then he went out on the platform and gulped air all the way to Grand Central, but his chest was still tight. Nor did his throat get moister or his chest get looser or his conscience get easier all that day. Not until he boarded the 5.29 back to Putnam's Landing and belted down his first I. W. Harper did a semblance of calm return to him.

He took his second drink to a quiet corner, sat down, and did some strong thinking. One thing was perfectly clear: infidelity was not his kind of work. Never again would he wander off the reservation. Never!

Next question: should he make a full confession to Grace? Answer: no. Why confess? It would only give Grace a lot of grief, and he had wronged the poor woman enough already.

The way to make things up to Grace was not by confession, but by trying to be the kind of husband she wanted him to be— mature, responsible, family-oriented, civic-minded. He highly resolved that starting today he would be precisely such a husband.

Correction: not starting *today*. Starting tomorrow. Before he put his feet on the straight and narrow path, he wanted one more whirl around the Maypole. With Grace, of course. Only with Grace. Tonight when he got home he would say to her, "Honey, you see before you a new man—mature, responsible, family-oriented, civic-minded. Let us celebrate this reformation. Let us go to a country inn and have a bird and a bottle. Then let us go upstairs and spend the night. Let us hold each other very tight and look upon the moonswept lawn and declare our love. Let us store up precious memories to sustain us in the busy days ahead."

Yes, thought Harry, nodding his head energetically, that was exactly what he would do—one last romantic fling at a country inn and then a lifetime of earnestness. And he would insist on a country inn tonight. No matter what plans Grace might have made, he would force her to cancel them. There would be plenty of other nights to be mature, responsible, family-oriented, and civic-minded. This night was for love, and love alone.

He had one more drink to shore up his determination, and he got off, and it was pouring rain, and Grace was not there to meet him.

She had never failed to show up before, and Harry was frankly worried. He waited fifteen minutes and then phoned home.

"Hello!" cried Grace in a frantic voice.

"Honey, what's the matter?"

"Oh, everything!" she replied angrily.

Harry felt a bolt of fear plunge through his belly. "It doesn't have anything to do with—with Angela Hoffa, does it?" he stammered.

"Angela Hoffa?" said Grace, puzzled. "Of course not. Why should it?"

Harry's heart came down from his glottis. "Then what's wrong?" he asked.

"I can't talk now. Get a cab, will you?"

"Yes, dear."

"Hurry!"

She clicked the phone down. Harry went over to the taxi stand. The cabs in Putnam's Landing were operated on a share-the-ride system. Six other passengers were dropped off before Harry, fuming with anxiety, reached his home a full hour later.

His anxiety was not lessened by the sight of three vehicles parked in front of his house: a truck bearing the legend MINTON EVANS—LANDSCAPER; another truck saying WALDO PIKE—HARDWARE; and a 1948 Studebaker sedan belonging to Dr. Magruder.

Harry paid the cab driver, got out in the rain, walked through his front gate, and found the lawn missing.

Missing. It was gone. There was no lawn.

Harry's house stood on the side of a hill that dropped steeply to a brook two hundred feet below. "How picturesque!" Grace had cried upon first seeing the location, and nothing would do except they buy this house.

Picturesque it was without a doubt. But there were certain shortcomings. For one thing there was not a level inch of ground for the kids to play on. Every time they went outside and threw a ball, it promptly rolled down the hill, into the brook, and out to sea. Harry figured that he had, at a conservative estimate, $500 worth of balls bobbing in Long Island Sound.

Then there was the problem of the lawn. A dozen times they had planted grass seed, only to have the first rain wash it down the hill. Finally they called in Minton Evans, who, at horrendous expense, gouged out a terrace fifty feet below the house and built a stout retaining wall that held the grass for almost three weeks. Then he built a stouter retaining wall that did the job for two whole summers. Then he decided that the trouble was not in the wall but in the grass, and he sold them a quarter acre of turf, which cost only a trifle more than broadloom carpeting.

Now Harry, his mouth agape with horror, stood in the drenching rain and stared at the raw brown earth which had been a lawn only this morning, and watched strips of turf slither sluggishly over the retaining wall and down the hill and into the brook.

Minton Evans, dressed in a yellow slicker and rainhat, looking like an elderly, cupidinous Uneeda Biscuit boy, came walking over to Harry. "It's that atom bomb," he said.

"*What?*" shrieked Harry. "An atom bomb fell here?"

"No, no, no," chuckled Minton. "I mean it's them atom bomb explosions that causes all this dang rain. I've lived in these parts, man and boy, for more than sixty years and never seen so much rain!"

"Listen," cried Harry furiously, "you told me that turf was going to hold! You *promised* me!"

"Mr. Bannerman," said Minton reasonably, "it ain't *me* settin' off all them atom bombs."

"Oh, God damn it!" screamed Harry, stamping his foot in the mire. "Oh, God damn it to hell!"

He slogged through the ooze and, ignoring the doormat, stormed into the house. Grace was sitting at the desk in the activities area writing a cheque, while Waldo Pike, hardware, stood behind her, his beady eyes bright with avarice.

"Now what?" yelled Harry.

"Oh, hello, dear," said Grace.

"Howdy, Mr. Bannerman," said Waldo, not quite tugging his forelock.

"What are you writing a cheque for?" roared Harry, brushing aside the greetings.

"A new washing machine," replied Grace.

"What?" whispered Harry, aghast.

"Well, dear," said Grace, "I just got sick and tired of Mr. Pike coming around every week to repair the old one."

"Oh, did you?" snarled Harry. "I rather looked forward to his visits."

"Ah, you're a card, Mr. Bannerman!" said Waldo appreciatively.

"And you're a thief!" yelled Harry. "This is the third time you've sold us a new washer. What the hell kind of machines are you bringing us?"

"Oh, the machines are all right," Waldo assured him. "It's the sand."

"What sand?"

"Your boys," explained Waldo. "They go out and play in the sandbox, and their pockets get full of sand, and then Mrs. Bannerman puts their overalls in the machines, and the sand gets in the camshaft."

"Yeah?" said Harry accusingly. "Last time you told us it was the soap flakes. What's it going to be next time—the water?"

"Yes, sir, you're a card!" said Waldo with an admiring smile. "Oh, by the way, when I was down the cellar, I noticed your power tool's gettin' pretty beat-up. Got some dandy new ones down at the store."

"You get out of here!" said Harry, advancing murderously on the hardware merchant.

"Well, good night," said Waldo and pocketed the cheque and departed.

"My, you're in a nice, pleasant mood," said Grace sharply to Harry.

"What kind of mood you expect me to be in when I come home and find myself teetering on the brink of bankruptcy?"

"And what about me?" said Grace hotly. "I'm the one who had to be here and suffer through all of it—the washer breaking, the lawn floating away, the boy getting sick——"

"What boy?" interrupted Harry.

"Peter."

"What's wrong with him?"

"I don't know. Dr. Magruder's upstairs with him now."

"Oh, grand!" growled Harry and raced up the staircase. Grace followed close behind.

Harry ran into Peter's bedroom. There at the bedside sat old Doc Magruder, looking more like a Norman Rockwell picture than ever. Peter, on the other hand, looked like the picture of Dorian Gray. His face was covered with hideous red bumps and blotches. But underneath the afflictions he was chipper enough. "Hello, Papa, dear," he said happily.

"What's the matter with him?" said Harry to Doc.

"Beats the dickens out of *me!*" answered Doc cheerfully.

"Well, what do you *think* it is?" demanded Harry. "Eczema? Impetigo? Poison Ivy? Psoriasis?"

"What's psoriasis?" asked Doc.

"Oh, for Christ's sake!" snarled Harry and went over and kicked the wall.

"Ain't really a heck of a lot we know about skin diseases," confessed Doc with a chuckle. "You've heard the old saying: some we treat *ex*ternally, some we treat *in*ternally, but most we treat *e*ternally."

Harry rumbled in his throat.

"Keep bringing the boy to my office every two, three days," said Doc to Grace. "We'll try everything. Something's bound to work sooner or later."

"Thank you, healer," said Harry with a tight smile.

"Forget it," replied Doc. "Well, better be going. Getting on to supper time."

Harry and Grace saw Doc to the door. Then Harry turned on his wife and said angrily, "Would you mind telling me why you called that old quack?"

"But everybody uses him," she answered.

"Sure!" cried Harry, waving his arms. "And everybody uses Minton Evans and everybody uses Waldo Pike! Patsies, that's what we are, the whole lot of us! And you know who's the biggest patsy of all? Me—for letting myself get into this mess!"

He turned on his heel, strode across the family area, into the activities area, and over to the bar. He yanked the cork savagely out of the first bottle that came to hand.

"That's right," said Grace, walking bellicosely towards him. "Get drunk. You didn't have enough on the train. Drink some more!"

Harry paused. The train. What happened to all the good resolutions he had made on the train? Had he not made up his mind to be mature, responsible, family-oriented, civic-minded? Was this a way to start—by diving into a bottle of booze?

He put the cork back in the bottle. "Grace, I'm sorry," he said quietly. "Forgive me. I shouldn't have lost my temper. After all, these little crises are part of being a father and home-owner and citizen, aren't they?"

"*Huh?*" said Grace, her mouth falling open.

Harry concentrated for a moment, remembering his pretty speech. "Honey," he said, "you see before you a new man— mature, responsible, family-oriented, civic-minded. So let's celebrate this reformation. Let's go to a country inn tonight and have a bird and a bottle, and then let's go upstairs and spend the night and hold each other very tight and store up memories to sustain us in the days ahead."

"Boy, you *are* loaded!"

"No, honey, I am perfectly serious. Is it a date?"

"What are you talking about?"

"Us. A country inn. Tonight."

"Have you taken leave of your senses?" she asked with considerable exasperation. "You know very well there's a special town meeting tonight to hear Guido di Maggio."

Harry felt a red tide of rage come pumping up from under his breastbone. Resolutely he pushed it back. "What do you say we skip it, huh, honey?" he said, smiling.

"Skip it!" she exclaimed. "*You*—of all people—to talk about skipping it? After we sent you down to Fort Totten to stop this thing, and you failed so dismally, do you think you can just wash your hands of the whole business?"

The rage would not stay down. "Grace, God damn it, I don't want to go to the town meeting! I want to make love to you tonight!"

"Quiet!" she hissed. "The children!"

"Grace," he said in a lower voice, "why won't you let me make love to you tonight?"

"All right, Harry, we'll go to the meeting and then we'll come home and make love when we go to bed."

"No!"

"Why not? Isn't that when people make love? When they go to bed?"

"I don't care what people do! I'm talking about you and me— and why the hell we can't ever get together."

Grace frowned. "Harry, I don't understand you. Are you trying to suggest that I'm frigid or something?"

"No, but——"

"But what? Have I ever refused you when you wanted me?"

"You're damn right!" said Harry stoutly. "Plenty of times."

"Sure," admitted Grace. "When the kids were pounding on the bedroom door. When there was an omelette on the stove. But I mean at night after we've gone to bed."

"I don't want you at night after we've gone to bed."

"In Heaven's name, why not?"

"Because," said Harry, "at night it's not *instead* of something."

"I don't follow you."

"All right, I'll spell it out. At night when we make love, it's just another item on the schedule. . . . Eight a.m.—get the kids to school. Ten a.m.—Red Cross. . . . Twelve noon—lunch. Seven p.m.—dinner. Twelve midnight—sleep with Harry. . . . Well, I don't want to be an item on a schedule, I want to be important enough to postpone things for, to re-arrange things, to drop them if you have to."

"Oh, Harry, grow up!" she begged. "Will you please, finally, at long last, grow up?"

"We have covered this subject too many times," said he coldly. "We will not go over it again. Just answer one question: will you come to a country inn with me tonight?"

"No."

"Grace," he said quietly, "I love you. I love you with all my heart. Will you please come with me?"

"Harry, stop being a damn schoolboy. There's an important meeting tonight, and we have an obligation."

The red rage came again. It filmed his eyes and constricted his chest so he could scarcely breathe. "All right!" He spat the words. "All right, God damn it!"

Out of the house he went. Hurling curses at his ex-lawn, he stomped over to the garage, got into the car, and zoomed out of the driveway like a projectile. Where he was going he knew not. But the car knew. It seemed to know also that Oscar Hoffa was away in Hollywood.

Within a quarter of an hour Harry was knocking on Angela's door. She opened the door. A triumphant smile lit her face. Harry stepped silently into the house. Angela closed the door. Harry reached for her, pulled her close, kissed her hard.

"Angela, I want to go to bed with you," he said, holding her.

"So do I, darling," she answered. "Oh, so do I!"

She kissed him fiercely, her mouth wild, her nails digging. She took his arm, led him to the couch, sat down beside him, kissed him again.

"I have to tell you something first," she said.

"Later."

"Now. I must."

"What?"

"I'm going away for a few weeks."

"Where?"

"Reno."

There is a process that freezes foods instantly. It cannot possibly work as fast as the chill which now shot through Harry, penetrating to the very marrow.

"I am going to divorce Oscar," she said.

"Now, now, now, now, now, now, now, now," said Harry, his tongue flapping like a pennant.

Angela laughed. "Don't be frightened, poor dear," she said, stroking his cheek. "You have no responsibility. You just happen to be the guy I fell in love with. It's my own fault—all mine. There's no need for you to feel any obligation whatsoever."

"Oh," said Harry, hearing distant noises of traps closing, nooses tightening, tumblers clicking shut.

"I love you and I'm stuck," said Angela with a brave little shrug. "It's my misfortune and none of your own."

"Uh-huh," said Harry. "Well, I guess I'll be shoving off. Big town meeting tonight!"

"You sweet idiot!" laughed Angela, placing herself athwart him. "You sweet, sexy idiot!"

"Don't be frightened," said Angela, working on his buttons. "Don't worry about a thing."

Thirteen

"TONIGHT," said the Moderator, "I am going to step down and turn the meeting over to Lieutenant Guido di Maggio of the 992nd Anti-Aircraft Missile Battalion."

The Moderator left the platform and took a seat in the audience. Guido walked to the lectern. No applause greeted him. There was, in fact, an almost tangible emanation of hostility from the assembly. Except for the di Maggio family and Maggie Larkin, sitting together in the back of the hall, not a friendly face could be seen.

Guido was not dismayed. He had prepared himself carefully for tonight's test, and he was full of quiet confidence. "Good evening," he said, not smiling. "I know you people pretty good, and I know you weren't born yesterday. I'm not going to try to con you with fancy speeches. You ask questions, I'll give you straight answers. Okay, who's first?"

The Moderator rose. "It's been a long time since I've been on this side of the platform, so if nobody objects, I'd like to get the ball rolling. Lieutenant, tell us why, with the whole countryside to choose from, the Army decided to put the Nike base smack in the middle of Putnam's Landing."

"We had to," said Guido. "We didn't want to, sir. We would have much preferred to pick some piece of land that nobody cared about. But you see, we're part of a ring around Bridgeport—a group of batteries that protect Bridgeport no matter where an enemy attack might come from. It's all figured out mathematically so that each battery overlaps the next one. You remove any one battery, you leave a great big hole in the defences."

"Isn't it better to have a hole in the defences," asked Willard

Beauchamp, "than to put nuclear warheads right in the centre of a heavily populated residential area?"

"Let me set your mind at rest about one thing," replied Guido. "It's true the Defense Department has announced the development of a Nike with a nuclear warhead. But we will definitely not have them at Putnam's Landing—not for several years at any rate. And when they do come—*if* they come—there will be adequate safeguards against radiation. . . . But that's for the future; right now all we've got is standard, conventional missiles."

"Isn't that bad enough?" asked Rodney O'Sheel. "High explosives, fuming acids—that's hardly the kind of thing we want in our community."

"Sir," replied Guido, "a Nike base is no more dangerous than a gas station. All our explosives are stored deep underground. We have concrete bunkers and earthen walls eight feet thick around the fuelling and firing areas. There is no danger whatsoever of injuring any property around the Nike base."

"No?" said Henry Steinberg. "How about the exhaust flames when you fire the Nike?"

"First of all," said Guido, "the Nike is never fired except in the event of an enemy attack. There is no practice firing. . . . I'll repeat that. There is *no practice firing*. The Nike will never be launched unless there are enemy planes overhead—and if it is launched, there is a five-hundred-foot safety zone around the launching site to take care of the exhaust flames."

The Moderator got up again. "All right, let's say that there is an enemy attack and you have to launch a Nike. As I understand it, Nike is a two-stage rocket. The first stage goes after the target, while the booster falls back to earth. Now what's going to prevent the booster from falling through somebody's roof?"

"The Nike is fired in a fixed trajectory," said Guido. "It is not aimed from the ground. We send it up to a pre-determined spot—in the case of Putnam's Landing, it will be somewhere over Long Island Sound—and then radar guides the missile to the target while the booster falls back into the Sound."

"What if the missile fails to hit the target and then goes flying around till it runs out of fuel?" asked Willard Beauchamp. "Doesn't it come crashing back to earth?"

"No," answered Guido. "If Nike runs out of fuel—or if it ever loses contact with radar control—it explodes itself automatically in the air."

Isaac Goodpasture rose and fixed Guido with a hard glare. "What you say is very impressive, young man. But I've been digging back in some old newspaper files. Isn't it a fact that in 1954 at Fort Meade, Maryland, a Nike took off all by itself and crashed right in the middle of the Washington-Baltimore highway?"

"Yes, sir, it's a fact," admitted Guido promptly. "It's a one-in-a-billion chance, but you're right—it happened. But I'll tell you two things: first, we've taken elaborate precautions to see that such a thing can never happen again. Second, when that runaway Nike landed on the Washington-Baltimore highway, it did *not* explode. A Nike will never explode unless it is sent up by radar control. It is not a weapon that detonates on contact. So in the fantastically unlikely event that a Nike ever gets loose again, you can be sure it will land without exploding."

"All right," said George Melvin, realtor. "We'll take your word for it that Nike isn't dangerous. But you can't tell me it's not dangerous to property values. Here in Putnam's Landing, we've got some of the finest, most valuable real estate in the whole country. What happens when the Army moves in with a big, ugly, noisy camp?"

"Sir," said Guido, "I can assure you that property values will not suffer one bit. You will hardly know the Nike base is here. The buildings will be neat, low, and inconspicuous. We will landscape the base to blend with the surrounding countryside. We will only have one hundred troops. There will be no noise, no smoke, no fumes, and no dust."

David Coleman got up. "Okay, Lieutenant, so Nike isn't dangerous and it won't hurt real estate values. But what good is it? I've been talking to some of my friends in the Air Force, and they tell me Nike couldn't hit the side of a barn."

"With all respect, sir," said Guido, "I beg to differ. Nike is a very effective weapon. I saw it with my own eyes bring down a B-17 at Red Canyon, New Meixco."

"Yeah?" said David. "But what if the Russians don't come in B-17s?"

"Nike can overtake and destroy any airplane in the world today—Russian, American or British—no matter what speed and altitude the airplane is flying at," said Guido flatly.

"What if the enemy plane stays out of range?" asked David. "What if it comes to about one hundred miles off the coast and sends in a guided bomb?"

"The Air Force is supposed to take care of enemy planes one hundred miles off the coast," countered Guido.

"All right," said David. "What if the enemy sends an intercontinental ballistic missile?"

"Then we're dead," admitted Guido. "Look, sir, Nike doesn't pretend to be anything but an anti-aircraft weapon. And it's a good one, no matter what the Air Force says. Sure, there'll be better missiles later, but meanwhile Nike is ready."

"Why not wait for the better missiles?" said Isaac Goodpasture. "Why waste all that taxpayers' money?"

"Because, sir, the enemy may not be willing to wait," answered Guido. "And besides, as weapons go, it isn't all that expensive. A Nike base—complete with buildings, launchers, rockets, radar, everything—does not cost very much more than one single jet airplane. And if an enemy attacks, one jet is in the hands of one man and can make one pass, while a Nike base has a hundred men and can send up an unlimited number of rockets."

Laura Beauchamp rose. "Lieutenant, I must be blunt," she said. "This is a quiet, homey village. Our daughters have been gently reared. What will happen to these pure, innocent girls when the town is full of soldiers?"

"Ma'am," said Guido mildly, "are you under the impression that a boy turns into a sex fiend the minute he puts on a uniform? Look at the kids who've gone into the Army from Putnam's Landing. Have they become rapists? Of course not. Well, the kids who are coming here will be American boys, just like yours, from American homes, just like yours. If your daughters have been brought up properly—and I know they have—you haven't got a thing to worry about."

Laura Beauchamp sat down, and nobody else got up. Guido looked intently at his audience. Their faces were no longer hostile; they were thoughtful now, wavering, even abashed. He decided the time had come to make his move.

"Folks," he said with great sincerity, "I know how you feel. I'm from Putnam's Landing too, and I don't like to see our town changed any more than you do. But, friends, our country has to be defended, and we all must do our bit.

"And besides," he continued, directing his glances at the merchants and tradesmen in the audience, "it won't be too bad having these kids around. Remember, they make good money, and they've got nothing to do except spend it. Fatso, I'll bet your diner will be doing more business than you ever dreamed of. Hank, you'll be moving used cars that have been sitting on your lot for ten years. Sol, that movie palace of yours will stop looking like a haunted house every night. Mr. Melvin, a lot of the guys are married and they'll be needing houses off the post. And, Mrs. Beauchamp, you can stop worrying about those amateur theatricals of yours. If you need anything at all—actors, props, stagehands—just call me.

"So what do you say, folks? Will you make these kids welcome and show them that you're good sports and good Americans? I know it means sacrifices on your part, but think of the sacrifices the soldiers are making. They're leaving their homes, their families, their schools, their girls. How will they feel if they come into a town full of hate and hostility? How would your own kids feel? Folks, listen to me. I grew up here, and I know you. You're fine, decent, generous people. I'm sure you're going to open up your hearts to these lonesome American kids far away from home. . . . Thank you."

Guido smiled sweetly at the audience, and suddenly everybody in the hall was smiling back. Then the applause began—a ripple at first, then a wave, then a thundering tide. Maggie Larkin bounced up and down in a transport of pride. Vittorio di Maggio turned in all directions, shouting, "Atsa my Guido! Atsa my boy!" Everybody rose and gave Guido a standing ovation.

When order was restored, Grace Bannerman stepped forward. "Lieutenant," she said, "I'd like to thank you for giving us a clear and interesting description of Nike, but more than that, I'd like to thank you for opening our eyes. We've been fools, all of us—selfish, inconsiderate fools—and I think I speak for everybody here when I say that we are thoroughly ashamed."

Heads nodded in agreement all over the hall.

"And," continued Grace, "I want to assure you, Lieutenant, that when the soldiers arrive, we will do our very best to make them feel at home, to make them a real part of our community!"

"Thank *you*, Mrs. Bannerman," said Guido. "And now, as a citizen of this town, I think I'm entitled to make a motion at this meeting, which I herewith do: I move that we appoint a Nike Hospitality Committee, and I nominate Mrs. Bannerman for chairman."

"Second the motion!" cried Maggie Larkin.

"Oh, no, no, no!" said Grace hastily. "I couldn't take the job. I have so many things already."

"Nonsense!" said Laura Beauchamp firmly. "All those in favour?"

"Aye!" came a resounding cry.

Grace flushed with pleasure. "All right," she said, laughing.

"My husband will kill me when he finds out, but thank you. I accept."

A mighty cheer was led by Maggie Larkin.

"Move we adjourn," said Manning Thaw, first selectman.

"Oh, darn!" cried Betty O'Sheel, plucking frantically at Grace's sleeve. "How about my garbage disposal plant?"

"Not tonight, dear," said Grace. "Some other time. Okay?"

"But I've waited so long," complained Betty, biting her lip.

"Tell you what," said Grace. "I'll put you on my Nike Hospitality Committee."

"Well, all right," said Betty, by no means mollified. "But when can I bring up the garbage?"

"Soon," said Grace, "soon."

"Second," said Isaac Goodpasture.

"A motion to adjourn has been made and seconded," said Guido. "All in favour?"

"Aye," said everybody.

"The meeting," said Guido, "is adjourned."

Fourteen

A GROUP of American boys sat in a troop train bound from Fort Bliss, Texas, to Putnam's Landing, Connecticut. They were young—eighteen or nineteen most of them—and their eyes were bright, and their bodies were fit, and as they sped to their new assignment in a faraway place, a sense of adventure filled their stout young hearts, a single question gripped all their keen young minds.

The question was voiced by Private William O. Wambess, a stalwart youth from Milwaukee, Wisconsin. "What," he asked, "are we going to do for broads in a jerkwater town like Putnam's Landing?"

"Let's face it: we're dead," said Private Roger Litwhiler, a broth of a lad from Boulder, Colorado. "It's tough enough getting broads in *any* small town, but in a *New England* small town—let's face it, boys: we're dead!"

"What a cruddy thing to do to us!" said Private Gustave Morrissette, a well-favoured stripling from San Diego, California. "Sending us to a cruddy no-action dump like Putnam's Landing!"

"Yeah," said the others and sighed and shook their heads mournfully—all but one. He laughed out loud. His name was Corporal Opie Dalrymple, and his home was Altus, Oklahoma. He was eighteen years old, five feet eleven inches tall, and growing. His hair was a tumble of chestnut curls; his face was fresh and full of wisdom.

He sat now among his colleagues, sprawled comfortably on his seat, his feet propped up on a barracks back in the aisle. Slung around his neck was a six-string Gibson guitar splendidly adorned with silver trimming, a picture of a palomino horse, and a legend in sequins: "MOTHER, I LOVE YOU." He struck a chord on the guitar, frowned slightly, adjusted the tuning pegs, tried the chord again, and nodded with satisfaction. Then he looked up at the distressed faces of his fellows and once more laughed out loud.

"What are you laughing at?" said Private William O. Wambess resentfully. "I don't think it's very funny—getting stuck in a hick town with no dames."

"Frinds," said Opie in accents that recalled hominy grits and sidemeat, "lemme tell you about hick towns. Ah ben in Nyawk, Nawlins, St. Louis, Chicago, and Hollywood, and Ah tell you the mortal truth, mah frinds, you'll find more poon per square inch in hick towns than in any big city on God's green earth!"

"Yeah?" said the others, crowding eagerly around Opie.

"It's a fack," Opie assured them. "You take a big city gal now. Night-time comes, she got thangs to do, places to go. But you take a little ole country gal. She ain't got but one thing to do at night: Ah mean poon."

"Maybe down where you come from," said Private Roger Litwhiler. "But we're heading for New England."

"Country's country," said Opie flatly. "Ah ben pickin' and sangin' all over these *U*nited States—north, south, east, and west—yeah, and Canada too—and wherever I ben, them little ole country gals all had the same thang on their mind."

"Poon?" asked Private Gustave Morrissette hopefully.

"Poon," affirmed Opie.

The young warriors, much heartened, returned to their seats. In the months of basic training, they had come to know that Opie was a man to be trusted. Here was no ordinary G.I.; here was a man broadened by travel, richened by experience, sharpened by show business—a man who, had not the Army nabbed him in mid-career, would surely today be a star of the magnitude of Ferlin Husky, or possibly even Ernest Tubb.

It had been, as a matter of fact, Mr. Tubb who first put Opie's feet on the steep, hard path to stardom. Mr. Tubb and a troupe of supporting artists gave a recital one evening in Altus, Oklahoma, and Opie, then six years old, was taken along by his mama and daddy. It was his first look at country music, and the effect was overwhelming. He sat through the concert as if in a trance, bulge-eyed and open-jawed. Only his little foot moved, solemnly beating time, and occasionally his tiny fingers twitched at the strings of an imaginary guitar.

At the end of the show his mama and daddy, in the friendly manner of country folk, went up to tell Mr. Tubb what a heap of enjoyment he had given them. Opie, hiding behind his mother's skirt, suddenly found courage, emerged from the dirndl, plucked at the white leather fringe on Mr. Tubb's handsome red and yellow cowboy jacket, and asked in a quavering but determined treble, "Mr. Tubb, how do Ah get to be a big stor like you?"

"Now, don't you bother Mr. Tubb," said Opie's daddy, fetching Opie a smart clout in the ear.

"Shucks, folks, Ah don't mind," said Mr. Tubb with a kindly chuckle. He tousled Opie's chestnut curls. "So you want to be a big stor, do you?" he asked.

"Yes, sir," said Opie fervently.

"Well, boy, here's what you got to do," said Mr. Tubb. He laid his hand over his cardiac region. "You got to sang from the hort, boy, you got to sang from the hort!"

Opie never forgot this fine advice. Whenever he sang, it was from the heart—direct from his heart to the hearts of the audience. But, of course, it was many years before he had an audience. In fact, it was many years before he even had a guitar. Opie's daddy, though mighty fond of country music, was not of a mind to encourage Opie's artistic aspirations. There were, after all, fifteen acres of unbounteous red dirt to farm, and only one son in the house. But Opie's mama, watching the boy sitting transfixed by the radio each night listening to the country disc jockeys, was filled with pity and saved her egg money and on

Opie's tenth birthday presented him with his very own Gibson guitar.

It cannot be said that Opie taught himself to play the guitar. The fact is, he never had to learn at all. The guitar was placed in his hands, and he straightaway ran off eighteen choruses of *My Bucket's Got a Hole in It.*

It was scarcely a month later that Opie wrote his first song. Standing in the half-filled silo where the acoustics provided a pleasant echo, he picked and sang a little ditty entitled *You Lied to Me Oncet Too Often.* It went like this:

> *You lied to me oncet too often,*
> *You broke off a piece of muh hort,*
> *You watched me rot and soften,*
> *You thought you was awful smort.*

> *You lied to me oncet too often,*
> *Muh love, it made you laugh,*
> *You near put me in a coffin,*
> *You branded me like a calf.*

> *You lied to me oncet too often,*
> *You never thought no more of me,*
> *Than a dirty old pig in a trough an'*
> *The fishes in the sea.*

> *You lied to me oncet too often,*
> *And now Ah hate yore guts,*
> *Ah may be weak and coughin',*
> *But Ah ain't completely nuts.*

Though Opie, at age ten, had no intimate acquaintance with the sorrows of love, he did sing his song from the heart, and his mama allowed that it was right pretty. His daddy was less impressed. "You keep out of that goddam silo, hear?" he said.

But Opie returned to the silo at every opportunity. In the next six years in addition to going to school, milking, ploughing, planting, haying, and chopping cotton, he wrote upwards of three thousand songs, including *On the Banks of the Fort Supply Reservoir; Red Eye Whisky Is My Buckler, but the Bible Is My Shield; Daughter's Gone to Dallas, a Car-Hop for to Be;* and *Dear God, I'm Glad You Took My Ethel, She Was Much Too Good for Me.*

Opie picked and sang his songs (from the heart) at dances, hoe-downs, barn raisings, and all other fiestas around Altus, Oklahoma, and the folks enjoyed them mightily, but no talent scouts came through town, and he finally decided that since fame was not coming after him, he would have to go after *it*. On his sixteenth birthday while his mama wept and his daddy hit him with an axe-handle, he took off for Oklahoma City to seek his fortune.

In the metropolis Opie discovered that he was not the only prodigy who had come boiling out of the hills. The waiting rooms of the radio stations were jammed with hundreds of guitar-slung young men, each with a huge repertory of home-made songs, each singing from the heart, each clawing for a chance to be heard. But Opie persisted and after several hungry months got an audition. The station manager and the station manager's assistant listened and looked at one another and nodded wisely. No doubt about it: this boy had the stuff—the twang, the whine, the heart.

From this point Opie's rise, if not meteoric, was certain and steady. He played around Oklahoma City for a while, then moved on to the other country music centres—Little Rock, Shreveport, Richmond—and finally he received the accolade: booking at the Grand Old Opry in Nashville, which is to country music what the Palace was to old time vaudeville.

In Nashville, Opie was truly initiated into the country music business—a fabulous business which accounts for forty per cent. of all phonograph record sales in the United States; a business whose stars—people like Ernest Tubb, Ferlin Husky, Red Foley, Carl Smith, Webb Pierce—are almost unknown in New York and Hollywood, but who nonetheless manage to earn a hundred thousand dollars and more every year; a business where every performer composes his own songs and then delivers them to the publishing house on a tape recording because not one of them can read or write music; a business where everybody drives a Cadillac, not for reasons of ostentation, but because it is quite common on tour to travel five, six, and seven hundred miles in a single day.

Opie's first tour (he got fifth billing in a troupe of five) took him north from Louisiana to the Dakotas, then into Canada to Winnipeg, Calgary, and Edmonton, then down to Bozeman, Montana, west to the State of Washington, south to California, and east through Arizona, New Mexico, and Texas. In all, he sang from his heart in forty-five towns, and in each of them the audience response was immensely gratifying.

Particularly the response from the girls in the audience. Young female fans of country music are not to be confused with their metropolitan sisters. The bobby soxers, for instance, who used to mob the Paramount to hear Frank Sinatra were filled with adulation to be sure, but adulation was all they had. Frankie to them was a star and, like a star, distant and unattainable; the best they could hope for was a shred of his clothing. But the girls at country concerts feel no such separation between themselves and the performers. That boy up on the stage singing to them from his heart is clearly country, even as they are, and they find it not at all unthinkable that he might be available for some close work after the show.

Opie did a sight of close work on his tour, all of which he thoroughly enjoyed, and he wrote a few new songs—not more than two or three hundred—and then came back to Nashville, bought himself a sky-blue Cadillac, made a second appearance on Grand Old Opry, recorded some songs, and left on another tour (third billing in a troupe of five this time) which took him east to the Carolinas, north to Vermont, and then back through New York State, Pennsylvania, and Ohio.

A notice from the draft board followed him all through this tour but did not catch up with him until he was back in Nashville. It could not have been more untimely, coming as it did when he was just beginning to get a foothold in country music, but it never occurred to Opie to ask for a postponement. Instead he got magnificently drunk and in the morning sent off his Cadillac to his daddy and reported quietly for military service.

There was a tiny bit of trouble during his first days in the Army. His barracks mates had some things to say about his sideburns, his buckskin fringed suits, and his guitar, all of which Opie bore with sweet patience until it became clear that direct measures were indicated. Then he cold-cocked his two principal tormentors with a short left and a short right respectively, and the ragging stopped.

Looking at Opie with new eyes—especially after his cowboy duds had been traded for khaki and a G.I. barber had darkened the floor with his sideburns—the boys in the barracks began to see that he was no rustic pantaloon, but a man of considerable parts. He was friendly, agreeable, and intelligent; he was no stranger to the world; he could drop a man with either his right or left hand; and he sang from the heart.

The mantle of leadership fell naturally upon Opie's shoulders, and he wore it with the lordly unconcern of the born commander. The company NCOs, also aware of Opie's quality, quickly promoted him to acting corporal. When the company was detailed to Putnam's Landing, the designation was made official.

Now Corporal Opie Dalrymple sat easily on the troop train clacking north by east and rested his feet on a barracks bag and struck soft chords on his guitar. He was content. He did not look back and curse the fate that had cut off a career full of bright promise; nor did he look forward with dismay to two years'

duty in a little New England backwater called Putnam's Landing.
"Country's country," he had said, and he felt with a serenity
based on accomplishment that no man need go loveless.

As he sat and anticipated a rich, full life in Putnam's Landing,
his muse, never distant, lighted on his shoulder and moved him
to composition. From the heart he sang and picked the following:

> *Ah'm a long gone soldier in a faraway land,*
> *And muh load of grief is great,*
> *But if you'll let me hold yore dear little hand,*
> *Ah'll be at Heaven's gate.*

Fifteen

"DADDY-O," said soft young Comfort Goodpasture to her hard old father Isaac, "what are you doing?"

"I am trying to write an editorial," replied Isaac, "and you do not lighten my task by humming *Love Me Tender* and rasping your fingernails. Is it possible that you might do those things in your own room?"

"But I want to talk to you," said Comfort.

"You do?" he said, mildly astonished. It had been many a long year since such a request had come from Comfort. "Is there anything wrong?"

"There certainly is!" declared Comfort. "Daddy-O, something awful is happening to me—something to do with sex."

"I knew it!" cried Isaac, going white. "I knew it was only a matter of time!"

"Oh, relax! It's not anything like *that*. It's just emotional."

"Glory be to God!" breathed Isaac, his colour returning.

"Well, it's nothing to celebrate," said Comfort resentfully. "I mean this thing has really got me bugged."

"*Bugged*," said Isaac, "is, I think, not an unusual condition for you."

"Not *this* bugged," she insisted. "Daddy-O, listen. Something weird has happened. All of a sudden, I like boys. I don't just *like* 'em; I mean I go ape when I think about 'em!"

"I see," said Isaac. "And when did this transformation take place?"

"I don't know. Three or four weeks ago, I guess. I first noticed it the night Grady Metcalf came round with his motor-cycle. You see, his fossils promised him a motor-cycle on his eighteenth birthday if he passed math, and——"

"By fossils," interrupted Isaac, "I presume you mean parents?"

"What else?" said Comfort. "Well, anyhow——"

"Excuse me," said Isaac, interrupting again. "Am I to understand that Grady Metcalf passed math?"

"Weirdsville, ain't it?" said Comfort.

"It is indeed," he agreed.

"Yeh," said Comfort. "Well, anyhow, Grady Metcalf, who is one of the really big meatballs of our generation, and I hate him like poison, he took me out riding on his motor-cycle, and you know what? All of a sudden he didn't seem like such a meatball! And you know what else? When I saw him in school next day, he looked even better!"

"Weirdsville," said Isaac solemnly.

"But that's not the worst of it!" cried Comfort. "*All* the boys looked good to me! I mean I went down the hall and saw twerps and gropers that I would just as soon step on 'em as look at 'em, and suddenly they didn't seem so bad after all. In fact, lately there's not more than fifteen or twenty boys in the whole school that I can't stand."

"Tell me," said Isaac nervously, "this new outlook of yours—has it made you, shall we say, more tractable?"

"Oh, don't worry, Daddy-O. I haven't *done* anything. They still call me 'The Iron Maiden' at school. . . . But I'll tell you the truth, Daddy-O: when I cope these days, my heart isn't really in it."

"You do, however, continue to cope?" asked Isaac hopefully.

"I do," sighed Comfort. "But it seems less important all the time. And that's what bugs me, Daddy-O. Why do I feel this way?"

Isaac was suddenly touched to the depths of his craggy heart. He rose from his desk, walked over to Comfort, and laid an awkward hand on her shoulder. "Comfort, child," he said softly, "if the Good Lord in His wisdom had not seen fit to take your mother, perhaps she could answer you. All I can say is, no matter how bewildering it all seems, it is quite natural, and soon everything will be in order again."

"Grand!" said Comfort unhappily. "What do I do in the meantime?"

"In the meantime," answered Isaac, "you've got three hundred years of Puritan blood in your veins. Listen to it."

The Putnam's Landing chapter of the Dean-Presley School of Juvenile Delinquency met nightly in the parking lot of Fatso's Diner. Here, starting at seven in the evening, they would stand beside their hybrid automobiles, tilt their pelvises, hug their elbows, smoke cigarettes, tell lies about their sex life, and spit. After a while they would go inside the diner, drink cokes, lean on the juke box and play Fats Domino, the Clef Tones, and, of course, Elvis. Toward midnight they would go home, where, during their absence, their fathers and mothers had been arguing violently, each mother contending that there was nothing wrong with the boy, he was just passing through a phase, and each father insisting that a good belt on the side of the head would send him through the phase a hell of a lot faster. As the boy slouched in the house, the mother would approach him with sweet propitiatory smile and say, "Would you like a glass of milk before you go to bed, dear?" By way of reply he would snarl, "Will you get off my back, fa Chrisake?" and lurch up to his bedroom while the mother bodily prevented the father from going after him and fracturing his skull.

Thus passed a typical evening of a typical New Delinquent—spitting, loitering, and addling his parents. No gas stations got held up, no stores got burgled, no citizens got mugged, no blood got spilled.

And no girls ruined. The sex life of the New Delinquent was wholly conversational. On week nights they had no dates at all; on Fridays and Saturdays they drove the local girls to dark places and made out. "Making out" was nothing more than what used to be called necking and petting. This activity, as older readers will recall, covered a good deal of territory, but always stopped short of fulfilment. The New Delinquents were in their hearts as scared of real sex as they were of real larceny.

Now on this night, while Comfort Goodpasture was having a heart-to-heart talk with her father, four New Delinquents were lounging around a fenderless, souped-up 1932 Ford in the parking lot of Fatso's Diner. Each wore a ducktail haircut and long, greasy sideburns, each held a king-size cigarette in his mouth, each was seventeen years old. They stood, this quartet of rebels without causes, these victims of the *Zeitgeist*, and made the following conversation:

"What's the scoop for tonight?" said the one called Wally.

"Same as last night—nothin'," said the one called Ed.

"Lousy burg is a lousy morgue," said the one called Charlie.

"Kee-rap," said the one called Fred.

All spat.

"They ought to have a youth centre in this burg," said Wally, "where a guy could pick up some tail."

"I could use some," said Ed. "It's been more'n a week."

"Kee-rap," said Fred.

"No, honest," said Ed. "Remember when my old lady took me to New York to see this head-shrinker? Well, I snuck away for a half-hour, see, and I'm walkin' down Fifth Avenue when I notice this dame givin' me the eye. She's about thirty-five, see, but she's still plenty good lookin'. So I just fall in step right next to her, and she don't say boo. She turns the corner, I turn with her. She goes into a hotel, I go right along. She don't say a word, see? So finally we get up to her room, and she lets me in and locks the door. Then she rips her clothes off, and of course I rip mine off too, and man, we went the whole route!"

"Kee-rap," said Fred.

"No, honest!" Ed insisted.

"Okay, let's drive to New York and get her," said Charlie.

"We can't, hey," said Ed. "I mean I promised her I'd never

come back. She's real hi-si, see, and if word ever got out about this, she'd be ruined with the Four Hundred."

"Kee-rap," said the other three.

They stood for a while expectorating morosely. Then Grady Metcalf roared into the lot on his big black Harley, and joy abruptly replaced dolour. They all broke into happy smiles and rushed to greet him.

Grady had always been their leader, but lately two developments had solidified his position. First, the motor-cycle. Second, now that he was eighteen, he had a draft card and could therefore buy beer across the New York State line.

"Grady, whaddya say? What's up? How ya makin'?" they cried, looking admiringly at this fine figure of a man in black denim trousers and motor-cycle boots and a black leather jacket with an eagle on the back.

Grady regarded them coldly through half-closed Presley-style eyelids, not replying, showing the disdain that became his station. He took out a cigarette, clicked a kitchen match on his thumbnail, lit up, dragged deeply, spat.

"How's the bike runnin', Grady?" asked Wally, laying a respectful hand on the flank of the Harley.

Grady deigned to speak. "Cuttin' out a little in third," he replied. "Havin' some trouble speed-shiftin'. Could be a plug."

The others listened in devout silence, as young seminarians to a bishop.

"But otherwise she's going pretty smooth," continued Grady. "Had her up to ninety-seven last night."

"Kee-rist!" said the others, awed.

Pleased by the response, Grady unbent a trifle. "What are you cats up to tonight?"

"Same as last night—nothin'," said Ed.

"Lousy burg is a lousy morgue," said Charlie.

"Kee-rap," said Fred.

"Hey, Grady, how about hittin' for New York State?" suggested Wally.

"Sure!" agreed Ed enthusiastically. "Let's go over to Beer Can Boulevard and get gassed!"

"No," said Grady.

"Well, then, how about we cruise around and see if we can find some tail?" said Charlie.

"Good idea," said Grady. "You do that."

"How about you?" asked Fred.

"I got mine," replied Grady.

They looked at him with delight and admiration. "Yeh, Grady?" asked Wally. "You on the scheme tonight?"

"That's right," he admitted.

"Who is she?" they asked as one man.

"Comfort Goodpasture," he answered.

Their faces fell. "Aw, Grady," said Charlie, "what for? You got this beautiful bike. You could pick up any broad in town. Why keep wastin' time on The Iron Maiden?"

"That's right, Grady," said Wally. "Why knock yourself out for nothin'? Nobody's ever made out with Comfort."

"Until tonight," said Grady confidently.

"What makes you so sure?" asked Fred.

"She's ready," replied Grady. "I feel it in my bones: she's ready!"

With this positive pronouncement, he kicked the starter on his Harley and blasted off. His disciples looked after him pensively. "If anybody can do it," said Ed, "it's Grady."

"Yeah," said Fred. "But nobody can do it."

Isaac Goodpasture had long ago learned that when a widower like himself raises a teen-age daughter like Comfort, the only possible principle to employ is *laissez faire*. Let her go where she wants, and depend on Providence and Yankee genes to bring her home intact.

But now as he stood at the window of his study and watched her roaring away on the back of Grady Metcalf's motor-cycle, her hair flying, her cheek flattened against Grady's leather jacket, Isaac wondered glumly whether the time had not come to drop *laissez faire* and try a set of leg-irons.

But no, thought he. Restraint would only make her wilder. Gentle suasion was the only answer—that and sneaking out some moonless night and slashing Grady's tyres.

He left the window and returned to his desk, resolutely putting thoughts of Comfort from his mind. He had a job to do—a job that had been thwarting his best efforts for many days. The following week Putnam's Landing was celebrating "Welcome Nike Day" and it was Isaac's task now to write an appropriately hospitable editorial for the *Gazette*.

But Isaac could not think of one solitary reason to welcome Nike. For a man who had dedicated his life to preserving the *status quo* in Putnam's Landing, the arrival of Nike was a pure calamity. Nor had he been comforted by Guido di Maggio's assurances at the town meeting. High explosives were high explosives, and soldiers were soldiers, and no amount of talk could convince Isaac that these two elements would fit snugly into the rustic pattern of Putnam's Landing.

Still, Nike was a fact, and it would be churlish—not to say unpatriotic—to rail against it now. There was nothing for it but to cast his mind about until he found some aspect, some angle, that would give him a properly cordial editorial.

So he sat and thought and cast. At last he found what he was looking for, and he wrote the following:

"To the officers and men of the Nike base, the Putnam's Landing Gazette extends a hearty welcome. We hope you will be content here.

"To those residents of Putnam's Landing who look upon the arrival of Nike with something less than delight, we offer this consolation: Nike has pre-empted for its use one hundred acres of Johnnycake Hill. If Nike had not come along and taken this land, it is certain that some developer would have grabbed it and constructed one hundred houses on the site. It is fair to estimate that the houses would have cost about $30,000 apiece, which means that

*property taxes accruing to the town from each house would have run
approximately $480 per annum.*

*"But before we mourn the loss of this revenue, let us consider
another aspect. These new houses would have all been sold to
commuters, who, as we have noted with no little dismay, proliferate
like rabbits. It cannot be doubted that a minimum of three children
would be born in each house—children who would have to be educated
in our public schools at a cost of $635 per head per year, thus bur-
dening the town with a net annual loss of $1,425 on each house!*

*"So we say, Welcome, Nike! And if the Air Force and the Navy
would also like to come in, welcome to them too!"*

Comfort and Grady sat on a bench at Tall Walnuts with the
motor-cycle parked nearby. There were stars in Comfort's eyes,
warmth in her bosom. She could feel the smash of the wind, the
roar of the exhaust, the road spinning dizzily underneath.

Grady, pretending casualness, reached over and picked up
her hand. She disengaged it with practised ease. "You start
groping," she said pleasantly, "and I'll put you in the hospital."

"Tell me somethin', hey," he asked. "What you got against
a little makin' out?"

"I just don't like people slobbering all over me, that's all."

"I don't slobber," he said. "I'll show you."

He gave her a quick, neat, unexpected kiss which to her im-
mense surprise, she found she was thoroughly glad to have
had.

"Was that bad?" he asked.

She shook her head dumbly, her eyes wide with wonder.

"Come here."

Without volition, it seemed, she slid closer to him. He raised
her head to kiss position and fell to work truly and well. She
relaxed in his embrace, all but her right hand, which swung in a
short, savage arc and slammed into the back of his neck. He
sprang away, howling with pain.

"Gee, I'm sorry, Grady," she said, genuinely contrite.

"What was that for?" he complained. "I thought you liked kissing."

"Oh, I do," she assured him. "Kissing is wonderful! It's *you* I can't stand."

"Thanks a lot," he mumbled huffily.

"Maybe you better take me home," said Comfort.

"Maybe I better."

Silently they mounted the Harley. Again, as they sped home, the good, wild, free feeling returned to Comfort. She hugged Grady tight, rubbed her cheek happily into his back, laughed with delight as they careened around corners.

They pulled up in front of Comfort's house. Grady helped her off, walked her to the door. "Well, so long," he said, offering her a tentative hand to shake.

"Don't you want to kiss me good night?" she asked.

"Do you think I'm nuts——?" he replied with feeling.

"I won't hit you," she promised. "Anyhow, I don't *think* I will."

"Well, I don't know——"

"Come on."

She turned her lips upwards. Apprehensively he bent over and gave a minimal kiss. When, however, no blows seemed to be coming, he increased the pressure.

"Ah!" she said, coming out of the clinch. "That was keen!"

Grady narrowed his half-drawn eyelids. "I don't dig you," he confessed.

"I don't dig myself," replied Comfort truthfully.

"Want another kiss?"

"Better not," she said. "I'm almost sure I'll hit you this time."

Grady scratched his head for a moment. "Well, good night," he said.

"Good night."

He walked towards his bike. He turned. "Hey, will you go out with me again?"

"No," she replied promptly.

"Why not?"

"Because you're such a creep!"

"So how come you kissed me?"

She shrugged. "You answer that one, chum, and you win the turkey."

He scratched his head some more. "Maybe I'll come around tomorrow. Okay?"

"Okay," said Comfort.

He stared at her in total confusion. "You are the *weirdest*!" he said.

She nodded. "Yeah. . . . Good night."

"Good night."

Thoughtfully they went their separate ways—Comfort up to her room to lie open-eyed on her bed while her antique blood went a few rounds with her contemporary endocrines; Grady home on his motor-cycle, feeling like a combination of Raffles and Pandora. He had managed to open the locked box all right, but, Kee-rist, what a mess of trouble had come flying out!

And yet, thought Grady as he rode, he *had* succeeded. Where every other expert at Webster High had failed, he had clearly scored. Sure, she was cuckoo and treacherous and strong as an ox, but all the same he *had* kissed her and he *had* been kissed back, and who else could make that statement?

Pride warmed his wind-whipped breast. It was no small thing to be the first victor over an adversary so formidable. She was Everest, and he was Tenzing, and this was no night to be slinking home, this was a night to celebrate!

He braked the bike, spun it around, and headed for Fatso's Diner to share his triumph with his loyal liegemen. They came running when Grady roared into the parking lot. "Well?" they cried eagerly. "Well? Well?"

"I'll give it to you in one word," said Grady. "*Jackpot!*"

A cheer rose from their throats. They shook his hand and pounded his back and tousled his hair.

"Hell," said Grady, concealing his pleasure. "Come on. Let's hit for Beer Can Boulevard."

He gunned his bike and raced away. The others piled into the hot-rod and followed.

"You know what he is?" said Ed as they rode.

"Grady?" said Charlie.

"Yeah," said Ed.

"What?" said Fred.

"An inspiration to us all," said Ed.

They nodded in solemn agreement and followed the big red tail-light on the big black Harley.

Sixteen

THE day was Tuesday, the time was fifteen minutes past noon, and the place was Oscar Hotta's office. Oscar sat behind his desk facing a half-dozen advertising agency executives, all dressed in funereal black that passes for chic on Madison Avenue. Oscar, who had a very tiny attention span for advertising executives, had not caught their names when they came in. He had a vague impression they were all called Dub Hotchkiss, and, indeed, they all seemed to answer to that name.

The topic of today's meeting was a television serial entitled *David and Bathsheba*, a biblical romance filled with action, passion, and godhead, which had a Trendex rating calculated to warm the heart of any sponsor. Yet the sponsor, the Crackle-Crunchies Corporation, was far from satisfied. In spite of the mounting popularity of *David and Bathsheba*, the sales of Crackle-Crunchies were showing no increase whatsoever, and, in fact, were declining sharply in some areas. To solve this paradox the agency executives were this day solemnly assembled.

"Just talking off the top of my head, of course," said the first Dub Hotchkiss, "but I think the kazoo here is product identification. This is only woodshed research, but my antenna tells me the public doesn't identify King David with Crackle-Crunchies."

"Right!" said the second Dub Hotchkiss. "Now we're getting down to where the rubber meets the road. Identification! That's the gizmo! Somehow we've got to tie up Crackle-Crunchies with King David."

"Well," said the third Dub Hotchkiss. "I've got a kind of crazy, off-beat idea. In fact, it's so far out in left field, I'm not sure I ought to bring it up."

"Nonsense, laddie," said the fourth Dub Hotchkiss. "Run it up the mast, and let's see if anybody salutes."

"All right then," said the third Dub Hotchkiss. "To get down to the short strokes, what I have in mind is a time machine. Every once in a while we put King David in the time machine and he pops into the twentieth century and has himself a bowl of Crackle-Crunchies."

"I don't know," said the fifth Dub Hotchkiss doubtfully. "We may be opening up a can of beans here. What do you think, Oscar?"

Oscar grunted. He had long ago learned to close his mind tight at meetings with agency people. Today it was especially easy, because today his mind was occupied by another topic: his wife Angela. Or—more properly—his *ex*-wife Angela.

Angela had come back from Reno five days earlier with her divorce, and since her return Oscar had been curiously unhappy. He had been happy enough to see her go. "Good riddance!" he had cried with characteristic gallantry. He had left her the Putnam's Landing house and moved into New York, thus cutting two hated hours of commuting from his day. He had worked as late as he liked, got up whenever he felt like it, kept television sets blaring in every room, answered to nobody for anything, and been better-tempered than he had been in years. But all the time he had clung secretly to a conviction that Angela would abandon the notion of a divorce before the six weeks were up and come slinking home for forgiveness.

But she had not. She had returned a free woman, and Oscar was filled with unaccustomed aches in unused regions. His pride hurt, and so did his heart, and even his conscience was stirring sluggishly. Not that he wanted Angela back; he recognised that a man like himself was far better off alone. But he still could not help wondering what had gone wrong, and how he could have prevented it, and what was in store for Angela now.

"Gentlemen," said the sixth Dub Hotchkiss, "hand me my

cross-cut saw; I'm going out on a limb. I am flatly against the time machine. It seems to me we're rooting around on the ground for acorns when we should be looking up to see where they're coming from. What's the biggest plus we've got on this programme? I'll tell you, gentlemen: it's *God*! We've established a fine, warm rapport between David and God over the last few weeks. Now, why can't we—reverently, of course—have God bring him a bowl of Crackle-Crunchies in a vision?"

"Too full of wrinkles," said the first Dub Hotchkiss, shaking his head gravely. "Some of those religious nuts might hop on it. Don't you think so, Oscar?"

Oscar grunted again. There had to be a guy, he was thinking. Angela wouldn't just go running off and get divorced unless there was a guy waiting somewhere. She was much too smart for such a bonehead play. But who was the guy? Where was he? And what did he have that Oscar didn't?

The intercom buzzed on Oscar's desk. "Yeah?" he snapped, pushing down the key.

"Mr. Stronghold on the phone," said his secretary.

Oscar, hardly a man for idle speculation, had not merely sat around and wondered who Angela's guy might be; he had engaged one Albert Stronghold, private investigator, to shadow Angela as soon as she got back from Reno. So far there had been no results, but this call, thought Oscar with a flutter of excitement, could be the jackpot. "Yeah?" he said into the phone.

"Subject left Putnam's Landing on the 10.07 train this morning," said Mr. Stronghold. "Subject registered at the Plaza Hotel at 11.54, checked into Room 921. Man came to room 921 at 12.15 p.m. and was admitted by subject. Man is tall, in midthirties, wearing tan topcoat and grey flannel suit, looked nervous, no distinguishing marks."

"Right!" cried Oscar jubilantly and banged down the phone. "Dub," he said collectively, "you guys mother-hen it, housebreak it, pressure-cook it, cross-pollinate it, blue-sky it, unglue it, run it down, and wrap it up. I'll see you around."

"But what about our problem?" cried the second Dub Hotchkiss in dismay. "How do we identify King David with Crackle-Crunchies?"

"Simple," said Oscar. "King David invents Crackle-Crunchies himself, see? But it's such a great delicacy that he don't want the common people to have it, so he keeps the formula a secret. When he dies, the formula is lost, and we don't find it till five thousand years later."

"Where do we find it?" asked the third Dub Hotchkiss.

"In the Dead Sea Scrolls," said Oscar. "Where else?"

All the Dub Hotchkisses looked at him with admiration bordering on awe.

"A barn-burner!" said one.

"This has *protein*!" said another.

"This *sings*!" said a third.

"Yeah," said Oscar. "Well, so long, Dub."

He leaped up from his desk and raced out of the office.

A tall man in his mid-thirties, wearing a tan topcoat and a grey flannel suit, looking nervous, and bearing no distinguishing marks, raised his knuckles to rap the door of Room 921 of the Plaza Hotel, and then changed his mind and stuck his hand in his pocket. Twice more he took out his hand, lifted it, put it away again. At length he shrugged and sighed and rapped.

The door opened instantly. "Harry!" cried Angela Hoffa. "Harry, darling!"

"Hello, Angela," said Harry with a faint smile. He extended his hand for a handshake.

"Well, aren't we formal!" said Angela jocularly. She took his hand, pulled him into the room, swung the door shut. "Take off your coat."

"No, thanks, Angela. I can't stay."

"Nonsense!" she said, moving around behind him and decoating him deftly.

"Honest, Angela, I've got to be going."

"Oh, don't be a goose." She picked up the phone. "Room service. . . . This is Mrs. Hoffa in 921. Will you please send up a bottle of White Label and some ice? . . . Thank you."

"Angela, thanks a lot, but I really don't care for a drink."

"I do," she said mildly. "Do you mind?"

"Sorry," he said. "Now, Angela, I agreed to meet you here today because——"

Angela gripped Harry by both arms and looked him full in the face. "Harry, how are you?" she asked in a voice throbbing with earnestness.

"Fine," he answered. "Now, as I was saying——"

"Aren't you going to ask how I am?" she said, gently reproachful. "After all, it's been seven weeks since you laid eyes on me."

"I'm sorry, Angela," he said contritely. "How are you?"

"That's better," she said with an approving nod. "I'm just dandy, thank you."

"I'm glad. Now, Angela——"

"Don't you want to ask me how Reno was?"

"All right," said Harry. "How was Reno?"

"It was hot and dry, and they pay ten to one on eight the hard way."

"I hope you won a lot of money," he said politely.

"Nope," sighed Angela. "I'm only lucky in love."

Harry quickly moved a few feet farther from her. "Angela, can I say what I came to say?"

"In a minute. How's Grace?"

"Grace? She's fine, thanks."

"Do you ever see her?"

"What?" said Harry, taken aback. "Of course I see her. Why?"

"Look, pal, I got back to Putnam's Landing almost a week ago and I've been hearing about nothing except the Nike Hospitality Committee. Day and night, isn't it?"

"Well," he said cautiously, "it does keep Grace pretty busy."

"You poor darling!" said Angela, giving Harry a compassionate look.

"Me? It's Grace who does all the work."

"While you stand by, poor lamb, and wonder what ever became of the girl you married."

"Angela, will you tell me something?" asked Harry earnestly. "Why do you keep after me? Haven't you got enough trouble?"

"Haven't *you*?" she countered.

"All I can use."

"Well then, why shouldn't we comfort each other?"

"*Comfort*? I can't face my wife. I can't face you. I can't face myself. You call that *comfort*?"

"You poor lamb!"

"I am not a lamb. What I am is a snake. . . . Or a rat. . . . Or a skunk. . . . I'm here to tell you we're through. I'm sorry you went to Reno on my account. I'm sorry about everything —sorry as hell. . . . But we're through."

"All right, darling. If we're through, we're through. But why such a long face? Let's keep it light. That's the way we started and that's the way we end."

"Oh, no! None of that! Please, none of that! Spare me the good-sport bit. If you've got a little pearl-handled revolver, by all means take it out and shoot me. But let's not have any smiling through tears. I can't stand it!"

"You *have* got a conscience, haven't you, poor darling?"

"I have."

"Poor darling!"

"And it's nothing we can repair by getting in bed again—in case that's what you're thinking of."

"As a matter of fact, it *had* crossed my mind."

"What for? There's no future in it."

"As a goodbye, then. As a proper goodbye."

"Angela, for God's sake, what do you want with me?

I'm a louse. What's more, I'm a *married* louse. . . . And the lousier I get, the more married I am. Don't you understand that?"

"You're not a louse, darling. You're just a poor, trapped, unhappy man. Why won't you let me help you?"

"Do yourself a favour, Angela. Go help someone else. . . . Here. Here's my hand. Give it a brisk shake, and then I'll take off while you sit here and thank your lucky stars you've seen the last of me."

She took his extended hand, slipped deftly inside his arm, pressed her soft, fragrant body against his, found his lips.

Suddenly there came a loud pounding on the door.

"Oh, my God!" quavered Harry, visions of house-detectives dancing through his brain.

"Relax!" laughed Angela. "It's room service."

"Pretty loud knock for room service," said Harry, not comforted.

She kissed him lightly. "You're a worrier," she said. She went to the door and opened it, and in came Oscar Hoffa like a wolf on the fold.

He ran over to Harry and looked at him with wild, total incredulity. "Oh, no!" he howled. "Oh, no! Not *you!*"

"What right have you got to come in here?" demanded Angela, her eyes crackling with wrath.

Oscar, unheeding, continued to gape at Harry. "Harry Bannerman, for Christ's sake!" he cried, smacking his forehead with the heel of his hand. "Oh, for Christ's sweet sake!"

"I'm asking you, Oscar," said Angela. "What do you want here?"

"Okay, okay," said Oscar to Angela. "Don't get a hæmorrhage. I'm not looking for revenge. I'm not sore at nobody. I didn't come to make trouble. . . . But I do think I'm entitled to see the guy who took you away from me." He looked again at Harry and shook his head in painted disbelief. "*Harry Bannerman*, for Christ's sake!"

"I'm not exactly sure of my rights in this situation," said Harry to Oscar, "but I can't say that I like your tone."

"No offence, buddy," said Oscar placatingly. "It's just that I always had you pegged for a hearth and home type. I'm sorry."

"That's okay," said Harry. "It's a natural mistake."

"But I still don't figure you with Angela," Oscar continued. "You ain't in love with her or anything like that?"

"Let's drop it. Okay, Oscar?" said Harry.

"Naah," said Oscar, answering his own question. "You ain't in love with Angela. You just got a case of the hots, that's all. So why pick Angela? She's nothin' but trouble. You want a broad, that's all. Well, I got broads. Any kind of broads you want—tall broads, short broads, thin broads, fat broads, young broads, old broads, white broads, black broads, pinto broads—you name it, buddy, I got it. . . . And be my guest. Just tell 'em to put you on my tab."

"Oscar, you get out of here this minute!" cried Angela shrilly.

"What are you gettin' sore about?" Oscar asked her. "I'm only thinking of you."

"That's a laugh," said Angela bitterly. "When did you ever think about me?"

"When I had time," answered Oscar.

"Thanks a lot."

"Angela, listen," said Oscar. "I don't know from love. If I had to tell a dame 'I love you' it would bust my jaw. But just the same I got a feeling for you, and a big one. Remember, kid, we had ten years together."

"I remember," she said grimly. "I remember well."

"Okay, so they were ten lousy years. But I'll tell you something: only a sonofabitch like me could have held you for ten years. If you want to get married again, good luck. But find somebody like me. Don't start up with guys like *this*." He jerked his thumb at Harry.

"I can pick my own men," said Angela furiously. "Now get out of here!"

"Angela, Bannerman's a *nice guy*. That's not for you. You marry him, you'll have him chewed to a pulp in six months. Then what? Back to Reno again. Then look for another Bannerman. Chew him up. Back to Reno. Is that the routine?"

"Oscar, butt out!" Her voice was a shriek and her eyes were swimming with tears.

"Angela, don't do it," said Oscar quietly. "Not Bannerman. I'm telling you this because, believe it or not, I really feel for you. Lay off Bannerman. You're a monster, Angela. Find another one."

Angela flew at Oscar, her claws out, her mouth working in a rage that was beyond words. Oscar grabbed her wrists and held her powerfully for a moment while he looked into her eyes. Then he released her, turned, and walked out of the room.

Harry stood in silence, pity and embarrassment keeping his gaze averted from Angela. "I'm sorry about this," he said. "About everything. . . . Goodbye, Angela."

"No!" cried Angela, bursting into tears. She rushed to Harry, threw her arms around him, pressed her heaving body against his. Clutching, trembling, weeping piteously, she begged, "Don't leave me! Please, Harry! Not just yet. Please stay awhile. Just a little while. Please!"

Gently Harry pried himself loose. "I'm going, Angela," he said as kindly as he could.

"Oh, God, I'm so alone!" she wailed, throwing her hands over her face. "I've lost everything—everybody! God, dear God, doesn't *anyone* care?"

Harry fought to keep his arms at his sides, to keep from gathering Angela to him to kiss her tears and stroke her shoulders and salve his guilt. "Goodbye," he said softly. "Believe me, it's best."

She turned her face to his. Mascara streaked her cheeks. Her mouth trembled. Desperation darted from her eyes. "A little while," she begged. "Please stay with me a little while. You owe me that much!"

Harry hung his head. "I'm sorry," he said, almost inaudibly. He picked up his coat, opened the door, and left without looking back.

He walked to the elevators and pressed the button. In a moment an elevator arrived. "Down," said the boy.

Harry stood rooted.

"Going down, sir?" said the boy.

"No," said Harry.

The elevator descended without him. He turned and walked slowly back to Angela's room.

Seventeen

PICTURE a dumb-bell, such as you would see in a gymnasium, but a very lopsided dumb-bell. This, roughly, is the shape of a Nike base. One bell of the dumb-bell contains about ten acres, the other contains about fifty acres, and connecting the two bells is a narrow bar approximately one mile long.

The ten-acre bell is called the IFC (Integrated Fire Control) Area. This is the brains of the Nike system. There are three radars here: one scans the skies; one tracks the target; one tracks the missile. There are also two vans, the size of trailer trucks, both jammed with electronic equipment. The RC (Radar Control) van operates the radars and gathers their data; the BC (Battery Control) van computes the data and sends the Nike up after the target.

The Nike takes off from the other bell—the fifty-acre Launching Area. This bell includes a large shed where the Nikes are assembled and ground-tested, a fuelling area behind eight-foot mounds of earth where the Nikes are filled with fuming acids, an LC (Launching Control) van which maintains contact with the IFC Area, and three concrete launching pits thirty feet deep. In these pits, the combat-ready Nikes are stored. When an alert is sounded, some quick last-minute adjustments are made to the Nikes, the steel doors on top of the pits yawn open, and the Nikes are hydraulically lifted to the surface for launching.

Joining the two bells is a mile-long strip, cleared of trees, hills, and buildings, so that the line of sight may be unbroken.

In both the IFC and Launching Areas are various administrative buildings, supply rooms, mess halls, bachelor officers' quarters, and barracks—all neat, low, cinder-block structures, painted to harmonise with the surrounding countryside.

In one of the barracks at the Nike base in Putnam's Landing on a Saturday morning in early spring, Corporal Opie Dalrymple, in his underwear, was handing down a pronouncement to several of his colleagues, also in their underwear. "Frinds," said Opie, "today, as evabody knows, is Welcome Nike Day. In a little while we're all goin' down to the Town Hall and drank some temperance punch and look over the poon. Now, frinds, they're gonna be lookin' us over too. So hear me good: Put on yore cleanest, newest, spankin'est uniforms. Shine yore buttons and make me a pretty little knot in yore necktie. Polish yore boots till you can see yourself in 'em. Walk tall. Suck in yore gut. Throw bock yore shoulders. Step along on yore tippy-toes. Look shorp. . . . You got that?"

"Yes, Opie," they said.

"All right," he continued. "That's half the secret: look shorp. Now Ah'll give you the other half: ack mis'able."

"Look sharp and act miserable?" asked Private William O. Wambess with a puzzled frown. "I don't get it."

"Ain't nothin' attracks a gal like a mis'able man," explained Opie. "But while yore ackin' mis'able, you got to look shorp. Otherwise there ain't no curiosity to it. Ah mean, if you stand around lookin' raggedy and beat-up, the gal ain't gonna wonder why yore ackin' mis'able. She'll figger anybody looks so mis'able jest naturally oughta *be* mis'able."

"Ah!" said the young warriors, comprehending.

"But don't stay mis'able too long," cautioned Opie. "Jest kinda *establish* it, and then git frisky and sparklin'. Tell her that heavy-laden though you be, you jest cain't stay sad with her around. Tell her she melts yore troubles like a summer sun burns off a mornin' mist. If that don't get her, she ain't worth havin'."

"Ah!" said the men-at-arms.

"Any questions?" said Opie.

"How do we convince them that we're miserable?" asked Private Roger Litwhiler.

"Easiest thang in the world," said Opie. "Tell 'em how lonesome you are for the gal you left back home."

"Tell the *new* girl about the *old* girl?" asked Private Ernest J. Hoffman incredulously.

"Why, shore," said Opie. "Then she knows she ain't scratchin' after a prize that nobody else wants."

"Ah!" said the citizen-soldiers.

"But what if you haven't got a girl back home?" asked Private Gustave Morrissette.

"Then lie," said Opie. "But lie *from the hort*!"

At this point someone at the end of the barracks hollered "Ten-hut!" Everybody popped to attention in his underwear, and Lieutenant Guido di Maggio came walking into the barracks.

"Oh, it's you, Lieutenant," said Opie, and everybody promptly stood at ease. The boys had been at Putnam's Landing only three days, but already they knew that Guido was not a man to dwell on rank. In fact, it embarrassed the hell out of him.

"Fellows," said Guido, "I guess you've all got some civilian clothes here, haven't you?"

"Yes, sir," they said.

"Good," said Guido. "I want you to wear them to the Welcome Nike party."

"Oh, but, sir," said Opie, "we was figgerin' on wearin' our uniforms. We're proud of our uniforms, sir. Mighty proud!"

"I am deeply moved," said Guido, "but you'll wear civvies to the party. This town hasn't been occupied since the Revolutionary War, and I'd just as soon not make the burghers any shakier than I have to."

"But, sir," Opie persisted, "we all shipped our good suits home. All we got is slacks and sports shirts. What Ah mean, sir, we'd look a heap more staunch and manly in our uniforms."

"I don't want you staunch and manly," said Guido. "I want

R.F.B.—6

you puny and boyish. I'm trying to persuade this town that you're just a bunch of sweet, harmless, freckle-faced American kids."

"Sir," said Opie sympathetically, "you shore got your work cut out for you."

"I have that," agreed Guido. "So I'd appreciate all the help you can give me today. When you meet the citizens, would you kind of gawk and shamble and say 'Shucks' whenever possible?"

"Ah can make my voice crack if you want," said Opie.

"We'd better not overdo it," answered Guido. "But thanks anyhow. . . . All right, get into your slacks and sports shirts. There'll be a truck in front of the orderly room at eleven-thirty. And please, when you get to Town Hall, try your very, very best not to goof. You see, gentlemen, I have been sent to Putnam's Landing on a trial basis to establish good public relations. If I don't, I will get my can shipped right out of here. And, believe me, gentlemen, no matter who they send in to replace me, you couldn't possibly have it *this* good!"

"Sir," said Opie, "we are fairly warned."

"See you," said Guido and waved and left.

Sadly the men gathered around Opie. "That sure takes care of our plans!" complained Private William O. Wambess.

"Man *pro*poses, God *dis*poses," said Opie philosophically. "But stay loose, frinds. We'll play it by ear."

Eighteen

THE Welcome Nike Party commenced promptly at noon in the meeting room of the Town Hall, and among those present were the following nervous persons:

> Guido di Maggio
> Grace Bannerman
> Harry Bannerman
> Comfort Goodpasture
> Manning Thaw

Guido di Maggio was nervous because he knew that if he did not make good as public relations officer, he would soon be on a shipping list to the frozen North, and standing not two feet away from him was one of the century's great hazards to public relations: Captain Walker Hoxie. Walker, it must be said, had not wanted to come to the party. He had, in fact, informed Guido that he would sooner dive into a tank of barracuda, but Guido had felt duty-bound to argue. "Sir," he had said, "you must come. The town has gone to a great deal of trouble to throw this big affair for us, and they won't take it very kindly if the commanding officer doesn't show up. Remember, sir, what Colonel Thorwald said about the importance of public relations, and I don't see how we can ever have good public relations unless you show a little bit of friendliness. I know, sir, that you do not have a very high opinion of civilians, but I assure you, sir, that this community is exceptional. All I ask is that you meet these people and talk to them and then make up your mind. That's only fair, isn't it, sir?" and Walker had said, "All right. All right, goddamit, I'll come to your goddam party," and Guido had been content because he had felt sure that Walker would be won over

when he met some of the delightful personalities with whom
Putnam's Landing abounded. Now, however, as he stood
beside Walker in the meeting room of the Town Hall and
looked at his flinty eyes and truculent mouth, he did not feel
one-quarter so sure.

Grace Bannerman was nervous because although she had
worked day and night as chairman of the Nike Hospitality
Committee, there were still many tasks which she had to delegate
to others, and she was not at all certain that everything was in
readiness. To be sure, most of the ladies on the committee had
done splendid work. For example, Minna Coleman, chairman of
the Sewing Sub-committee, had run up some terribly attractive
dotted swiss curtains for the barracks; Doris Steinberg, chairman
of the Dayroom Furnishing Sub-committee, had succeeded in
obtaining twelve gilt chairs and the complete works of Jane
Austen; Eleanor Milburn, chairman of the Hobby Shop Sub-
committee, had gone down to the railroad station and passed
out one hundred notices to commuters, asking whether they had
any power tools they wanted to donate to the Nike base, and
ninety-one had said yes; Monica Farquhar, chairman of the Re-
creation Sub-committee, had obtained for the soldiers free
memberships to the YMCA and an invitation to the Purim dance
at Temple Israel; Lucy Weisskopf, chairman of the Housing
Sub-committee, had, for the benefit of married officers and men
who wished to live out of post with their wives, managed to
locate several attractive rentals—the gatehouse of the McAllister
estate containing four rooms and a bath for $300 a month, the
upstairs of the Owl Garage containing two and a half rooms and
a stall shower for $175 a month, and a number of furnished
rooms, some as low as $80 a month with kitchen privileges; and
other workers had done equally brilliantly. It was chiefly Betty
O'Sheel who troubled Grace. Seeking to lift Betty's morale
after the second tabling of the garbage plant proposal, Grace
had given her the important job of chairman of the Refreshment
Sub-committee for the Welcome Nike party. It had not worked.

Sulky and vague, Betty had piled error upon error, and now, with the noon hour struck and the room full of hungry soldiers and citizens, Grace could see no sign either of refreshments or Betty O'Sheel.

Harry Bannerman was nervous because he had just spotted Angela Hoffa across the meeting room. She had spotted him too and was already knifing through the crowd after him. Harry sidled rapidly away in an opposite direction. Since that over-charged afternoon at the Plaza Hotel, he had managed to avoid Angela by staying close to Grace. Unfortunately, the only way anyone could stay close to Grace in the last few weeks had been by joining the Nike Hospitality Committee, so Harry had devoted his leisure hours to draping bunting, hanging Japanese lanterns, cranking mimeographs, delivering messages, fetching and carrying, pulling and hauling, lifting and toting—none of which made him what you would call merry in his heart. But, all the same, he preferred it to another ramble with Angela. Each new encounter with Angela brought a new bundle of guilt, and he already had more than a man could carry.

Comfort Goodpasture was nervous because today was the day she had to give Grady Metcalf an answer. Since the first night she had let him kiss her, he had been pestering her to go steady until she was practically wigsville! She had told him no a million times. She had called him a drip, a creep, and a primate and had said that the best thing he could do for her was to join the French Foreign Legion. Still, she continued to let him kiss her, and sometimes when he held her gently and the moon was high, a tide of sweetness came over her, a rush of warmth that pinkened her cheeks and parted her lips and placed a single tear in each eye. But then she would look at Grady, and the spell would fall off with a thudsville. If only, thought Comfort with many a sad sigh, if only she could find a boy who would not merely kindle the spark but also keep it burning bright! But where was there such a dreamsville boy? Surely not at Webster High School. Of that sorry lot, Grady, dunce though he was,

was clearly the pick. And now he stood in the meeting room of the Town Hall in his black motor-cycle jacket and looked at Comfort through half-lidded eyes and waited for the answer she had promised faithfully to give him this day. And Comfort, *faute de mieuxville*, was deciding to say yes.

Manning Thaw, first selectman of Putnam's Landing, was nervous because today was Saturday. Ordinarily on Saturday he closed the Town Hall at noon. He turned down the thermostat before he left, and it was not turned up again until eight o'clock Monday morning, thus saving the town a tidy amount on fuel. But today, what with the Welcome Nike party going on in the meeting room, he couldn't very well turn down the thermostat. And here's the tragedy: there was only one thermostat in the whole building, so heat was not only rushing to the meeting room but also to all the empty offices upstairs. And to afflict Manning's Yankee soul further, damn fool latecomers kept opening all the outside doors and letting in a steady flow of cold air. He wouldn't be a bit surprised, thought he grimly, if forty dollars' worth of oil went up the chimney before this dang party was over!

Manning had to admit, however, that except for the oil, the party wasn't costing the town one cent. The Nike Hospitality Committee had raised all the money themselves. And a pretty penny it must have been! thought Manning, looking around the meeting room. Everybody in town had showed up, and everybody from the Nike base too. In sixty years of freeloading, Manning did not remember such a turn-out.

As yet the party was in its early, quiet stage. Intermingling had not started. Everyone stood in a group of his own kind. Manning was with the Yankee clippers: George Melvin, Doc Magruder, Waldo Pike, Isaac Goodpasture, and other such worthy men.

Next to them were the Italians, clustered around Vittorio di Maggio, undisputed chief of the Italian colony since his son Guido had brought new prestige to the name.

Next were the commuters, talking animatedly of topics that occupy the commuter mind: Neilsen ratings, sheep manure, penis envy, vermouth, and the like.

Then came a dazzling group composed of Grady Metcalf and the New Delinquents. Like their revered mentor Grady, all the boys were now wearing black leather motor-cycle jackets, each jacket gleaming in front with an astonishing number of chromium zippers, and adorned in back with a picture of a red and white eagle, its claws full of blue lightning bolts. Their hair was gooey with brilliantine, their sideburns bisected their cheeks, their lips languidly held king size cigarettes. Clinging to their calves were black denims pegged to fourteen inches, and on their feet were motor-cycle boots.

Their attention was fixed on another group of young men across the room—the troops from the Nike base. Slowly, warily, the New Delinquents examined the soldiers, and then, their eyes filled with cool contempt, they turned away. There was manifestly nothing to fear from these clean-cut, crew-cut types in their little cotton sports shirts and their un-pegged slacks. Squares—that's all they were: government issue squares.

Next to Grady and his cohorts stood the maidens of the town, Comfort Goodpasture at their centre. They, too, were casing the soldiers and finding them pallid. So boyish they looked, so artless, so inexperienced, so nowhere! "Dullsville!" said Comfort, reflecting the consensus, and the girls all nodded and turned their backs on the soldiers and their fronts towards the New Delinquents.

Across the room the soldiers were casting covetous eyes upon the girls. "That's mighty nice poon," said Private William O. Wambess.

"Yeh," said Private Roger Litwhiler. "Let's go get some. What do you say, Opie?"

But Opie, whose eyes were just as covetous as his comrades', and twice as astute, had seen that the situation was not hopeful.

"Frinds," he said, "it ain't no use. We're givin' away too much weight."

"Do you mean those punks in the black leather jackets?" said Private Ernest J. Hoffman contemptuously.

"They're punks shore enough," allowed Opie. "But where's *yore* black leather jacket?"

"Ah," said the men, the sad truth emerging.

"Trouble is," said Opie, "we all look like somebody's little brother."

"I'll bet we'd get that poon easy if we had our uniforms on!" said Private Gustave Morrissette.

"Frind, that's zackly what Ah'm thankin'," said Opie. "So Ah'll tell you what we're goin' to do: We're goin' back to base and put on our uniforms and our shiny-bright high-top boots. We are also puttin' on our jingly Marksman medals. Then we are comin' back here, all creased and shorp and jingly, and we are goin' to march in, walkin' tall, and we are goin' to buzz through that poon like seven year locusts through yella bantam corn!"

"Hurrah!" shouted the men, hope colouring their sturdy young heads.

"But Lieutenant di Maggio said we had to wear civvies," said Private William O. Wambess.

"Ah am goin' to straighten him out," said Opie. "Y'all wait right here."

Opie went to look for Guido di Maggio, who was standing near the front of the room nervously trying to soothe Walker Hoxie's savage breast. "You'll love these Putnam's Landing folks!" Guido was saying earnestly. "You'll be crazy about 'em once you meet 'em."

"All right, all right," said Walker impatiently. "Let's get it over with."

"Yes, sir," said Guido. He cast his eye around the room, looking for some especially winsome personalities to captivate Walker. He spotted a hale fellow named Jerry Tupper, a Broadway director by profession, who was widely acknowledged to have one of the most fetching characters on the Eastern seaboard. He walked over to Mr. Tupper, took his arms, and brought him back to Walker.

"Sir," he said, "I'd like you to meet one of our leading citizens, the famous director, Jerry Tupper."

"Well, well, well, this is a *real* pleasure!" said Mr. Tupper, giving Walker a manly handshake, and a smile that would melt a stone. Guido smiled too, certain that Mr. Tupper could not but win the heart of Captain Hoxie, and he went off to find more charmers.

"How long have you been in the Army, sir?" asked Mr. Tupper.

"Twenty-two years," replied Walker.

"And still a *captain*?" asked Mr. Tupper incredulously.

"That's right," said Walker.

"Well," said Mr. Tupper, chuckling and draping an affectionate arm around Walker's neck, "you must be a bigger goof-up than I was! Hell, I was the sorriest excuse for a soldier that ever put on a uniform, and I made lieutenant colonel in sixteen months!"

"Oh?" said Walker.

"I was in the last one," explained Mr. Tupper. "Signal Corps Motion Picture Unit out in Long Island—'Funland,' we called it. What a war we had! Reveille in the Stork Club, chambermaids in the barracks, a weekly shuttle to Hollywood! Man, I never drew a sober breath! They had me working on a movie called *Care of the M-1 Rifle*. Catchy title, huh? Well, I worked on that little opus for two years, and I bet I spent more money than de Mille ever heard of. Never did finish it, either. I swear I never had it so good!"

"Heh-heh," said Walker.

"You got it made, Walker," said Mr. Tupper, tousling the Captain's hair. "You got the right idea, boy: stay on the government tit. Why not? Three squares and a flop, nothing to do, free medical care, free trips, plenty of time off, and a pension when you're ready to hang up the gloves! Why go out in the world where you have to produce? You're smart, kid: stick with your Uncle Sugar!"

"Uh-huh," said Walker.

"Let's get together and shoot the breeze sometime," said Mr. Tupper. "I got a story that'll kill you—about the time the General showed up for inspection and found the Copa line shacked up in the BOQ!"

"Nice to have met you," said Walker, and as Mr. Tupper was giving him a final handshake, Guido came back with another merry Andrew to enchant the Captain.

"Sir," said Guido, "I'd like you to meet Mr. Arthur Waterford."

"I have been looking forward to this meeting with keen anticipation, sir," said Mr. Waterford, giving Walker a warm hand-clasp and a smile bright with bonhomie. Guido, feeling better by the minute, went off to find yet another endearing personage.

"How long have you been in the Army, Captain?" asked Mr. Waterford.

"Twenty-two years," said Walker.

"Too lazy to steal?" asked Mr. Waterford, giving a guffaw and thumping Walker jovially on the back.

"Heh-heh," said Walker.

"Only kidding," said Mr. Waterford, linking his arm amicably in Walker's. "The Army's a marvellous outfit. Simply marvellous!"

"I appreciate that," said Walker.

"But, of course, a man doesn't want to spend his whole life in it, now does he?"

"Doesn't he?" said Walker.

"Of course not!" said Mr. Waterford firmly. "Man's got to have a little ambition too. Now, I happen to be in the electronics game. Fellow like you, with all your Nike experience, we'd be willing to start you at a mighty attractive salary."

"I don't think so, thank you," said Walker.

"Inside of two, three years, you'd be making twenty thousand," said Mr. Waterford. "And then, who knows? Money's no object in the electronics game. What the hell! The government pays the freight!"

"I don't think so, thank you," said Walker again.

"You mull it over," said Mr. Waterford. "If it's your pension you're worried about, we've got a plan that makes the Army's look pretty puny. Call me sometime and we'll have a good chin. I'm in the book. Arthur Waterford."

"I'll do that," said Walker.

"Meanwhile," said Mr. Waterford, "if you want to pick up a few bob, keep your eyes peeled for promising youngsters in your battery. You send us a few talented kids, we'll make it worth your while."

"That's very kind," said Walker and shook Mr. Waterford's hand, and Guido came walking up with a large, animated lady.

"Sir," said Guido, "I'd like you to meet Mrs. Laura Beauchamp."

"Delighted!" said Laura, mashing the Captain's knuckles. "I must confess, Captain, that at first I was appalled at the notion of quartering soldiers in Putnam's Landing. You know how quickly the military can declass a town. Look at Newport."

"Uh-huh," said Walker.

"But I have quite changed my mind," continued Laura. "I regard you now as nothing less than a Godsend!"

"That's nice," said Walker.

"I was at my wits' end," admitted Laura, "until Lieutenant di Maggio generously offered me fifty boys."

"It was nothing," said Guido modestly.

"Fifty boys for what?" asked Walker.

"The folk drama," said Laura. "Surely you know about the folk drama?"

"I've been busy," said Walker.

"Well," said Laura, "in 1778 the British tried a landing here on Ram's Head Beach and were repulsed by the Minutemen. Next Fourth of July we are going to re-enact that battle right on the very spot! The local high school boys will play the Minutemen, and your boys will play the Redcoats."

"Let me get this straight," said Walker. "*My* troops are going to fight *against* the Americans?"

"Yes," said Laura.

"I see," said Walker.

"Next fall I may try Thermopylæ," said Laura. "I'll let you know."

"Nice to have met you," said Walker.

"Very talented lady," said Guido to the Captain when Laura had moved on.

"Uh-huh," said Walker.

"This town is full of bright people," said Guido. "And the wonderful thing is how friendly they are. Don't you think so, sir?"

"Princes," said Walker. "The lot of 'em."

"I'll go bring you some more," said Guido and made another sortie into the crowd. But before he could select his next offering, Corporal Opie Dalrymple caught him by the sleeve.

"Excuse me, sir," said Opie, "but Ah got to tell you somethin'. Me and the boys are goin' back to the base and git rid of these here clothes and put on our uniforms."

"But you can't," cried Guido. "I ordered you to wear civvies."

"No, sir," said Opie. "You didn't *order*. What you did was you *suggested*. Army regulations says plain as day that the Army got to clothe the troops from their underdrawers to their overcoats, so Ah don't guess ennabody can *order* a sojer to wear ennathang the Army didn't issue to him."

"Oh," said Guido.

"The boys set a great deal of store by you, sir," said Opie, "and we'd shore admire to do like you *suggested*, but, sir, we'd just feel a whole lot better in our uniforms."

"Oh, well, I guess it won't do any harm," said Guido.

"Thank you, sir," said Opie. "We'll be back right soon."

Opie left, and Guido continued his search for more entrancing citizens to delight Walker Hoxie. He came across Grace Bannerman. "Mrs. Bannerman," he said, "I'd like to have you meet Captain Hoxie."

"I'd love to, Lieutenant," replied Grace, "but not right now. I'm looking for Betty O'Sheel. You haven't seen her by any chance, have—— Oh, there she is! Excuse me, Lieutenant."

Grace rushed over to Betty O'Sheel, who was leading a procession of pink, puffing ladies, each bearing a large carton of food. "Betty, you're *hours* late!" cried Grace. "Where in the world have you been?"

"Well, if you want to know," replied Betty with considerable heat, "I've been on the phone with Mr. Emil Wetkus."

"*Who?*"

"Mr. Emil Wetkus, president of the Garba-Crunch Corporation," replied Betty, glaring at Grace, "who called to say that he must have a decision soon from Putnam's Landing because the Garba-Crunch Corporation is besieged with orders from forward-looking communities the length and breadth of the land!"

"Oh, for Heaven's sake!" groaned Grace.

"Well, I happen to think sanitary garbage disposal is important, even if other people tend to forget it," declared Betty, her lip trembling.

"All right, dear. All right, all right," said Grace, giving Betty a flurry of placating pats. "Now, come on, girls, let's get set up."

Grace led the ladies to a long trestle table in the rear of the room and proceeded to deploy them. "Frankfurters, right here . . . Buns, over here. . . . Potato chips, over here. . Pickles and mustard——" Grace paused and looked around with a frown. "Who's got the pickles and mustard?" she asked.

"Gee, I don't know," said Betty.

"Well, who's your Relish Chairman?" asked Grace.

"It was Margie Klein," answered Betty, "but her water broke."

"Didn't you appoint another one?" asked Grace, fighting to keep her sanity.

"I forgot," mumbled Betty.

"Oh, Betty, *really*!"

"Well, you'd forget things too if Mr. Wetkus kept calling you all the time," said Betty defensively.

Grace counted ten. "All right," she sighed, "who'll run out and pick up some pickles and mustard?"

"I will, dear," said Harry Bannerman, appearing suddenly at Grace's side with Angela Hoffa not ten feet behind him.

"Oh, thank you, sweetie," said Grace. "Go to Sammy's Delicatessen. He'll know what to give you. And hurry back!"

"Yes, dear," said Harry.

He made a quick start, took five steps, and found Angela standing squarely across his path.

"Got you!" she said triumphantly.

"Hi, Angela," said Harry, looking frantically for an escape route. "I've got to go for pickles and mustard."

"I'll come with you," she said.

"No, no, no, no, no!" he cried.

"All right, boy, relax!" she said soothingly. "And quit running, will you? This thing is getting too ridiculous. What are we—Laurel and Hardy or something?"

"Angela, they need the pickles right away."

"Oh, stop this nonsense! We're big kids now. We don't run. We *discuss*."

"Angela, not *now*!"

"Okay. When?"

"I don't know. Soon. I'll call you."

"Don't wait too long, will you, darling?" said Angela sweetly. "A girl gets lonely all by herself at the end of a burned bridge."

She gave him a brave, wry smile, turned, and left.

"Oh, God!" whimpered Harry and took his guilt-flattened psyche to Sammy's Delicatessen for pickles and mustard.

The ladies, whipped into a froth of activity by Grace, had lunch all ready when Harry returned. "Attention, everybody!" called Grace, clapping her hands sharply. "Attention, please! Luncheon is now being served."

Led by Manning Thaw, the crowd fell to ingesting hot dogs with many a laugh and a cheer. But in the midst of the noisy repast, suddenly everyone was still, for into the chamber marched a platoon of uniformed soldiers, walking tall, looking so trim and military, so staunch and manly, so keen, alert, fine-honed, and capable, that not a breast in the vast and varied throng remained unstirred.

Especially the breasts of the maidens of the town. They saw in a flash of truth that these soldier boys were not, as they had first thought, dullsville; they were, indeed, *sharpsville*; and as the troop wheeled in their direction, clearly intent on establishing a beach-head, they tingled with anticipation, every mother's daughter.

Leading the wave, Corporal Opie Dalrymple deftly out-flanked Grady Metcalf and his black jacketed irregulars and drew up in front of the girls. "Howdy, ladies," he said. "Ah and muh men would be proud to help you to some refreshments."

"A Southern accent!" cried Comfort Goodpasture, clapping her hands in glee. "Man, I go ape when I hear a Southern accent!"

"Ah'm glad," said Opie, offering her his arm and leading her to the refreshment table.

Behind him came the other G.I.s, each with a local belle in tow, and back in a corner stood Grady Metcalf and his cohorts, glowering villainously and wishing they were outside so they could spit.

"What can Ah get you, Miss?" said Opie to Comfort.

"Just a couple of hot dogs," she answered. "I already ate."

He fetched her a snack and something a bit more substantial for himself.

"How do you like Putnam's Landing?" asked Comfort.

"It's a right nice town," he said. "But of course," he added with a mournful sigh, "*she* ain't here."

"*She?*"

"Muh girl back home."

"Oh," said Comfort respectfully.

Opie sighed some more.

"How long since you've seen her?" asked Comfort.

"Months."

"How long till you see her again?"

"Months."

"She might not even be yours any more," said Comfort hopefully.

"True," sighed Opie.

"You poor thing," said Comfort, remembering her manners.

"Well, Ah s'pose Ah am," said Opie, breaking into a sudden smile. "But somehow around you, Ah cain't feel *too* blue. What Ah mean, Miss, you melt muh troubles like the summer sun burns off a mornin' mist."

"Oh, that's crazy!" exclaimed Comfort, full of admiration. "I mean's it's real poetry. It's like I got a girl friend named Gloria Coleman, she wrote a poem once to Elvis Presley which I sent him."

"Elvis musta thoroughly enjoyed that," said Opie. "He told me many a time how much a good pome tickled him."

Comfort's eyes widened wildly. "Do you *know* Elvis?" she asked in an awed whisper.

"Not as well as Ah'd like to," replied Opie. "Trouble is, we was always playin' different towns."

"You," she said weakly, hanging on to his sleeve, "are in show business?"

"Ah'm a stor," he said simply.

"Oh, this is too much," cried Comfort, flinging up her arms in a transport of ecstasy. "This is the *endsville*!"

"Hey," said Grady Metcalf, appearing behind Comfort and tapping her on the shoulder, "I gotta talk to you."

"Oh, flake off!" said Comfort impatiently.

"Come on, hey," said Grady, taking her arm. "You and I got a little question you're gonna answer today. Remember?"

"Go away, little man!" said Comfort, yanking loose. "Shoo!"

"All right, hey. Let's just can the comedy and come on, huh?" said Grady.

"Frind," said Opie pleasantly, "Ah don't believe the young lady wants to go with you."

"What's it to you, Army?" snarled Grady.

"Now why don't you jest be a good fella and flake off?" said Opie.

"Yeah?" said Grady.

"Yeah," said Opie.

A group of black jackets came drifting up behind Grady. "Yeah?" said Grady, more strongly this time.

"Yeah," said Opie as several soldiers gathered quietly behind him.

Grady looked at Opie's hard, watchful face. He looked at the soldiers standing back of him, silent and ready. He turned to his own minions and saw their eyes wavering, their foreheads starting to bead. He wheeled and walked away, his colleagues dragging along behind.

The New Delinquents stopped on the other side of the room and formed a bitter caucus. "If them guys think they can come waltzin' into this town and grab off our broads, they got another think comin'," said Grady menacingly.

"You damn right!" said Charlie and Wally and Ed and Fred.

"Nobody does nothin' like that to *us*!" said Grady.

"You betcher butt," said Charlie and Wally and Ed and Fred.

"If they're lookin' for trouble, by God, we'll give it to 'em!" said Grady.

"Yeh," said Charlie and Wally and Fred, but Ed, who was a shade more cautious, asked, "Give 'em what, hey?"

"A rumble!" declared Grady.

"Oh," said the others with a large lack of enthusiasm.

"You ain't chicken?" asked Grady, looking hard at his crew.

"Of course not," said Charlie. "Hell, I *love* a good rumble. But who needs it with these guys? What I mean, our broads'll be runnin' back to us before you know it. I mean, this is only the first time they seen these Army cats. Wait'll the novelty wears off."

"Sure!" cried Wally and Ed and Fred, embracing the argument.

"Yeh?" said Grady doubtfully.

"Sure!" said all with great positiveness.

"Well, maybe you're right," Grady allowed. "But," he added grimly, "it better not take too long. Otherwise there's gonna be blood spilt—G.I. blood!"

"Hello, fellows." Lieutenant Guido di Maggio strolled by. "Did you get enough to eat?"

"Yeh," they said.

"That's nice," said Guido and strolled on and came upon Maggie Larkin, who was working at the punch bowl.

"Hi, hon," he said with a loving smile.

"Hi, dear," said Maggie, smiling back. "What a wonderful party!"

"It is, isn't it?" Guido agreed. "I was kind of worried at first."

"About Captain Hoxie?" said Maggie. "Oh, he's a perfect lamb. I've been watching him. He stands there and talks to everybody just as nice as pie!"

"I knew he'd like the people if he gave them half a chance," said Guido.

"And your soldier boys are darling!" said Maggie. "Just darling!"

"Yes," nodded Guido. "A dandy group."

"As far as public relations is concerned, you haven't got a thing to worry about," said Maggie.

"You know something?" said Guido, smiling like the Mask of Comedy. "I believe you're right!"

Nineteen

GUIDO DI MAGGIO, frowning like the Mask of Tragedy, crouched in front of the dug-out at the Little League Field on Ram's Head Beach. The Mask of Comedy had not stayed with him long. It had, in fact, slipped off the very day after the Welcome Nike party when Guido, still jovial, had come into Captain Walker Hoxie's office and had said cheerily, "Well, sir, that was quite a little shindig, yesterday, wasn't it?"

"Grn," Walker had said.

"It's like I felt from the beginning," Guido had continued. "There's nothing basically incompatible between us and the town. We give a little, they give a little—that's all it takes."

"Rowr," Walker had said.

"A lot of people asked me yesterday when they could come out and see the base," Guido had said. "When do you think we should have an Open House, sir?"

"How about two days after I die?" Walker had said.

"Ha, ha," Guido had said. "But seriously, sir, I promised them an Open House, so we better set a date."

"Listen, sonny," Walker had said, "and listen good. You do whatever you want with those cruddy feather merchants, but let's get one thing straight: they are never going to set foot on my Army post. *Never!* You got that?"

"But, sir——" Guido had said.

"You mention Open House once more and you will be the first commissioned officer in history to pull permanent K.P." Walker had said. "Now get out of here."

That had been the initial step in Guido's decline. Then, a couple of weeks later, had come the Tall Walnuts affair.

Walker had summoned Guido into the BC van one afternoon.

"Look at this radarscope," he had said. "There's some funny blips about a quarter of a mile north of here."

Guido had looked. "Ah!" he had said. "That must be Tall Walnuts."

"What's Tall Walnuts?" Walker had said.

"It's a park, sir," Guido had replied. "The pride and joy of Putnam's Landing. It's got the finest walnut trees in all New England. Nearly a hundred feet tall, some of them."

"They got to come down," Walker had said.

"*What?*" Guido had gasped, blanching.

"They're interfering with our radars, you damn fool!" Walker had said.

"Well, sir," Guido had said, licking his lips, "couldn't we build our radars a little higher?"

"No!" Walker had roared. "Now you go tell those cruddy feather merchants to lower those trees or I'll send a work detail over and chop 'em right down to the ground."

"Yes, sir," Guido had said mournfully, feeling certain that public relations would not be conspicuously improved when the town's beloved Tall Wallnuts became Truncated Walnuts.

The next blow to Guido's reeling *esprit* had been due to Little League. This time it had been Maggie Larkin, not Walker Hoxie, who had lowered the boom.

Guido had been uneasy about Maggie from the very beginning of the Little League season. True to her word, she had been his enthusiastic collaborator from the day he organised the Rockets, as his team was inevitably called. She had served as score-keeper, cheer-leader, and house mother, and the boys, duly inspired, had responded with a series of six straight wins.

But all the time Guido felt a gnawing certainty that there would be trouble. When you put together such a volatile combination as Maggie and children, an explosion was inevitable.

And it had come. At first there had been some warning rumbles—frowns and coldness from Maggie, a steady diminishing of enthusiasm. She had stopped keeping score, then stopped cheering, then stopped giving pep talks, and finally stopped coming to the games altogether.

"What's the matter, hon?" Guido had asked, dreading the answer.

"I don't want to talk about it," she had replied stiffly.

"But you're going to," he had said. "So it might as well be now."

"Very well," she had said and turned to him with eyes brimming with tears. "Guido, I know I promised to help you with the Little League, and I tried. I tried with all my heart! I closed my eyes as long as I could to all the ghastly things that were going on. . . . But no more! I'm finished. I can no longer stand by and watch you traumatise those children."

"What are you talking about?" he had said, astounded. "They're the happiest team in Little League! They're in first place!"

"Are all of them happy?" she had asked. "Even the poor little tykes who sit on the bench game after game, developing a festering inferiority?"

"Oh, come on now," Guido had protested. "I give everybody a chance to play."

"Sure!" she had replied bitterly. "When the team is so far ahead that it doesn't matter, you let the poor little bench-warmers come in for an inning or two. Oh, Guido, can't you see what you're doing to their plastic young souls? Can't you see that you're giving them scars they will carry all their lives?"

"Aw, Maggie," Guido had said, "didn't you promise me you were giving up all that nonsense about child psychology?"

"I do not call it nonsense," she had said coldly, "to protect little children from being warped. Either you let everybody play an equal number of innings, or I'm through!"

"Through with Little League, you mean?" Guido had asked hopefully.

"Through with *you*!" she had declared.

Guido had looked at her determined eyes, her uncompromising mouth, her hard chin. Then he had looked at the soft expanse below, and he had known that he could not say her nay.

"Okay," he had said, sighing, and from that day forward, at the end of the third inning, which is the mid-point in a Little League game, he had benched his regulars and sent in his scrubs, and as a result, the Rockets had been creamed the next three times in a row.

As a further result Guido had created a brand-new set of enemies for the United States Army—namely, the parents of his regulars. Though Guido had carefully explained to them that he was benching their sons in order to keep the psyches of the scrubs free from trauma, he had met with a signal lack of under-standing. All they had done was mutter and grow tight around the corners of the mouth. With each succeeding loss their tempers had shortened; lately they had taken to baring their teeth whenever they saw Guido.

Now as Guido crouched in front of the dug-out at the Little League Field on Ram's Head Beach, the Rockets were in the process of dropping still another game. It was the bottom of the sixth and final inning, the score was Mustangs 4—Rockets 3, and Guido's scrubs were at bat. The first man up, Daniel Bannerman by name, drew a walk. (This is not strange when you consider that Daniel was only thirty-six inches high and batted from a crouch.) Guido flashed a bunt sign to the next batter, Jimmy Armitage. (The bunt sign was quite simple; Guido just held up a sign which said "BUNT!") Jimmy obediently dropped a bunt down the third base line. ("Dropped" is perhaps a misnomer; the ball went fifteen feet up in the air.) The third baseman, hav-ing cleverly stolen the bunt sign, charged in and was waiting with outstretched glove as the ball descended.

The second out was made by Daniel Bannerman, who got tagged off first base when he wandered into short right field to pick up a daisy. The last out was scored by an athlete named Dickie Sutphen, who went down swinging at three consecutive fast balls, each fifteen inches over his head.

Maggie Larkin, bright as the dawn, came bustling into the Rockets' dug-out. "It's all right, boys," she chirped, distributing loving pats all round. "You tried your best. After all, it isn't winning that counts. It's playing the game! Isn't that right, Guido?"

"Grn," said Guido, fighting off a shiver. The parents of the regulars were filing past the dug-out, giving him looks that frosted his bones. Soon now, he was thinking, Colonel Thorwald would be coming to Putnam's Landing to look over the state of public relations. It was not impossible he would find that Guido had turned the town into the anti-military capital of America. Guido shivered again, a sudden vision of Alaska looming frigidly in his mind.

"And now, boys," said Maggie, clapping her hands merrily, "let's all go get some ice-cream."

"Just," muttered Guido, "what I need."

Three hundred yards away on another part of Ram's Head Beach, Laura Beauchamp was rehearsing her folk drama.

Laura sat on a high lifeguard's chair, shouting through a megaphone and deploying her mammoth cast. "Places!" she called. "Places for the last act, everybody! Minutemen, get behind the breastworks. Redcoats, into the longboats. Quickly, please."

The high school boys, led by Grady Metcalf, took their positions behind a rampart of sand which had been heaped up on the beach. The soldiers, led by Opie Dalrymple, clambered into a flotilla of three rowboats moored in the lee of a projecting dune. "All right," shouted Laura. "Quiet, please. Enter Goodwife Putnam."

Goodwife Putnam, played by Comfort Goodpasture, emerged from behind the bath-house and ran to Grady Metcalf. "Oh, Ethan," she cried, "have a care, for the King's hated militia are well known for their prowess with the long rifle!"

"I fear not," replied Grady Metcalf. "If my blood contribute to the seed-time of this new nation of free men, I count it well spent, hey."

"Longboats!" shouted Laura. "Come in, longboats!"

The rowboats lurched sluggishly around the dune. Standing in the prow of the lead boat was Lord Cornwallis, played by Opie Dalrymple.

"Heave ho, muh horties," said Opie. "Let us show this here rabble that His Majesty's sojers shall not cringe before ennathang!"

"Beach the longboats and form a hollow square!" shouted Laura.

They did.

"Now advance on the breastworks!" called Laura. "Keep in formation. . . . Minutemen, wait until they get as far as the trash can before you open fire. . . . Oh, that's splendid. Very tense! Very effective! . . . All right, Minutemen: FIRE!"

"Bang, bang, bang, bang, bang," said Grady Metcalf and his Minutemen, pointing index fingers at the advancing Redcoats.

The British started to die in droves. Every other man clutched his breast and fell to the ground, kicking and twitching extravagantly.

Opie, however, stayed erect and led the surviving soldiers right up to the edge of the rampart. Then he looked around and saw that his forces had been decimated. "Sound retreat, drummer boy," said Opie. "Ah have gravely underestimated the mettle of these formers and ortisans."

"Yes, sir," said Private William O. Wambess. "Brrm, brrm, brrm," he said, beating a roll on an imaginary drum, and the remnants of the invading army turned and ran ignominiously for the boats. They piled in and paddled away.

"Thus always to tyrants!" cried Comfort, coming out from behind the bath-house.

"Huzzah!" cried the Minutemen.

"Excellent, excellent!" shouted Laura Beauchamp. "Of course it will go much better when we get our costumes and props.

... Take five minutes now, and then we'll run through it again from the top."

The actors broke for a brief recess. They broke neatly into two distinct groups: Grady Metcalf and the high school boys went over and lounged against the bath-house; Opie Dalrymple and the G.I.s sprawled on a dune.

Then a third group came into the scene—a gaggle of high school girls who had been observing the rehearsal from the road at the top of the beach. They walked down from the road now, clustered around Comfort, and then, all together, headed for the dune and the G.I.s. On the way they passed the townies who glared at them balefully, but the girls chattered and giggled and did not even turn their heads.

The girls and the soldiers exchanged hilarious greetings and proceeded to pair off—Comfort, of course, with Opie. "Hi," said she.

"Howdy, honey," said he.

"Did you do it?" said she.

"Ah said Ah would, didn't Ah?" said he.

"I thought you might have been kiddin'," said she.

"No, ma'am!" said he, giving her an earnest look. "Ah don't kid about important thangs like that."

"Gee!" she said, wriggling with delight. "I bet I'm the only girl in Webster High who ever had a song written to her."

"Wanna hear it?" asked Opie. "Ah brought muh git-fiddle." He slung his gorgeously decorated guitar around his neck.

"Now?" said Comfort, somewhat dismayed. "You mean in front of all these people?"

"Why not?" said Opie.

"Well, golly, I thought it was kind of—you know—*private*."

"Honey, do you know the wonderful thang about love?" he asked. "The wonderful thang about love is the more you tell the world about it, the more it's *yores*."

"I never thought of it quite that way," confessed Comfort.

Opie struck a loud chord on his guitar. "Frinds," said he to all assembled. "Ah'd like to sang a little song Ah wrote—*from the hort*—to this charmin' young lady by muh side."

"Pshaw!" said Comfort, reddening with pleasure.

Opie ran off a few introductory measures and began:

> *Ah lost muh hort in Putnam's Landin'*
> *By old Long Island Sound.*
> *Ah loved you when Ah saw you standin'*
> *So purty on the ground.*
>
> *Ah lost muh hort in Putnam's Landin'*
> *In old Connecticut State.*
> *Yore so sweet and undemandin'*
> *And you weigh a perfeck weight.*
>
> *Together we'll grow old.*
> *We won't never scold.*
> *We'll nicely kiss*
> *And yodel like the Swiss*
> *As the years unfold.*
>
> *Ah lost muh hort in Putnam's Landin'*
> *Neath the old New England sky,*
> *Ah found me a gal that's real outstandin',*
> *Yippee-o, yippee-ay, yippee-I.*

Comfort listened entranced, her lips parted, her eyes gleaming. All around Opie couples stood with arms circling waists, swaying gently as he hummed a second chorus, and then they were all humming together, their hearts full, their young voices drifting sweet and clear across the still water.

And lounging against the bath-house wall, their sideburns like brackets enclosing blobs of hate, sat Grady Metcalf and the New Delinquents. "Sure," snarled Grady to the others. "You cats are so damn smart. Them Army guys are only a novelty, huh?

The broads'll come runnin' back to us as soon as the novelty wears off, huh— . . .

The rest, having no answer, were silent.

"I told you right from the beginning," continued Grady hotly. "A rumble! That's the only way. Now are you cats chicken, or are you with me?"

"Jees, Grady," said Charlie, "it ain't a question of bein' chicken. It's just that I wouldn't feel right about beltin' an Army guy. I mean it's a little un-American, ain't it?"

"Yeh," said Wally and Ed and Fred.

"Chicken!" said Grady, rejecting their argument whole. "You're scared of them Army cats. That's what it is."

"No, hey," insisted all.

"Yeah, you're scared," continued Grady. "I don't know why you should be. Hell, they're only eighteen, and you guys are seventeen and a half. How much stronger can they get in six lousy months?"

"That ain't the point," said Wally. "The point is what's the use of gettin' into a rumble when we don't need to? I mean the broads are bound to come back to us when the novelty wears off. Let's just sweat it out a little longer."

"Yeh," said Charlie and Ed and Fred.

"I'll clue you," said Grady. "There's gotta be a rumble. You cats keep on dreamin' if you wanna, but sooner or later, mark my words, it's comin' to a rumble!"

"Places!" shouted Laura Beauchamp. "Places, children!"

Twenty

*The following events occurred in Putnam's Landing on the
Fourth of July:*

At five a.m. an unidentified citizen, full of Blatz and patriotic
fervour, threw a large firecracker from a speeding car. It ex-
ploded in front of the house of Mrs. Angela Hoffa. Angela sat
bolt upright in bed, shrieking and clutching her heart. In a
moment she realised it was only a firecracker and tried to go back
to sleep. Sleep, however, would not come, nor would the panic
leave her bosom.

After tossing for an hour she abandoned the pursuit of sleep,
switched on the bedlamp, lit a cigarette, and gave herself up to
despair. A fine kettle of fish, thought she blackly. Here she was
—thirty-eight years old and stuck in Putnam's Landing with no
husband nor prospects of any. Oscar was gone and Harry was
unavailable, and it was nobody's fault but her own. How could
she have been so stupid? How could she have made such a
thundering booboo as to cut Oscar loose before she had Harry
properly hooked?

And now what to do? Go back to Oscar? It was, she supposed, not impossible, but what sense did it make? Does a
butterfly go looking for a lepidopterist? Does a cow run to
Swift and Co? Does the Count of Monte Cristo tunnel back
into the Chateau d'If?

No, she'd had Oscar—ten grinding years of him—and she
wanted no more. What she wanted was Harry Bannerman.
This, too, was not impossible. In fact, it was downright easy—
if she could only get him alone long enough to apply a few elementary holds.

But how in the world could she get Harry alone? The way
he clung to Grace these days was positively marsupial! Each
night he ran right from the office to Grace, got a firm grip on her,
and never let go until he went back to the office the next day.
Phone calls from Angela were ignored, notes were unanswered.
And it was no use following him around Putnam's Landing; if
he didn't actually have Grace by the hand, she was always within
hailing distance.

No, there was no way to pry Harry loose from Grace. But,
thought Angela suddenly sitting up straight in bed, there *was* a
way to pry Grace loose from Harry. Not a pleasant way, to be
sure, but neither was Angela in a pleasant situation. Her bridges
were burned, her back was against the wall, her clock was running
out, and her canoe was up the well-known creek. Was this a
time to think of pleasantries?

Of course not. She must use the remedy which had now
occurred to her—a drastic measure, but a sound one: She must
go to Grace and confess that she and Harry had become
lovers.

Yes, thought Angela with a determined nod, that was the
ticket. That would surely drive a wedge between Grace and
Harry—if not permanently, at least for a little while. And that's
all Angela wanted: a little while. Just a short time in which to
catch Harry away from the pouch and twine herself around him
and show him where his happiness truly lay.

Angela glanced at her watch. Six-thirty; a trifle early for
phone calls. She switched off the bedlamp and slipped back
under the covers. She lay awake refining her plans until eight
o'clock. Then she picked up the pink telephone and dialled.

"Grace? . . . I hope I didn't wake you, sweetie. It's Angela.
. . . Yes, I'm afraid there is something the matter. . . . Honey,
I don't mean to sound so *misterioso*, but could you come over
here for a few minutes? It's terribly important. . . . No, I'm
sorry, I can't tell you about it now. . . . Thank you, dear. Oh,
one more thing: please don't tell Harry you're coming over.

Okay? . . . That's a lamb. . . . I'll make some coffee. How do you like it? . . . Black and bitter? That's how you'll get it. . . . I'll be waiting. . . ."

At 8.34 a.m. on the Fourth of July there was a practice alert on the Nike base. It was a routine training exercise, such as were carried on at unspecified hours every day in order to keep the men on their toes. Captain Walker Hoxie pressed a button, a siren started screaming, troops poured out of the mess hall, barracks, and orderly room and ran on the double to their battle stations. Walker sat at a control board in the darkened BC van with Guido di Maggio by his side. Radarscopes scanned the skies endlessly. A panel of lights told the state of readiness of each missile at the launching pits a mile away. Guido watched the panel. When the lights along the top were all red, he consulted his wrist-watch. "Fourteen-oh-nine, sir," he said to Walker, meaning that in fourteen minutes and nine seconds from the time of the alert, the launchers were all in firing position.

"Gotta do better than that," growled Walker, but since he did not swear Guido knew he was satisfied.

Walker secured the troops from alert and, with Guido, went out of the gloomy van and into the bright sunshine.

"Beautiful day for the Fourth of July celebration," said Guido, cocking an eye at the cloudless sky.

"I'm going with you," said Walker.

"It usually rains on the Fourth and—You're *what*?" cried Guido, doing a double-take of almost professional quality. Walker was going to the Fourth of July celebration? Walker, who had not set foot on the civil soil of Putnam's Landing since the Welcome Nike party; Walker, who had instructed his sentries to shoot to kill if anyone in mufti came within ten feet of the gate; this same Walker was now *voluntarily* going out to mingle with civilians?

"Sir!" said Guido. "*Why?*"

"A good question," Walker allowed. "I'll answer it. I'm

going because Colonel Thorwald called this morning and said he's coming up from Fort Totten."

A hot, expanding ball of fear was suddenly born in Guido's stomach. So it had arrived at last. D-Day. H-Hour. The moment of truth. Today the Colonel would come and inspect and decide: Guido warm in the arms of Maggie Larkin, or Guido frigid on the trackless tundra. Which?

"What time will he be here?" asked Guido anxiously.

"This afternoon around two or three. He's got to review a parade at Fort Totten at noon, and then he's driving up here."

"Thank you, sir," said Guido and saluted and got into the jeep and drove to the apartment of Maggie Larkin.

"Maggie," he said, mopping his brow, "Colonel Thorwald will be here today."

"Is that bad?" she asked.

"It could be fatal," he replied grimly. "However, there's one very big thing in my favour. Today is the Fourth of July and everybody will be loaded with patriotism. I wouldn't think they'd pick a day like this to gripe to the Colonel."

"So what are you worried about?"

"One thing—and that's why I'm here. . . . Maggie, the Rockets have a Little League game this afternoon, and I want to make it perfectly clear to you right now that I am *not* sending my scrubs in after the third inning. I am keeping them on the bench all through the game."

"What?" she cried, aghast.

"Today," said Guido, "we are playing the Cougars, who are in second place, just a half game behind us. If I blow this game, then the Cougars are in first place and the Rockets are in second place, and the parents of the Rockets will come to the dug-out and stone me. Now, Maggie, how is that going to look to the Colonel?"

"Guido, I am shocked!" she declared. "Today—the Fourth of July—the stands jammed with people—the most important game of the year—and you are going to keep those poor little boys on the bench? How can you, Guido? How *can* you? Why don't you just take a hot iron and brand them *'Inferior'* —*'Second-rate'*—*'Unworthy!'* "

"Maggie——"

"Today of all days, you must not reject those children!"

"Maggie, sweetheart, lover," he pleaded, "the Colonel will ship me to *Alaska*!"

"Oh, pish!" scoffed Maggie. "Certainly a man who reaches the rank of colonel in the United States Army must have a high degree of intelligence."

"Hah!" said Guido.

"Just you stop worrying about Alaska. Remember that you have *souls* in your care. You cannot fail them now!"

"This, I suppose, is your last word?"

"Yes, Guido."

"Well, goodbye," he sighed and started away.

"Where are you going?"

"Home," said Guido, "to pack my longies."

At nine-fifteen a.m. on the Fourth of July, Harry Bannerman came downstairs, walked into the kitchen area, and found his three sons seated at the breakfast bar with three empty bowls in front of them and the table covered with spilt milk, bits of cereal, and various gooey substances.

"Good morning, Papa!" they cried and kissed him from three sides.

"Good morning, boys. Where's your mother?"

"She had to go out for a while," said Bud.

"We fixed our own breakfast," said Peter.

"I had Sugar Pops with chocolate chips and brown sugar," said Daniel.

"I had Rice Krispies with honey and after-dinner mints," said Bud.

"I just had a Hershey bar with jelly," said Peter.

"On behalf of our family dentist, I thank you," said Harry.

"Do you want us to fix *your* breakfast, Papa?" said Dan.

"No, thanks," said Harry hastily. "I'll get it myself."

He found the Chemex coffee pot and a box of paper filters. He took out a filter and folded it as he had seen Grace do a thousand times. For him, however, it came out more like a paper hat. He shrugged and tried another. This time he got a paper airplane. A third attempt produced something roughly in the shape of a Maltese cross.

"Ah, the hell with it," said Harry and went to the refrigerator and poured himself a glass of milk.

Grace came into the house.

"Good morning, dear," said Harry cheerfully. Then he saw her face. A spot of colour burned high on each cheek; the rest was dead-white. Her lips were drawn tight. Her eyes were narrow and strange.

Harry rushed to her side. "What's wrong, Grace?" he said in alarm.

She turned away, eluding his grasp. "Children," she said in a strained voice, "I want you to go outside and play."

"But, Mama, I want to read my history book," said Bud. "It's the Fourth of July."

"Outside!" snapped Grace. "All of you! Now!"

The boys looked at her in bewilderment. "Yes, Mama," they whispered and padded quickly out, casting nervous glances over their shoulders.

"Grace, for God's sake, what is it?" demanded Harry.

She faced him. Her eyes bored into his. "I've just come from Angela Hoffa's house," she said.

A sadness descended on Harry—a sadness such as he had never known. "What did Angela say?" he asked, and his voice seemed to be coming from far away.

"She told me she has been having an affair with you," replied Grace evenly. "She said it has been going on for several weeks and in several places. She said that you and she were in love and that you wanted to divorce me and marry her."

"That's a lie!" shouted Harry.

"*What's* a lie?"

"Grace, I don't want to divorce you! I wouldn't dream of divorcing you. I love you!"

"And the rest?"

"The *rest?*" he said, not comprehending.

"The rest of Angela's statement. Is that a lie too?"

He looked into Grace's hard, searching eyes. He turned up his palms helplessly.

"I see," she said quietly. "Thank you."

"Grace, I can explain."

"I hope so. I devoutly hope so."

Harry paused, thought how to begin, then shook his head. "No," he said. "I can't explain. I thought I had some justification, but it's no good."

"May I hear it?"

"It's childish. I got sore because of all your activities—the house, the kids, the clubs, politics. Maybe I was jealous. Or maybe I had to prove I was still a man, even if *you* didn't seem to need me. I don't know. . . . Anyhow, it's no justification."

"As a matter of fact, it *is*," said Grace. "I can't say that I *approve* it, but I certainly understand it. I pushed you too far, and you felt you had to do something. All right. I accept that."

"You *do?*" said Harry, hope returning.

"I do *once!*" she replied sharply. "If this had happened only once, well, I guess I'd just lick my wounds and try to forget it. But we're not talking about *once*, are we? We're talking about habitual and systematic adultery—and *that*, Harry, I have not got coming!"

"Grace, I swear it!" cried Harry. "After the first time, I never intended to come near Angela again. I swear it! But somehow I just couldn't get away."

"I see," said Grace coldly. "What did Angela have? A gun? An ether cone? What?"

"Please listen to me. No matter how bad things look, you've

got to believe I love you. Believe me, I take my oath, I love you, only you, nobody but you, and never for one minute have I stopped loving you!"

"Even in Angela's arms?"

"You're making it awfully tough, Grace."

"Did you expect a gold watch?"

"Let me say it once more: I love you. This business with Angela, I regret more than you will ever know. I can't justify it, not in any particular. I can only hope that you will forgive me. I love you, Grace, with all my heart. I'll never give you cause again to doubt it."

"Now I'll make *my* speech," said Grace. "It's a simple one. Small matters are sometimes complicated, but fundamental things like this are always simple. When Angela told me the news this morning, I knew immediately what had to be done. It came almost like a reflex: first the problem; then, automatically, the solution. There's only one, you know—only one solution."

"Yes?"

"You are leaving here, Harry," said Grace steadily. "I don't want to be married to you any more."

"Grace! In God's name, what are you saying? I love you!"

"I can't believe that—not ever again—and if I can't then I can't be your wife. You see? I told you it was simple."

"Grace, listen to me!"

"No. This is nothing we can patch up with promises. There's no trust left. It's gone."

"If you'll only listen——"

"Harry, please! I have somehow managed to hold myself together, but one more second of this and I am going to fly into hysterics! Now please, please for the sake of the children, will you leave quickly and quietly and without another word?"

He stood rooted for a moment, looking into her eyes.

"Please," she whispered.

He nodded and left by the kitchen door, taking care to stay out of sight of his sons.

Grace stood quite still, squeezing her hands together hard, clenching her teeth.

Peter came bursting in from outside. "I gotta wee," he announced.

"All right, dear," said Grace.

"Where's Papa?"

"He—he had to go to New York."

"Oh," said Peter. "But we're going to the beach anyhow, aren't we?"

"Yes, dear."

"Poor Papa! He'll miss everything."

Grace turned her back abruptly on the boy. Her shoulders were perfectly still, her head was erect, her arms were at her sides, not a sound came from her throat. Only her eyes were weeping.

At 2.59 p.m. on the Fourth of July, Guido di Maggio's Rockets were tied o—o with the Cougars at the end of three innings of a hard fought ball game on the Little League Field at Ram's Head Beach.

Guido, sighing, went into the dug-out to bench his regulars and send out his scrubs for the beginning of the fourth inning. It meant, of course, throwing away the game because the Cougars were a tough and determined team. But so was Maggie Larkin tough and determined, and she was sitting right now in the nearby bleachers fixing Guido with an implacable eye. Well, thought Guido, clinging to any consolation, however tiny, at least Colonel Thorwald had not yet arrived, and it was conceivable that the Cougars could make short work of his bench-warmers and that the game would be over before the Colonel got there. On the other hand, thought Guido with a sudden trembling in the extremities, it was equally conceivable that the Cougars could bat all night.

Guido dragged himself over to his bench. "Boys," he said, looking without joy at the collection of puny limbs, baby fat, and spongy tissue there assembled, "go in and play."

The scrubs, their heads averted, remained seated.

"Didn't you hear me?" said Guido. "It's time for you to go in."

Daniel Bannerman, smallest of the scrubs, rose. "Sir," he said, "we've been talking it over. We don't want to go in. We want to win the game and stay in first place."

A wave of exultation came over Guido—came and went. Naturally he wanted to win the game—for the sake of the team, for the sake of his job. But he could feel Maggie's eyes drilling into his back. "Sorry, fellows," he said. "You have to go in."

"Please!" begged Daniel. "Please don't make us play!"

"You have to," said Guido. "You'll get your psyche all scarred."

"Oh, sir, please, please, please!" cried Daniel, his eyes filling with tears. "It's so *wonderful* to be in first place!"

And Guido—Maggie Larkin to the contrary notwithstanding —saw clearly in which direction lay mental health. "Okay," he said, coming to a decision. "You guys stay on the bench. Regulars, go back in!"

The first team ran happily out on the field. Guido shot a look at Maggie in the stands. He saw her eyes and mouth widen with stunned disbelief; then he saw them narrow with rage. She rose and started walking out of the ball park with wrathful, rapid strides.

"Hey, Maggie!" Guido shouted after her. "It was the kids' idea, not mine. Honest to God, Maggie, I didn't do it on account of the Colonel. He isn't even here!"

But Maggie was not able to hear Guido because the parents of Guido's regulars, who were under the bleachers forming a lynching party in case Guido benched their sons again, were splitting the air with great, joyous cheers.

"Play ball!" called the umpire.

Guido squatted by his dug-out and watched Maggie's stiff back retreating in the distance. Mad again, thought he morosely. And when she got mad, it took forever to make her glad.

Oh well, he thought, brightening somewhat, at least he would be in Putnam's Landing to carry on the gladdening of Maggie. Because he was going to win today's ball game; of that he was confident. And at the end of the game—by which time the Colonel would certainly have arrived—the parents of the Rockets would come rushing to Guido to clasp his hand and pound his back, and the Colonel, observing this touching scene, would surely conclude that Guido was the right man in the right place!

And so it was. Guido won the ball game 1—o with a daring triple steal in the sixth inning, and the parents not only shook his hand and thumped his back, but actually carried him twice around the field on their shoulders.

Only trouble was that the Colonel had still not arrived.

At 5.07 p.m. on the Fourth of July the second act of *Sweet Land of Liberty*, a three-act folk drama written, directed and produced by Laura Beauchamp, ended to tumultuous applause before a capacity audience on Ram's Head Beach.

The bleachers, which had been moved over from the Little League Field and set up in a semi-circle on the beach, were filled with appreciative theatre-lovers who clapped their hands wildly —except for two. These were Captain Walker Hoxie and Lieutenant Guido di Maggio. They sat in mopish silence, nursing their private sorrows.

Guido spoke first. "I wish the Colonel would get here already," he said querulously.

"*You* wish he'd get here?" cried Walker. "If I'd known he was going to be this late, do you think I'd have spent the last three hours with these cruddy feather merchants?"

"Attention! Attention, please!" called Laura Beauchamp, perched in the high lifeguard's chair with her megaphone. "In just a few moments, you will see the last act of *Sweet Land of Liberty*. But that, good people, is not the end of today's festivities! Far from it! At six o'clock we will have our traditional

Independence Day clambake, sponsored by the Men's Auxiliary of the Women's Club, and then, of course, at eight o'clock we will have our traditional fireworks display, sponsored by Volunteer Hose Company No. 4. . . . So don't go 'way, anybody!"

Laura stepped down from the lifeguard's chair and went into the bath-house to see whether her large cast was ready for Act Three.

On one side of the bath-house were Opie Dalrymple and the soldiers, feeling very foolish in Redcoat uniforms that fitted them randomly and powdered wigs that kept sliding over their eyes. On the other side of the bath-house were Grady Metcalf and his friends, looking like Early American hub-cap thieves in their linsey-woolsey and buckskin. The only lady in the cast, Comfort Goodpasture, somehow managing to look sexy in a Mother Hubbard, sat in front of an improvised dressing-table and fiddled with her make-up.

Grady Metcalf came up behind Comfort.

"Go away," she said promptly.

"Listen, hey," said Grady, "I been thinkin', see, and I'm willin' to let bygones be bygones, know what I mean? So what do you say you and me hop on the Harley tonight and do a little cruisin'?"

"No," said Comfort. "N-O-E. No."

"I don't care about the goin' steady bit," said Grady. "I mean, if you don't wanna go steady, that's okay with me. But I don't see no reason why we can't get together once in a while and buddy it up a little. How about it?"

"No."

"Aw, why not, hey?"

"You really wanna know?"

"Yeh."

"All right," said Comfort. "Come closer. I'll show you something." She unbuttoned the three top buttons on her Mother Hubbard.

But underneath the Mother Hubbard Comfort was wearing a baby-blue sweater and on the sweater was a jingly, shiny object.

"This," she explained, "is Opie Dalrymple's Marksman's Medal. He pinned me last night. *Now* will you flake off?"

Grady's face darkened with rage. His eyes narrowed, his lips drew back, his hands curled into fists. Without a word, he wheeled and walked away.

"Places, chaps!" called Laura Beauchamp. "Places for the last act!"

The actors filed out of the bath-house. Opie Dalrymple and the Redcoats went behind the dune where the long boats were moored. Grady Metcalf and the Minutemen took their positions in back of the rampart. The audience fell silent as a flourish of hautboys, played by Laura Beauchamp and her husband Willard, announced the beginning of Act Three.

Comfort entered and warned Grady of the Redcoats' prowess with the long rifle. Grady replied that he was entirely willing to contribute his blood to the seed-time of the Republic. The long-boats hove into view. Opie exhorted his men to show no fear before the rabble. The Redcoats beached their craft, formed a hollow square and advanced on the rampart. When the Redcoats were well within range the Minutemen opened fire. The Redcoats started dropping like flies, but Opie, never breaking stride, continued to lead the survivors towards the rampart. The Minutemen loaded and fired, loaded and fired.

Except Grady. He stood silently, his neck corded, his temples throbbing, his eyes homicidal, and watched Opie Dalrymple move steadily closer. "A rumble!" rasped Grady. "Now!"

"What did you say, hey?" asked his friend Wally.

"I say we're gonna have a rumble right now!" cried Grady, turning to his followers. "Who's with me?"

"Aw, gee, Grady," said Fred and Ed and Charlie.

"Chicken!" spat Grady. "That's what you are—chicken!"

"I wouldn't put it that way, hey," said Wally.

"Chicken! Chicken! Chicken!" repeated Grady furiously. "Just stand there and take it while these Army crud steal your broads! Well, I ain't chicken."

"What are you gonna do, Grady," asked Fred.

"I'm goin' after that bastard Dalrymple!" declared Grady.

"Yeh?" said Ed and Charlie and Wally.

"Whoever ain't chicken can come along. But I'm goin' anyhow. And," said Grady with a sudden shout, "*here I go!*"

With that he leaped over the rampart. Opie, still advancing, was only a few feet away. Grady drew back his fist, charged Opie, and gave him a tremendous smash in the jaw. Opie toppled to the ground like a felled redwood.

With a savage cry of triumph, Grady turned to his men. "Come on!" he yelled.

Courage came flooding into their narrow chests. They jumped over the rampart and descended upon the surprised soldiers like engines of destruction. In a twinkling, every soldier lay on the ground.

From the audience came a spontaneous burst of applause. "How realistic!" said one. "How authentic!" said another. "Best play-acting I ever saw!" said a third.

"Whatever are they doing?" said Laura Beauchamp to Willard.

Opie Dalrymple rose to his knees and shook his head to clear it. He looked around and saw the beach littered with his fallen comrades. "Up!" he cried, suddenly alert. "Git up and fight!"

He bounded to his feet and sailed into Grady Metcalf. He gave him a left to the belly, a right to the belly, another left to the belly, and then a right to the jaw that knocked him all the way over the rampart.

Inspirited by Opie's example, the Redcoats scrambled to their feet and fell upon the Minutemen. Back surged the tide of battle, back to the rampart.

From the bleachers came mounting applause. "Marvellous!" said one. "Terrific!" said another. "That Laura Beauchamp is a regular Gadge Kazan!" said a third.

"What *can* they be thinking of?" said Laura Beauchamp to Willard.

Behind the rampart Grady Metcalf rallied his disordered forces. "Come on, hey!" he yelled. "Rack 'em back!"

The Minutemen charged over the rampart, fists churning. The line of Redcoats sagged; then stiffened and held. Toe to toe the opposing warriors stood, neither side giving, neither side relenting. Then slowly, inexorably the Redcoats began to drive the Minutemen backward. Back to the rampart, over the rampart, behind the rampart, Opie Dalrymple's men slugged and clobbered the foe. Opie was everywhere—deploying his forces, raising the fallen, felling the risen, ignoring all pleas for quarter, smiting the enemy with vigour, precision, and unholy glee.

Now the applause in the bleachers stopped. Smiles vanished from faces. Frowns appeared. "You know what," said Guido di Maggio in a horrified whisper. "It's a rumble!"

"Yup!" said Walker Hoxie, grinning with vast enjoyment.

"Our guys'll kill those high school kids," said Guido frantically.

"I do believe they will," agreed Walker, chuckling like old Saint Nick.

Guido leaped to his feet. "I've got to stop 'em!"

Walker grabbed his wrist and yanked him down. "You sit right here!" he snapped.

"Captain, it's a slaughter!" cried Guido.

"It's a tonic," said Walker, beaming. "That's what it is."

"I heard that!" said Clement R. Metcalf, father to Grady, a large, beetling man who was sitting directly behind Walker Hoxie.

Walker turned and looked up at Mr. Metcalf. "Would you care to do anything about it?" he asked amiably.

"Yes, by God!" replied Mr. Metcalf and gave Walker a shot in the eye that sent him toppling over several rows of people in front of him.

"Now see here!" exclaimed Guido, rising.

"And you too!" yelled Mr. Metcalf. He threw a punch at Guido's head. Guido automatically ducked and automatically countered. He caught Mr. Metcalf on the point of the chin, and Mr. Metcalf fell backwards. As Mr. Metcalf had been sitting in the top row of the bleachers, this was rather a long fall.

Then Mr. Metcalf's brother, Robert Lewis Metcalf, hit Guido in the side of the head and sent him sprawling down into the crowd below.

Then Guido's brothers, Pete, Bruno, Carmen, and Dominic, came scrambling up the bleachers and took hold of Robert Lewis Metcalf and threw him down on top of Clement R. Metcalf.

Then four brother Elks of Clement R. and Robert Lewis Metcalf proceeded to grapple with the di Maggios. This contest, unlike the others, lacked compactness. It surged and rolled in many directions, and a goodly number of bystanders were drawn into the fray, but on which side, no man could say.

And at the bottom of the bleachers, Walker Hoxie, having failed to push his way back to the top, selected the handiest target—the electronics tycoon, Mr. Arthur Waterford—and gave him a resounding clout in the ear. Mr. Waterford, a gentleman boxer, riposted with a series of smart combinations to Walker's nose.

And Mr. Brooks Cathcart, a tiny, bald man with a goatee and gold-rimmed glasses, by profession an expert in rare books, who had purchased a house in 1948 from the real estate dealer George Melvin—a house which had started settling immediately and continued to settle at the rate of fourteen inches every year—looked around him now, saw that the melee was general, and took this opportunity to walk up quietly behind George Melvin and hit him in the back of the neck with his little, pointy fist.

And Guido di Maggio ran back and forth crying "Peace! Peace!" but there was no peace. People kept belting him, and he was forced, regretfully, to deck quite a number of prominent citizens.

And women shrieked, men cursed, babies cried, girls squealed, gulls screamed, fish jumped, fists crunched, sleeves ripped, noses bled, teeth dropped, eyes blacked, ears rang, and the battle sputtered through the bleachers and burgeoned on the beach.

And Colonel Thorwald, who had been delayed on the Merritt Parkway by heavy holiday traffic, arrived to inspect the status of public relations in Putnam's Landing.

Twenty One

HARRY BANNERMAN, having been turned out of his hearth and home, went, of course, to look for a bar.

But it was not yet ten o'clock in the morning, and it was the Fourth of July to boot, and Harry could not find a bar open. Up and down the Post Road he went, a pathetic figure rattling doorknobs and peering in windows and plaintively calling, "Anybody here?"

Finally, on the very edge of town, he came upon an establishment named The Pilgrim's Pride Bar and Grill. It was seedy, squalid, filthy, dismal, dank—but it was open. Gratefully Harry plunged inside.

The bartender, a man with a three-day beard and a copy of *Confidential*, looked up incuriously as Harry entered. "Whisky," said Harry. Without conversation, the bartender poured a shot, placed a small glass of beer beside it, took fifty cents, and returned to his reading. Harry mounted a stool of red plastic and chromium, found a fairly dry place on the bar for his elbows, and had his drink.

He was having his twenty-first—his twenty-*fifth*, if you count the four he spilled—when out of the gathering dusk three soldiers with split lips and blackened eyes came walking into the bar.

"I can't serve you guys," said the bartender to the soldiers. "I'm off limits."

"There's no other bar in town open," said Guido di Maggio.

"I'm off limits, I tell you," said the bartender. "You guys'll get in trouble."

"Hah!" said the three soldiers as one man. What more trouble could they get into? each one was thinking. Guido di

Maggio was being shipped to Alaska first thing in the morning and thus losing any chance of ever squaring things with Maggie. Opie Dalrymple was up for court-martial on charges of violating several Articles of War, several local ordinances of Putnam's Landing, and possibly the Kellogg-Briand Pact. And Walker Hoxie had been dealt the unkindest cut of all: Colonel Thorwald was busting him down to second lieutenant but making him stay in Putnam's Landing!

"Aw, come on, give us a drink," said Guido to the bartender.

"I can't, hey," he answered. "I'll lose my licence."

"You'll lose your eye, you cruddy feather merchant, if you don't stop this crap," said Walker, looming large over the bar.

The bartender took a good look at Walker, swallowed, and said, "What'll you have?"

"Three whiskies," said Walker.

"Ah'll have three whiskies too, please, sir," said Opie.

"What the hell," said Guido, shrugging. "Make mine the same."

"Aw, no, fellas!" begged the bartender. "I'm closin' up in a little while. I'm goin' down to the beach to see the fireworks."

Walker leaned forward and grabbed the bartender by his leatherette bow-tie. "Okay, okay!" said the bartender. "Okay, okay, okay!"

Walker released the bartender. In front of each soldier he placed three shots of whisky and a schooner of beer. They fell to work with dispatch and in five minutes had ordered a second round.

From his stool at the end of the bar Harry Bannerman tried to get the three new-comers in focus—slow work. At last he succeeded. "Aha!" he said thickly. "Nike soldiers. Hadn't been for you bastards, I'd still be married!"

He slid off his stool and weaved belligerently towards them. Guido was the closest. He threw a tremendous right uppercut, which Guido ducked without haste. Guido pinned Harry's arms gently to his side. "Please, Mr. Bannerman," he said earnestly, "please don't start up with us tonight. We got a *lot* of trouble!"

"Leggo, you professional killer!" mumbled Harry. "Leggo and fight."

"Mr. Bannerman," said Guido, holding firm, "you want to sit here nicely and drink with us? Huh, Mr. Bannerman?"

Harry thought it over. "All right," he said. "I'll drink with *you*. . . . But not with *him*," he added, pointing at Walker Hoxie. "You know why? 'Cause he represents the resurgence of the brute mind, is why."

"All right," said Guido, helping Harry up on the stool next to his. "You drink with me. Bartender, three whiskies."

"All around," said Opie.

The bartender groaned but complied.

The four men sat and drank in silence, the glasses in front of them emptying rapidly—Harry's rather more rapidly than the others, because he kept missing his mouth.

"I got an idea," said Harry, after a while. "Let's sing *When Johnny comes marching home again, hurrah, hurrah, we'll give him a hearty welcome then hurrah, hurrah, the men will cheer the boys will shout the ladies they will all turn out and we'll all feel gay when Johnny comes marching home*."

"How does it go?" said Opie.

"Shut up," said Walker. "I don't want any goddam singing."

Guido looked thoughtfully at his whisky glasses. One was still full. He knocked it back. "Hoxie," he said, "you know something? Bannerman's right. You *do* represent the resurgence of the brute mind."

"That's a fack, sir," agreed Opie. "You got no refinement a-tall."

Walker gripped the edge of the bar and started to rise in anger. But half-way up he stopped. He settled back slowly. "You fellas really think so?" he asked in a small voice.

"Absolutely!" said Guido. "Why can't you try to get along with people? I mean civilians. They're people too, you know."

"They're people," Walker admitted. "But they ain't *military* people. They're *civilian* people. That's two entirely different things, like oil and water. They don't mix."

"I'll tell you what don't mix," said Harry. "Men and women don't mix. That's what don't mix."

"Frinds," said Opie, "the world is full of thangs that don't mix, but somethin' holds it together anyhow. That somethin', frinds, is love. You got to do like the Book says: love thy neighbour. Open your horts, frinds, and chase away them scarey shadows with love and understandin'."

"That's beautiful!" breathed the bartender.

All fell into a pensive silence.

Walker spoke first. "I thought it over," he said, "and I don't believe it."

"You ain't drunk enough," said Opie. "Bartender, three whiskies all round."

"Aw, fellas," he pleaded, "the fireworks are gonna start in a few minutes. I gotta close up!"

"Whisky!" roared Walker, banging on the bar with his big red fist.

"Tell you what," said the bartender. "I ain't supposed to do this, but I'll sell you a couple of bottles to take out."

Walker lunged for him. The bartender ducked. When he came up he had two bottles in his hands. "I'll *give* you a couple of bottles!" he cried. "Okay, fellas, okay?"

"Thank you, frind," said Opie. He relieved the bartender of the whisky and turned to Lieutenant di Maggio. "Guido, buddy, where shall we go?" he asked.

Guido scratched his head. "I'd invite you to my house," he said, "but it's full of people."

"I ain't got a house," said Harry, choking back a sob.

Walker patted him clumsily on the back. "That's all right, pal. We'll go my place. It's nice and cosy."

Linking arms, the four troubled souls went off to Walker's nice, cosy room in the Bachelor Officers' Quarters on the Nike base.

On Colonel Thorwald's plate there were six clams, a two-and-a-half-pound lobster, a fillet of flounder, a baked potato, and two ears of sweet corn, all done to a turn by the Men's Auxiliary of the Women's Club for the traditional Putnam's Landing Independence Day clambake. But the Colonel had no appetite. Ever since he had arrived at Ram's Head Beach and stopped the rumble and handed down his terrible, swift judgments on Guido, Walker, and Opie, he had been besieged by irate townsmen who came around to register complaints against the United States Army. To all of them the Colonel had replied with soft answers and promises of reform, but they had not been noticeably mollified.

Now the Colonel stood with his hands full of sea-food and tried to patch things up with the real powers of Putnam's Landing—Manning Thaw, Isaac Goodpasture, George Melvin, and their coteries. "Gentlemen," he said, smiling strenuously, "naturally there are bound to be little frictions in a situation of this kind, but don't you worry, we'll work them out. The important thing, as you know, is that we've established a combat-ready base here—a vital link in our chain of national defences."

"How would we know that?" asked Isaac Goodpasture. "We've never been allowed to set foot on your Nike base."

"Why, that's terrible!" cried the Colonel. "Would you like to see the base?"

"We got a right to, ain't we?" said Manning Thaw. "It's part of our town, ain't it?"

"It most certainly is!" declared the Colonel. "That's exactly the way I want you to feel: the Nike base is a part of *your* town."

"Let's go see it then," said Isaac.

"Now?" said the Colonel.

"Why not?" said George Melvin.

"But aren't the fireworks starting soon?" said the Colonel.

"We *seen* fireworks," said Manning Thaw. "What we ain't seen is the Nike base."

"Very well, gentlemen," said the Colonel, setting down his plate. "Let's go!"

Walker Hoxie's lodgings at the Bachelor Officers' Quarters were furnished with Spartan simplicity—just an army cot, a wooden chair, and a pine chest—but there was plenty of room on the floor, and that is where the four unfortunates now lay.

They were conducting a species of musicale, anti-phonal and loud. Harry was singing *Small Hotel*, Walker was singing *The Caissons Go Rolling Along*, Guido was singing *Baby, It's Cold Outside*, and Opie was singing his own composition *The Floyd Collins Polka* and at the same time accompanying himself and all the others on his guitar.

There was a knocking on the door. It continued for several minutes, but nobody heard. At length the door opened and Private Roger Litwhiler, wearing a helmet liner and carrying a carbine, stepped inside. "Sirs," he said nervously. "Sirs! Sirs! Oh, sirs!"

"Howdy, hoss," said Opie genially. "Have a snort." He extended a bottle of whisky to Private Roger Litwhiler.

Private Roger Litwhiler drew back in horror. "Oh, no!" he said. "I'm pulling guard. I'm supposed to be at the gate right now. Please listen to me, everybody. I've got to get back to my post. Please listen!"

"Gimme your gun," said Harry, snatching the carbine. "There's somebody I wanna kill."

Private Roger Litwhiler retrieved his weapon. "Please!" he shouted desperately. "Listen to me! Colonel Thorwald just drove in with a bunch of people. He's over in the IFC Area now, showing 'em around. Then he's coming back here to the Launching Area. You guys better get out before he gets here!"

"Is that the way to report to an officer?" said Walker, flat on his back. "Take off your hat and salute."

"Or take off your salute and hat," said Guido, giggling.

They all found this a delicious piece of badinage and laughed for upwards of sixty seconds, rolling over and over on the floor.

"Look, I can't stay away from my post any longer!" said Private Roger Litwhiler frantically. "Opie, for God's sake, get these guys out of here before you all end up in Leavenworth—and me too!"

He pulled Opie to his feet and slapped his face a dozen times, Opie grinning immensely through all of it. "Okay, okay, hoss, Ah'll git 'em out," said Opie amiably.

Private Roger Litwhiler ran back to his post, and Opie raised up his three comrades and propped them against the wall. "Frinds," he said, "we got to hide."

"Not it!" said Harry.

"Now come along," said Opie. "Y'all get a holt of me."

He fastened their limp hands to his shirt and led them stumbling and lurching out of the BOQ. Once outside he looked around for a hiding-place. To go off the post was clearly impossible; the gate was almost a hundred yards away. It would have to be some place closer. Opie swivelled his head around, trying to get the landscape to stop waving. His companions, meanwhile, sang a medley of *Oh, Susannah*, the *Hut-Sut Song*, and *A Mighty Fortress Is My Lord*.

Then Opie saw the launching-pits where the Nikes were stored. "Perfeck!" said he enthusiastically. "Dork and deep and quiet. Frinds, into the pits!"

He pushed, rolled, and hefted them over to a steep metal staircase that descended thirty feet to the bottom of the pit. Once he got them to the head of the stairs, the rest was easy; he simply released them and listened to them bounce softly down. Then he went down himself, giggling happily as he thumped along the stairs.

The pit was a huge concrete box. Overhead were massive steel doors, now closed. On the floor directly beneath each set of doors was a steel platform that could be raised hydraulically to the surface. On each platform was a rocket launcher. On each launcher, lying flat, was a slim, white Nike, gleaming eerily in a shaft of moonlight coming down the staircase.

"What's those ugly things?" asked Harry, pointing at the Nikes.

"*Ugly!*" cried Walker, outraged. "They're *beautiful!* Most beautiful damn things I ever saw in my life," he said tenderly and went and put his arms around a Nike and laid his cheek on the cold white skin.

"Yeah?" said Harry, and went and put *his* arms around a Nike and laid *his* cheek on the cold white skin.

"Beautiful!" repeated Walker. "Ain't it beautiful?"

"I don't think it's so beautiful," said Harry.

"You're drunk!" Walker said and turned away from Harry in disgust. "Anybody bring a bottle?" he asked.

"I got one," said Guido.

"Where are you? It's dark in here," said Walker.

"Over here," said Guido, and Walker went stumbling over to him.

"*Not* beautiful," muttered Harry, looking over his Nike. "Ugly.... And dirty too," he added, flicking a greasy red tag on the Nike's nose. There were three other such tags along the length of the Nike. "Tell you what I'll do," said Harry to the Nike. "I'll clean you up a little and see how you look." He removed the four red tags and examined the Nike again. "Still ugly," he pronounced.

"Gimme a drink, Guido," said Walker to Guido.

"I'm Opie," said Opie to Walker.

"Where's Guido?" said Walker to Opie.

"Over here," said Guido to Walker.

Walker found him in the darkness. "Gimme a drink," he said.

"First tell me what you are," said Guido.

"I forget," said Walker.

"Think," said Guido.

Walker thought. "Oh, now I remember.... I am a resurgence of the brute mind."

"Good boy!" said Guido and handed Walker a bottle.

Walker tilted it back.

"Hey, Walker," called Harry, still clutching the Nike. "You wanna know something? Nike's ugly! Ugly, d'you hear? *Ugly!*"

"Oh, for Chrisake!" exclaimed Walker. "I leave it to you guys. Is Nike beautiful?"

"Purty as a colt," said Opie.

"Gorgeous," said Guido.

"I don't see it," said Harry.

"Of course you don't see it!" said Walker. "Too goddam dark down here. Let's get it up where you can get a look at it."

He lurched to a control board behind a bunker and pressed the button that operated the hydraulic lift. The steel doors at the top of the pit yawned open. The platform, carrying Harry and the missile, moved slowly upward to the surface. As the platform rose—and Harry watched goggled-eyed—the launcher automatically elevated itself. By the time the platform reached the top, the Nike stood in its almost vertical take-off position. "I'll be damned!" muttered Harry admiringly.

"Hey!" came Walker's faint voice, calling up the staircase. "What do you think now?"

Harry walked away, closed one eye, and made a careful study of the Nike, standing tall and slender and white against the starry sky.

"I changed my mind," yelled Harry. "It's *beautiful!*"

"You goddam right!" called Walker up the staircase.

"This, gentlemen," said Colonel Thorwald, conducting the Yankees on a tour of the IFC Area, "is called the BC van—the Battery Control van. Here is where the Nike is actually fired. It takes off from the other area, a mile away, but the trigger, so to speak, is right here—this little switch."

He pointed at an ordinary toggle switch on the control board.

"Hey, careful!" cried George Melvin nervously. "You almost touched that thing."

The Colonel chuckled. "It wouldn't matter if I did," he said.

"Nike has one of the most foolproof safety systems ever devised. First of all, in order to launch a missile, the battery must be on what is called 'Red Alert'—and we are never on 'Red Alert' unless enemy planes have actually been identified in the vicinity. . . . However, I want to show you just how safe Nike is. For a few seconds, I'm going to put the battery on 'Red Alert'." The Colonel punched the RED button on the control board. Instantly sirens screamed, lights flashed, and the radarscopes sprang into life.

The Yankees huddled together, looking extremely perturbed.

"It's all right, gentlemen," said the Colonel soothingly, "I just want to prove to you that you have nothing to fear from Nike. We are now on 'Red Alert'. But still a missile cannot be launched. Why? Because nobody over in the Launching Area has raised a missile to the surface. . . . But let us say that somebody, through some incredible error, had raised a Nike to launching position. It still would not take off. Do you know why?

"Because," said the Colonel, "as a final, foolproof, last-minute precaution, there are four red tags on each Nike that have to be removed *by hand* before the Nike can take off!"

"Sounds pretty safe," said Manning Thaw.

"Foolproof!" said the Colonel firmly. "Go ahead, Mr. Thaw. Push the button yourself."

"Oh, I don't really care to," said Manning, drawing back.

"Go ahead," insisted the Colonel. "I want you to reassure yourself."

"Well——" said Manning.

"Go ahead," said the Colonel.

"Oh, all right," said Manning and flipped the switch.

And in the bleachers on Ram's Head Beach the folks were sitting and watching the traditional Fourth of July fireworks display sponsored by Volunteer Hose Company No. 4.

First there were the set pieces—flaming flags and Washington crossing the Delaware and other patriotic scenes. Then came the pinwheels and fountains. And then, best of all, came the sky-rockets.

The first rocket was a bombshell of blue and yellow and white.

"Ah!" said the crowd.

Next came a starburst of red, green, and orange, followed by a second burst of dazzling white.

"Aaah!" said the crowd.

Next came a double shower of green, pink and gold on the one side and lavender, yellow and white on the other.

"Aaaaaaah!" said the crowd.

Next came a spreader star that threw out every colour of the rainbow in a series of multiplying bursts.

"Aaaaaaaaaaaaaah!" said the crowd.

And then came something never seen in the memory of the oldest inhabitant. It started from the ground, throwing out a huge, wide flare-path of white with red and blue edges, and it went up, up, up, never dimming, never diminishing, and it climbed higher and higher and higher, still glowing, and up and up it went, up, up, up, blazing all the way, up, up, up, still burning, and up some more, higher than any sky-rocket had ever gone, higher than any aeroplane, igniting the summer sky, flaming like a comet, rising higher and higher and still higher and still higher, blazing, blazing, burning bright, and climbing up and up and up and up and out of sight.

"Aaaaaaaaaaaaaaaaaaaaaaaaaaaaaaaaaaaaaaaaaaaaaaaaaaaaaaaaaaaaaa aaaaaaaaaaaaaah! said the crowd.

Epilogue

AND so, with the night sky blazing, our drama crunches to a close.

And what of the souls roiled and tumbled in the maelstrom? Eh? What of them?

Well, sir, here is what happened.

Three days after the Fourth of July, Maggie Larkin, carrying a suitcase, was on the way to the railroad station to catch a train home to her mother and father when she came upon young Daniel Bannerman skipping down the street.

"Hello, Daniel," said she.

"Hi, Miss Larkin," said he.

"How are you?" said she.

"Oh, I am *so* happy!" he cried, his earnest young eyes aglow. "We're in first place, you know!"

He then proceeded to tell her how the scrubs had persuaded Guido not to send them into the ball game on the Fourth of July, and Maggie, learning the truth for the first time, was filled with shame and pity. She thought how unfair, how cruel, she had been to Guido. She had refused to open the door for him when he came around to explain, refused to answer the phone. She had sent the poor wretch off to the tundras of Alaska without so much as a goodbye.

So heavy was Maggie's heart when she arrived at the railroad station, so laden with contrition, that she did not take a train to the home of her family, but went instead to New York City and boarded an airliner for Alaska that very same day and fell into Guido's arms and tearfully begged his forgiveness.

It was, of course, forthcoming. Three days later they were

married and today they live in a quonset hut and are without doubt one of the most devoted couples north of Moose Jaw.

On August 8th, Harry Bannerman, aching with loneliness after five weeks' separation from Grace, was sitting in his dreary hotel room in Manhattan when the telephone rang. He reached for it reluctantly. Angela Hoffa had been calling him every evening without fail; also without success. But this time it was not Angela phoning. It was Grace.

"Grace, honey, baby!" he shouted joyfully.

"I would like you to come home, please," she said in a quiet, expressionless voice. "Bring your things."

"Oh, wonderful!" he cried, scarcely able to contain himself. "Wonderful!"

But the minute he came bursting into his house in Putnam's Landing, Grace put a damper on his enthusiasm. "Let's get one thing straight immediately," she said, holding him at arm's length. "I haven't asked you home to forgive and forget. I still feel exactly the way I felt when I sent you away. That hasn't changed one bit. . . . However, something new has come up, and I'd like you to move back into the house—temporarily, I mean."

"What's come up?" asked Harry.

"I found out this morning that I'm pregnant," said Grace.

"Oh," said Harry.

"After the baby is born," she continued, "we can work out a permanent separation, but until then I'm afraid I'm going to need your help around here—if you're willing, that is."

"Of course," said Harry.

"You understand that this is in no way a reconciliation?"

"You mean I'm to stay out of your bed."

"I do."

"All right, Grace. Any way you want it."

"Thank you."

"You're welcome."

So for the next six months Harry, true to his word, lived with

Grace as her nominal husband. To the world, to their children, they presented a front of solid connubiality; in private they kept their distance. At first Harry attempted an occasional tender overture—a sigh, a sidelong glance, a batting of the lashes—but Grace always replied with such a frost that he finally gave it up.

But all the time Grace's resolution was weakening. Externally she was adamant; on the inside there was galloping erosion. More and more she doubted her own doubts. Was it *really* possible that Harry did not love her? In spite of all his transgressions, could that light in his eyes be anything but true, deep, abiding devotion?

On January 19th she went to the Putnam's Landing Hospital and gave birth to the baby—their first daughter, for whom the name Martha had long been waiting—and when Grace was brought down from the delivery-room and found Harry leaning over her, kissing her hands, weeping with joy and relief, she was once and for all convinced. This man loved her; this foolish, antic, mercurial, man-type man loved her beyond the doubting of it.

Grace did a heap of thinking in the hospital, and she came home with a very intelligent plan. "Harry," she said, "you and I are going to have a little holiday, just the two of us."

"Oh, wonderful!" cried Harry jubilantly. "Let's go to the Concord and have a good rest and swim in the indoor pool and eat some of that wonderful food."

"Yes," said Grace, "the Concord is very nice and the food is divine, but I had something a bit more ambitious in mind."

"Yes?" said Harry.

"As you know," she continued, "my mother sent me a nice cheque when the baby was born, and I think, as an investment in our future, we ought to spend it on a real vacation."

Harry's eyes widened. "Where will we go?" he asked.

She produced the travel section of the *Sunday Times*. "I studied this very carefully in the hospital," she said, "and here's something that sounds just perfect. In Cuba there's a place called

Veradero Beach—fifteen miles of soft, clean, white sand—and right on Veradero Beach there's a beautiful new resort called the Oasis. It's got the sea on one side and a salt-water pool on the other, big air-conditioned rooms, superb cuisine, water ski-ing, fishing, palm trees, trade winds, tropical sun, tropical moon, tropical stars, mambo and cha-cha, planter's punch, and siesta every afternoon!"

"Just a minute, I'll get my hat," said Harry, and did, and ran to the nearest travel agent, and flew with Grace the following week to Veradero Beach and checked into the Oasis which was, indeed, beautiful and new and air-conditioned, and had the sea on one side and a salt-water pool on the other, and the cuisine was superb, and the breezes were balmy, and the punches were planter's, and Grace and Harry, dancing under the tropical moon, toasting in the warm white sand, having siesta in the still afternoon, laughed often and held one another tight and exchanged kisses both ardent and tender and were happier than they had ever been, even in the first days in Greenwich Village.

Then they came home. Grace, with her heart in her mouth, watched to see whether Harry was finally ready to settle down after this big fling. At first there were no changes, and Grace was filled with despair. Then, little by little, things began to happen. One evening Harry came home with a copy of *Good House-keeping*. "What's *that*?" cried Grace, astounded. "I happened to pick it up in my dentist's office this afternoon," explained Harry. "Look here," he said, pointing to a page in the magazine. "Why can't *we* have a barbecue like this? It doesn't look too hard to build." And—what do you know—he went and built it!

Another evening Harry was at a PTA meeting with Grace when, suddenly, to everyone's astonishment, he leaped to his feet and made a passionate plea for a stop-and-go sign at the school crossing on Main and Locust. The Yankees, of course, opposed it, but Harry argued so cogently, so forcefully—indeed, so tiresomely—that he finally pushed it through.

And another time—it was four o'clock in the morning—

Grace heard voices in the house and woke up. She reached over to shake Harry, but he was not in bed. Then it occurred to her the the voices in the house belonged to Harry and Martha—then eight months old. Grace sat up and listened. She heard Harry explain to Martha that there was really nothing to cry about, wet pants were a common enough hazard and easily repaired. There, he said, didn't that feel better? And wasn't that powder nice and soft? And wasn't Martha the sweetest, handsomest, brightest child ever born? And didn't she love her old dad? And wouldn't it be fine soon when she learned how to walk and her old dad would put her in a pretty yellow dress and take her down the street and everybody would gnash their teeth with envy because *they* didn't have a daughter so beautiful, intelligent, winsome, fetching, graceful, charming, virtuous, seemly, and wholly estimable? Grace listened and chuckled silently and dropped a tear or two and when, after thirty minutes of this conversation, Harry came back to bed, Grace slid under the covers and pretended she was asleep.

Just the other night when Grace and Harry were reading before the fire, she suddenly put down her book and said: "Harry?"

"Yes?" he said.

"I love you," she said.

"That's nice," he said.

"You've changed, you know," she said.

"In what way?" he said.

"The best way," she said. "After all these years you've finally acquired maturity."

"Like hell I have," replied Harry with a horrendous scowl. "What I've finally acquired is senility," he said, "and I'll thank you not to talk about it."

"Yes, dear."

"There's a lesson here," continued Harry, "for you and for all womankind. If your husband isn't shaping up the way you like, just be patient. Always remember that time is on *your* side."

"Yes, dear," said Grace solemnly and climbed into his lap.

Oscar Hoffa is happy too—or, at any rate, as happy as Oscar Hoffa gets. Six out of the top ten TV shows last month were his, but, actually, the show that made him happiest ranked so low that it wasn't even in the listings. This was a programme called "The Life of the Mind"—a cultural hour featuring such *divertissements* as sonatas by Hindemith, readings from *Finnegans Wake*, and discussions of the art of Jackson Pollock. Oscar, with violent reluctance, had agreed to produce the programme for only one reason: the Federal Communications Commission has a rule that a certain number of hours per week must be devoted to non-profit broadcasts in the public interest.

So what happened? Last June, Oscar, giggling wildly, got called up to Brandeis University and presented with an honorary Doctor of Humane Letters degree.

He still wears his academic robes around the office sometimes.

Angela Hoffa got just what she deserved: she ended up as Mrs. Walker Hoxie.

She ran into Walker on the Merritt Parkway one September afternoon. Literally, that is. She drove her Coupe de Ville up the back of his jeep, and he came running at her with such cursing and glowering that for a moment she thought it was Oscar reborn.

There followed a long, abrasive courtship, but she finally wore him down. They live today in Angela's house in Putnam's Landing without a television set. They fight most of the time—chiefly because Walker keeps trying to persuade Angela to join the WAC.

Grady Metcalf was sent off to an excellent military academy in Massachusetts. It is now the only military academy on the Eastern seaboard with sideburns.

Opie Dalrymple and Comfort Goodpasture are going steady, united in a love so deep, so lyrical, so wholesome, that even Isaac cannot object to it.

Opie never did get court-martialled. Shortly after the night of the runaway Nike, there was a kind of general amnesty, and Opie, among others, was pardoned.

What brought about this new era of good feeling was some fast footwork by Colonel Thorwald. The town, of course, was wild with rage after the Nike ran away. Wildest of all was George Melvin, realtor, because when the Nike came back to earth, it landed smack in the old Yarbro property on the Shore Road—a property belonging to George Melvin.

The Nike did not explode when it landed, but all the same a ton of metal falling from 70,000 feet digs itself rather a commodious hole. George Melvin screamed blue murder. He was suing everybody, he cried, from the President on down.

Colonel Thorwald, recognising the need for dramatic counter-measures, flew to the Pentagon and got an authorisation to purchase the old Yarbro place from George Melvin—at George Melvin's price. This pacified George Melvin. Then the Colonel turned around and presented the old Yarbro place to the town of Putnam's Landing. This pacified the town—especially after Betty O'Sheel leapt up in town meeting and demanded the old Yarbro place for the new garbage disposal plant. This time Betty had the votes, and today Putnam's Landing, thanks to Betty O'Sheel, the United States Army, and the Garba-Crunch Corporation, has one of the slickest, quickest, cheapest systems of putrescible and non-putrescible waste disposal in all of this great, broad, free land of America.